Taylor Made

Carly Peake

Cover by Jim Haywood

For Beatrice & Bean

I had come to the conclusion that babies were a bit like marmite. At least for some people anyway. I mean, the majority of the population could probably go either way on their thoughts on bringing a tiny, totally dependent on you for literally everything, life into the world. But then there were people who absolutely knew that they were made to be a parent, and contrary to this, those who were definitely not.

For me, it had been an 'on the fence' situation for most of my twenties. I liked my life, my freedom, and I loved my family, which consisted of a niece and nephew that arguably gave me the best parts of parenthood without the responsibility. However. This was not the case any longer. I wanted to hear a tiny little voice call out to me 'mama', and I wanted to hold a baby in my arms that I didn't have to hand back before walking out of the door. The problem I had now, was I couldn't quite make my dream a reality using the more traditional methods of baby making.

Somewhere deep down, I had always known that I preferred the idea of 'happily ever after' being with a woman. I always panicked more for Scully being abducted by aliens than Mulder. I preferred the Spice Girls to Take That (specifically, Geri Halliwell to Robbie Williams). I was jubilant when Kate Winslet let Leonardo DiCaprio sink in Titanic, and I love P!nk for more than her extraordinary and emotive voice. It wasn't anything I hid down any longer, (not since I was nineteen and had taken Daisy Rose to my parent's anniversary party). I was out and proud and I even had the rainbow striped socks to prove it. You don't get those as an initiation into the LGBT community or anything, they were a Christmas present from my best friend.

People presume that you'll end up with dungarees, a buzz cut and ten cats or half a dozen dogs if you're a lesbian. I do own dungarees. They're comfy. I do not have a buzz cut, nor do I have any pets. I could see cats and dogs in my future, but I also saw babies in my future too.

As we sat now in my living room, I looked at my best friend; Kate's, ever growing bump and gave it a little rub. I swore I'd never be one of those people that randomly touched other women's pregnant bellies, but here I was. Although Kate wasn't a random woman, we'd been friends since we were five years old (she was responsible for the rainbow socks, and my rainbow salt and pepper shakers with matching egg cups) and it was perfectly acceptable for me to lean in and make silly noises into her tummy.

"You could always go for Emily Junior," I couldn't see the harm in putting my own name on the table.

"Ha! Not going to happen my friend," Kate laughed, and I rolled my eyes. Maybe I wasn't fully appreciating the mammoth responsibility that comes with naming a child. I was mulling over my next suggestion, eager to receive something other than an eye roll from Kate, when the door opened.

"What are you two talking about?" I looked up to see my girlfriend, Beth, walk in and beamed up at her as she leaned down for an affectionate little peck on the lips.

"Baby names," Kate brought Beth up to speed. "I've not got long left to make Tom think that whatever name I pick was actually his idea," Kate couldn't help but smile as she said her loving and devoted husband's name to us. They had been together for five years and this was their first little Tom-Kat to begin their family together.

"Mm," Beth pondered. "I like a name that can be shortened or can have a cute little nick-name associated with it," she had always been grateful for being able to shorten Elizabeth to 'Beth'. "I don't like names like Ruth or Liam, they're too sharp," she sat down opposite Kate and I and thought for a moment. "A good solid Samantha that can become Sam or William shortened to Will."

"So how did you come to a decision to choose a name for Olivia?" Kate directed her question at Beth, and I winced, masking it with an inquisitive gaze in Beth's direction. I pretended I hadn't heard this story before, and that it didn't make my heart ache every time I thought of Beth raising a child without me by her side.

"Well, *he* wasn't really bothered, so it kind of got left to me. Olivia was always at the top of my list for a girl, and now she's Liv," I listened attentively to Beth's response and then I heard the front door open. An "ooey, it's only me," from my mother, followed by a "for feck's sake, Jane will you not screech like a banshee as soon as I get through the door, I'm not feckin' deaf yet," from my gran.

I stood up and went to greet them both.

"Hi Gran," I kissed her cheek and she wiped it off immediately.

"I don't want feckin' germs from them little gobshites you work with now Emily, what's the matter with you," I laughed at her reference to the fact I worked as a teacher in a primary school and kissed my mum's cheek before leading us all back into the living room. Kate tried to stand up but without a fork-lift truck that was going to be difficult.

"No, you stay where you are, Kate," my mum sat beside her and placed her hand on the bump. It was weirder when she did it. "How long now?"

"I've got three weeks left."

"Oh, it's exciting isn't it!"

"I feel a bit faint, Emily, I think it's the dehydration. Have you put the kettle on yet?" I rolled my eyes at my gran and helped her to sit down.

"I'll do it now, anyone else?" two shakes and a nod and I turned to go to the kitchen.

"When you get back you can check out my latest twoot on this twatter."

"Gran! It's TWITTER! How many times!"

"That's what I said. I've twelve followers now you know."

"Yes, and I believe you're either related to them all or they sit with you and have their hair permed every Friday morning whilst you send 'twoots' under the driers," she waved her hand dismissively, pretending she wasn't listening. She did that a lot.

"I've got Pip too," she added.

"Who?"

"The silver fox himself, that Willoughbooby is no match for me," a little laughter rippled around the room.

"Gran, Philip Schofield does not follow you on Twa… Twitter."

"He feckin' does!"

"Gran…"

"I'll show you, come and look at this twoot."

"Tweet," Gran rolled her eyes at me and opened her handbag. She pulled out three mobile phones, an iPod, a Kindle Fire and two digital cameras.

"Jesus, Nancy, have you got any watches in there as well? I bet you do a roaring trade on the Sunday market," Beth and Kate laughed but tried to disguise how genuinely amused they were.

"I shouldn't take the piss now Beth, one day my fortune will be yours and Emily's, now which one is he on…" Gran balanced her glasses on the end of her nose and perused her electronic items whilst I dashed out to put the kettle on.

At this point I feel I should point out a few things. My gran (Nancy) was Irish, if you hadn't managed to pick up on that, and my mum (Jane) was one of seven children. Which meant that I had enough cousins, aunts and uncles to populate my own country (although that would cause some serious issues with inbreeding and produce a peculiar race of offspring.) My mum didn't grow up in Ireland, she's the youngest of the seven and was the only one born in England, which she claims makes her unique and I claim makes her the milk man's.

I loved my family more than anything in the world, but I was seriously concerned for Gran's safety on the black market with her never ending supply of electronics and, occasionally, white goods. I also worried that if she kept referring to Twitter as 'Twatter' she'd end up getting beaten up. She would never cope with a quiet life. She had lived on her own for twenty years and for a woman rather indeterminate of age she was doing just fine.

I brewed the tea and entered the living room to find Gran and Kate having an arm wrestle. I told you. An ordinary life would be wasted on her. I looked at Beth and she shook her head and shrugged.

"Don't ask Babe," was Beth's only remark. I put the tray of tea and biscuits down on the coffee table (a selection of Bourbon creams and Chocolate digestives) and sat beside my mum.

"Mum, for God's sake make her stop!"

"Are you mad? I'm not getting involved," I was about to intervene myself when Kate's arm was finally forced down and Gran was crowned champion. She simply reached for her cup of tea, took one of each biscuit and sat back in her chair.

"I warned you, I trained to interrogate terrorists with MI5, an arm wrestle is like stepping on an army of ants."

"Gran..."

"I did! This country owes me, full of feckin' foreigners now, would never have happened in my day!"

"Mother!" Everyone was struggling to hold back their amusement at my gran's behaviour, particularly as she herself was technically not born and bred in the UK, but it was nothing that we hadn't all heard from her before. My mum never did like to hear her talking like that, I sometimes wondered how they were related, they were nothing like each other, and I didn't really remember my granddad all that well to know if my mum was like him. Gran said that she was 'her father's daughter', maybe I'm right about the whole milkman thing...

Just then there was a car horn outside, and Kate began to make it look like she was attempting some sort of manoeuvre to regain an upright position, it was like watching a Teletubby try and get off its back.

"That'll be my chauffeur, he said he'd stop and pick me up on his way home from work," I helped Kate stand and picked her bag up for her. "Was a pleasure to see you all, as always. Nancy, you've got some muscles girl!"

"You were a strong competitor; it was a fair fight. I was never about to go easy on you because of the whole baby thing. Life's tough, nothing wrong with teaching that now before the little one meets all the eejits out there."

"Ha, ha! Thanks, my unborn child and I appreciate the lesson," everyone else waved and air kissed goodbye, I walked with Kate to the door. I helped her put her coat on and gave her a big squeeze.

"Thank you for coming over."

"A pleasure as always, but I still think there's something you're not telling me, pregnancy has thrown me off my game, but I'll figure it out," she raised an eyebrow at me as she straightened the collar on her latest Joules purchase.

"I'm fine!" I lied. I didn't know how I could expect her to buy that when I was barely convincing myself that I was 'fine'.

"Well for the record, I don't believe you. I'll find out eventually, you know I will."

"I know, no stone left unturned until you're satisfied. But you'll be a Mummy soon and that'll be the end of it, you'll be far too busy to enquire into the lives of others!" I assured her.

"You must be joking, I'm going to live vicariously through the experiences of others to give me a break from nappies, bottles, baby grows and nursery rhymes! You are going to be my conduit to the life I'm leaving behind," I laughed. "I'm serious!" I kissed her cheek and opened the door.

"Go on, before your lovely husband thinks I'm keeping you hostage," I gave Tom a wave and he saluted back.

"I'll see you soon," Kate squeezed my arm and then wobbled out to the car. I waited until they had driven off down the road and took a deep breath. If only she knew. If only she knew how desperately conflicted my emotions were with total joy at her impending motherhood and complete envy at wishing it was me.

I took a deep, steadying breath and walked back into the living room to re-join everyone. I sat next to Beth, and she placed her arm around my waist. I loved her, of this I was certain, but for me there was something missing. Olivia, Beth's daughter, was nine years old and I loved her with all my heart. She took her parents split completely in her stride and it didn't seem to affect her socially or academically. She was a complete whiz at school and her confidence had grown enormously (she was now in the school drama club, my dramatic flair being the underlying influence there). However, Olivia had a mum and a dad, and a step-mum.

There's a Mother's Day and there's a Father's Day, there's no 'Mum's Lesbian Life Partner Day'. When Beth and I first got together, we discussed the fact that she had Olivia to think about, and I've always pushed for her needs being at the forefront of everything we do. At the time I just didn't see having children of my own in my future, as I said, I was very much on the fence about parenthood. But then I fell in love, and everything changes when that happens.

"You okay?" Beth spoke in a quiet voice, and I looked down at her realising I'd been in my own little world since Kate had left. I smiled and nodded.

"I'm just tired."

"We don't have to go out tonight if you don't want to? It is a school night."

"I do want to go, besides, we can't cancel now, Gran would never forgive me, she's wanted to see this since she saw Chicago with Richard Gere singing 'razzle dazzle'."

"I still think it's a bit weird that we're going out with your mum and grandma to see a Burlesque show. She does realise that Richard Gere won't be on the stage? Or any man for that matter!"

"I think she's planning on trying out some of the moves in a bid to seduce the 'Silver Fox'," I laughed and drew Mum and Gran's attention over.

"What are you two eejits laughing at?" such a way with words.

"Nothing, Gran. We were just saying we should change and get ready to go."

"Now that's the smartest thing you've said since I got here, go on now, you're not going out looking like that."

Beth and I stood up and made our way upstairs to get changed. I knew everything would be okay. I had all that I needed, I was loved by so many people, and I was grateful for everyone who I held dear. My friends and family were the best and most supportive I could ask for. It was just getting more difficult to reconcile the thought that this could be it, this was who I was for the rest of my life. I would never be 'Mum'.

When we arrived at the theatre, I looked around at the other patrons and shared a sideways glance with Mum. There were lots of rather interesting outfits being modelled by several women (and men), which meant only one thing. More material for Gran than she could handle. We swiftly ushered her through to the bar area, which seemed to be where the more, how can I put it, discreetly dressed people, were sitting. It was a safety zone for Gran's zero filter commentary. I ordered a round of drinks and we sat down on the big comfy red chairs.

"Jesus, Mary and Joseph, I feel like I'm talking to Big Brother. Where's the feckin' cameras and Davina?" Gran laughed at herself as she disappeared into the chair. "Look at me, I'm shorter now than the day I was born!"

"Mother! Will you please watch your mouth!"

"How the feck do I do that now, Jane? Does anyone have a mirror? What's my mouth going to do? Is it part of the show tonight? I knew I'd see some lips, just didn't expect it to be my own!" I snorted and miraculously managed to swallow the mouthful of wine I had with a choke and my mum just buried her head in her hands, her face the same colour as the 'Big Brother' chairs.

As it turns out the show was very tastefully done and apart from Gran rustling a bag within two minutes of it starting to ask if anyone would like a mint humbug, she behaved very well. I saw her as she watched people walk by dressed in stockings and suspenders, corsets and basques, and she almost didn't bat an eyelid. During the interval she bumped into someone from her Zumba class (yes, she does Zumba. It's a special class for the over 60s, and she didn't appreciate when I pointed out that she was pushing it thinking she could handle a class for the over 60. It got worse when I asked if they would consider an over 80s class, I think she was prepared to disown me as a granddaughter at that point).

So, she spent the interval discussing whether or not the woman who works in the corner shop would be able to get any of those 'tassel things' and whether they had batteries in to make them twirl in circles as her boobs were too low now for her to have any control over what they do. In her words: "I'd have to send a long distance telegram from my brain to my nipples to get them to feckin' move around on my tits." The worst thing she managed to do after that was turn and ask Beth if she could get her leg up by the side of her head and whether she knew where she could get a giant martini glass from.

The drive home was short, but Gran still managed to fall asleep. Much to my mum's delight and pure enjoyment – she and Gran lived next door to each other, so we dropped them both off, arguing all the way down the path about whether it was too late to have a fry up and too early to call it breakfast. Apparently semi-naked women made Gran hungry.

Chapter 2

I am not a morning person. I am least of all a morning person on a Monday. I find it difficult to get up and get myself ready, never mind hold down a conversation. Beth is unfortunately the complete opposite. She gets up as soon as the alarm goes off (I need at least two snoozes) and then she starts talking to me straight away about work or something she wants to suggest about work or something that happened at work last week that she forgot to tell me. Her brain switches straight into work mode and I have to remind myself I have a career and a mortgage to pay that requires my attendance at my job.

I like to cling on to the weekend for as long as humanly possible. I cannot bring myself to discuss what the caretaker said about one of the cleaners, or what one of the parent helpers said to one of the other mums on the playground, or how a student on their work placement tried to tell her what to do and how she had better not do it again. I considered it successful if by eight o'clock I was clothed, had managed to do something with my hair and didn't have toothpaste round my mouth.

Beth and I worked in the same school, and we had been there for six years. She was a teaching assistant, and I was a teacher. She was actually my teaching assistant when we first got together. Not ideal circumstances, but there was literally nothing that either one of us could have done about it. We didn't plan it, we both knew it was wrong to start anything between us, and in the beginning, it was only a kiss. One brief kiss in her living room after we had been working for hours on a display for the classroom and consumed a LOT of wine. It may have been just a kiss, and we may have been a little tipsy, but we had both known it was coming. We had known for weeks; it just took one of us being brave enough to act upon it.

We would have Olivia back from her dad's after school today, and those times were always my favourite. When I could sit and talk to her about her day and help her with her homework. Or we could dance around to songs from musicals and play board games (although she always cheated). Those were the best days, and although I always had way too much work to keep on top of, I always had time for Olivia.

We had crossed paths throughout the years she had been on roll at school, but I had never taught Olivia, our relationship only strengthened once Beth and I had moved in together. We were the ones who preferred the Harry Potter books to the films and who would rather be out jumping in puddles than sitting indoors, and we often had *'don't tell mum conversations'*. I would do anything for Olivia, and I loved how much she trusted me. For most of the time, seven days a week we were a happy and 'normal' family.

My last *'don't tell Mum'* discussion with Olivia had been about how much she wanted a pet. She didn't mind what sort, but we had then spent an hour looking at puppies and kittens on the internet whilst Beth did the ironing. It was Olivia's tenth birthday in a month's time, and I was desperately and discreetly working on the pet subject, it would be the perfect gift.

"Morning Em!" I turned around to see a colleague coming towards me down the corridor.

"Morning, Lucy, good weekend?" She followed me into my classroom, and I dropped my bags onto the nearest table. A Saturday night of marking meant a heavy load on a Monday morning.

"Yeah, you know, the usual. Housework, school work, tidying up after the useless shit that sat playing on his PlayStation all weekend," she laughed. Lucy had a very rocky relationship with her boyfriend, one minute they were off, the next they were on; she was often sat in the staff room crying on a Monday morning because of another 'trial separation', which usually lasted a day or two, ready for it to all repeat a few weeks later.

"No rest for the wicked as they say," I smiled and turned on my computer, thinking that she would now leave me to get ready for the day ahead. She didn't.

"I just wanted to remind you about the Mother's Day cards," she continued. "We looked at the templates from last year and we're going for the same thing again, a flower with each child's face in the centre. That okay?"

"Yes, that sounds perfect."

"Excellent, I've got a new college student starting with me today, so I'll get her to cut us all out a set of templates and we can get them done and out of the way then," I nodded and Lucy finally left.

Mother's Day. I love my mum more than anything, and my gran (deep down I knew my mum loved Gran more than she let on too) but Mother's Day was getting harder and harder to deal with each year.

I try to blank it out as much as I can, until I have to face that it's here, that it's literally on the doorstep about to ring the doorbell and come in for a cup of tea and a garibaldi. Olivia wasn't one for making a fuss and she would never bring up the fact that it was Mother's Day, but I would have to take her to get a card and choose some token gift or another.

After I managed to push Mother's Day out of my head, I threw myself into work and kept busy until the doors opened at 8:50am. As soon as I was surrounded by the 30 children who were depending on me to keep a level head and educate them, then it was like the weight of the world had been lifted from my shoulders.

"Miss Taylor!" I liked to think of that as my superhero code name, "Miss Taylor, guess what!"

"Yes, George?"

"It's 21 days until my birthday!"

"Wow, is it really?!"

"Do you want to come to my party?" he said with a mouthful of chocolate brioche.

I smiled, beamed actually, from ear to ear. "That's very kind of you," George's mum appeared at the door and walked in, "morning." She huffed and puffed with George's lunch box, book bag and coat, as well as a replica of the same items for his little sister.

"Morning," she handed me a small white envelope and half rolled her eyes. Although, now I'm saying that I'm not actually sure how a person 'half' rolls their eyes, but if such an ability existed then that's what she did. "I had to write you one, he's not stopped pestering me all weekend," ah, she was referring to the party invitation.

"Aww, that's very sweet, thank you."

"He'll have forgotten about it by the time it's his birthday, but anything for a quiet life now."

"I completely agree, I won't mention it," I smiled, and George's mum did a full roll of her eyes and then she laughed, kissed her son goodbye and off she went.

"Miss Taylor! I went to Peppa Pig World on Saturday! Look!" I turned around to see Hannah showing me the biggest Peppa Pig I had ever seen in my life, it was supposed to be a key ring, but it looked like I could sit on its back and ride around the playground on it.

"Wow! She is great! Did you have a good time?"

"It was amazing! I went on a ride that went round and round, Mummy came on it too and then she felt sick, so we had to go and sit down in a café and Mummy was sick in a box of chips!" Hannah found this highly entertaining and giggled as she skipped to put her lunch box away.

"Miss Taylor! Look at my knee!"

"Oh my goodness, what on Earth have you been doing, Kyle?"

"I went on my big brother's quad bike, and it went really fast, and I fell off it!" it alarmed me somewhat how hyped and impressed Kyle seemed with his news, especially as I looked down and saw the big cut across his knee, the bruises on his other knee and the grazes going all the way up both arms. "Mummy thought I'd broke my arm, but I haven't, I wanted to have one of them things though so everyone could write on it."

"Trust me, Kyle, you don't want to have your arm in a cast – it's not a very sensible thing to want to happen to yourself, now come on – put your things away and settle down with your book."

I moved towards my desk and logged on to the computer to take the register as the children settled for their early morning reading session. I glanced around to see if we looked ready to start but as I took a breath to say the first name on the list, I felt a poke on my hip and looked down to see Poppy waving a piece of paper at me.

"Thank you, Poppy, is this for me?" she nodded and skipped back to her chair. It was a home-made card with a picture of a cat under a rainbow and it read the following:

Mis Taila

yoo ar ml faivrut teecha

I luv yoo

fom Poppy

All around the writing were love hearts, flowers and butterflies. I loved it when my kids did stuff like this for me at home, and I pinned it to my notice board with a few other pictures and colourings that had been given to me over the months. Then feeling incredibly lucky to be entrusted with these thirty little people's minds every day, I completed the morning register.

By lunch time I was so snowed under that I was ready for the weekend to be here again in order to do some catching up. I had a meeting with the headteacher and deputy head after school, so I was not going to be getting home anytime soon, nor returning to my scrumptiously comfy bed. I was just about to tuck into a sandwich whilst marking the spelling test we had done this morning, when my phone starting buzzing across the table. I looked at the name on the screen 'Mum'.

"Hey, Mum, everything okay?"

"No, everything is not okay, I'm at the hospital."

"What? Why? Is it Gran?" it wasn't that I suspected her of being likely to fall ill or be involved in a mishap, but the odds were high.

"Yes of course it's Gran," it was at this point I heard Gran's voice in the background.

"Give me the feckin' phone, Jane."

"Mother get back into the bed."

"I can speak for myself, I'm not a complete eejit."

"Really? Are you sure? Have you forgotten why we're here?!"

"Mum! What is going on?" I didn't mean to shout, but sometimes that was the only way to communicate with the two of them. My mum took a deep breath, and I could almost hear her slump into a chair and put her head in her hands in despair.

"Your gran has burnt her lips," I waited for more, but it didn't come.

"Pardon?"

"No, it's okay, you heard me right. She and her friend from Zumba heard from someone else that their grandson's best friend's brother said you could get high from smoking a banana skin," oh God. I didn't need to hear the rest, I knew where this was going. "So, your gran and her friend decided to give it a try…"

"No fecker told us you have to dry out the skins first!"

"Dry or wet it was the most ridiculous thing I have ever heard in my life, Mother!"

"Well a bunch of bananas is cheaper than Marijuana! Have you seen what they charge on the street for that these days? It's feckin' criminal!"

"Yes, Mother, it is!" In my head my mum was making the sign of the cross and was wishing that she had been an orphan, I felt a little sorry for her as she carried on trying to tell me about the whole incident. "Anyway, they are both very lucky that they didn't set their faces on fire, now your gran's been checked over and aside from some mild burns on her lips and singeing her moustache, she's fine."

"You cheeky little gobshite, moustache? Have you looked in a mirror lately, Jane? You look like you're going to extreme lengths to audition for a Freddie Mercury tribute with the lip line you've yourself!" I had to stifle a laugh and I knew I needed to round this up quickly.

"So, is everyone involved in the, umm, unfortunate accident, okay?" I tried to stay serious, but it was tricky. Mum sighed.

"Yes. Everyone is fine, I just thought you'd want to know."

"Absolutely I want to know, I'll call you later, let me know if there's anything I can do."

"Okay, Emily love."

"Bye Mum," I hung up and looked around the room, half wishing someone had been able to bear witness to what I had just heard. Then I burst out laughing, proper from the depths of your stomach, tears rolling down your cheeks, uncontrollable laughing. My gran. Smoked an actual real-life banana skin. Priceless.

By the time 3:15pm arrived I didn't know where the day had gone. It felt like a matter of minutes since I had welcomed my class in, and now I was seeing them out of the door. I was greeted most afternoons by a queue of parents with endless questions, not much of which regarded their child's education.

"Miss Taylor, did he go to the toilet much today? It's just that he was weeing a lot over the weekend, and I didn't know whether to take him to the doctors or not, what do you think?" I was almost certain that most parents thought that as well as being qualified to educate their child, teachers also held a PHD and could offer medical advice on a daily basis.

Next question.

"Miss Taylor, how's he been today?" I looked at the worried face of the mother stood in front of me and the small boy hiding behind her legs. Ryan. He had a few anger issues and occasionally struggled to not take them out on the other children.

"Hello, he's not been too bad in the classroom, but he did get sent out of PE," I hated relaying stories like this. His poor mother gasped with horror, so like ripping off a plaster as quickly as possible, I continued to explain. "We were playing cricket and another little boy threw the ball to Ryan, but he didn't like the way it was thrown to him, so he hit the other boy across the head with the cricket bat." I watched as Ryan slunk even further behind his mum and she turned to look at him. I wanted to add that it was a plastic bat, but I didn't think that held much consolation. It certainly hadn't consoled the boy who had the bat wrapped around his head.

"You told me you had been good today, why did you lie to me Ryan?" there was no response; I would never have expected one. "I'm really sorry Miss Taylor."

"Don't worry, you've nothing to apologise for. He said sorry eventually, he did miss out on the rest of the PE lesson, which was a shame, but we talked it through, and he's had some time out this afternoon in the sensory room, so he's been alright."

"Okay, well thank you."

"No problem, see you in the morning, bye Ryan," he gave me a sheepish look from behind his mum's leg and then ran off, his mum shouted after him and legged it to catch him up.

With all 30 children gone I turned to go back into my classroom as Olivia headed towards me down the corridor.

"Hey, Livvy," I gave her a hug and she walked into my classroom with me, "how was your day?"

"It was okay. I've got a letter about a trip in my bag. It's to Euro Disney for two nights next year, I'll be in Year 6 then, I'll definitely be old enough to go, we spend a whole day going around the Disney Park!"

"Wow! Do they need any adult helpers?" I grinned and she laughed.

"You can't go!"

"Why not?"

"Because you work here and you're not a mum of anyone who will be going," she laughed innocently and fished the letter out of her bag before standing up from the table she had temporarily parked herself on. "Is Mum in her room?" I nodded and she skipped off out the door, trailing the letter behind her. She didn't even think it warranted my reading it, school letters, school reports, information about Cub camps, trips – none of it needed bringing to my attention because I wasn't her mum.

I gathered my notebook and pen and scooted upstairs to the head's office for my meeting. I often enjoyed meetings with the leadership team, it made me feel like I was making a wider difference to the children's lives at school, beyond those in my class. But tonight's was a long meeting, and we all left the building together just before six o'clock. I was looking forward to a peaceful evening and an early night.

When I got home, Beth and Olivia had already eaten, as was quite often the case, so I zapped my dinner in the microwave for a couple of minutes and sat down at the table. It was at this point that Beth walked in.

"Hey Babe," she kissed the top of my head as I stuffed Spaghetti Bolognese in my mouth (some might say around my mouth as I was rather renowned for wearing a meal such as this one rather than eat it). "You're home late."

"Yeah," I shovelled another fork of food into my mouth.

"Did Olivia tell you about her trip?" I nodded, "she said she'd seen you before she came in this afternoon. I've text Adam," Olivia's dad, "he said that he's got to wait until Sarah gets home to discuss it with her as they're saving for the wedding," Sarah was Adam's fiancée, they had been together for almost the same amount of time as Beth and me (I had used the word 'rebound' a lot at first, but it seems to have stuck).

I could detect in her tone that Beth wasn't happy, and she verified this as she continued speaking, so I continued shovelling. "I don't know what it has to do with her, it's Adam and I that will be paying for it, it's got nothing to do with Sarah. I mean I wouldn't have asked you or felt the need to discuss it with you first, I know I want her to go."

Ouch. That stung. I paused mid-chew and Beth looked at me.

"Why do I feel like I should stop talking?" she was walking a path that I didn't want to go down. I swallowed and tried to remain nonchalant.

"I don't know what you mean, Adam wishes to discuss it with his partner and make sure that they can afford it, I don't see anything wrong with that," I looked at her as I stopped talking and she sort of nervously smirked, she knew that I didn't like how she had just cast me aside. Suddenly my appetite had gone.

"I'm her mum and Adam is her dad, and that should be all that matters."

"Some might say that Olivia is very lucky to have two sets of parents who care for and love her, who want the best for her. Who would love for her to be able to go on a school trip to Euro Disney," I scraped the rest of the meal into the bin and put my plate in the dishwasher. When I turned back around, Beth was still watching me.

"I didn't mean to upset you."

"I'm not upset."

"Well then I didn't mean to offend you."

"I'm not offended."

"Well then what are you?"

"I'm nothing, that's the whole point isn't it," it was a little below the belt, but I was hurt. Beth moved to come towards me just as Olivia walked in.

"Mum, it's Dad, he says he wants to talk to you," she handed Beth the phone and sat down at the dinner table to watch expectantly as her parents spoke. I left the room and closed the door firmly behind me.

Chapter 3

I was about to call Mum and see how Gran was, when my phone rang in my hand. It was my sister, Charlotte. She is twenty-seven, five years younger than me and married to her childhood sweetheart, Chris, with two beautiful children. We also have a younger brother, Luke, who is about to turn twenty-one. Their lives are so perfectly 'normal' and seem to have followed the exact paths that they should have, there are never any dramas (other than those that involve Gran, which we've often no choice in being dragged into).

I've often thought that the reason there is such a big gap between our ages is because my mum grew up with six brothers and sisters, and she wanted to see how she coped with each one until it was of an age where it was a little more independent before she had another one. So, as the eldest I had always felt a sense of duty to be a good role model, but as it turned out, it had been completely the other way around.

"Hi, Charlotte."

"Oh thank God you answered, have you heard about Gran?"

"Yep."

"Absolutely hilarious. I told Chris and he snorted mashed potato down his nose," she laughed. Charlotte and Chris have been together since they were fourteen years old and got married when they both turned eighteen. They now had my gorgeous niece Amy who was five, and my handsome nephew Charlie, who was three.

"I haven't had chance to tell Beth yet, but it was absolutely priceless listening to the pair of them in the hospital bickering with one another."

"I wish I could say I was shocked, but in all honesty when you weigh it up, it isn't that much of a shock at all."

"This is true. So, to what do I owe the pleasure of your call this evening?" I arranged myself comfortably on the bed to listen to more funny anecdotes regarding Amy and Charlie.

"Just checking in, Chris is bathing the kids and I used Gran as an excuse to call you and leave him to it, is that bad?"

"Not at all, he needs to pitch in with the kids, it's ingenious."

"I thought so. There is one thing I wanted to ask though. What are you going to get for Luke for his birthday?" Luke lived away at university at the minute, using his student loan to build up his Funko Pop Vinyl collection. I wasn't even sure what that meant but he was very excited last Christmas when Gran produced a 'limited edition' Skeletor figurine that I'm still not convinced he didn't take himself away to have a little cry over. He was a good lad and had a heart made of pure adorable geek.

"I don't know. Are we still going up to surprise him at the weekend? Because I'm not so sure that's a good idea," Mum had thought it would be 'nice' for the whole family to travel up to see Luke (in Sunderland, we lived in Derby, it wasn't exactly up the road for a pint of lager and a beige finger food buffet). It wasn't Mum's worst conceived plan, but it wasn't one of her best either. As soon as she realised that his birthday was the day after Mother's Day then it was absolutely the best idea she had ever had, and this meant that we all had to do exactly as we were being told.

The worst part was that Luke had no clue whatsoever that we were on our way up, and I just couldn't get the image of catching him in some sort of compromising position out of my head.

"Well, he's either going to be drunk or re-enacting the final battle from Game of Thrones with his geeky roommates."

"Or high on banana skins," we both laughed.

"Honestly, Em, what did we do to land a family like this one? Or is everyone's family like this but people just don't talk about it?"

I smiled, "oh absolutely not, we are in a very unique position to have one Mrs Nancy Byrne as the matriarch of our family. There can't possibly be other families out there like ours. Indeed, we are truly blessed."

"Blessed my arse." Charlotte paused. "Wouldn't change any of it though."

"No. Me either." I loved my sister, I worried about our brother being so far away from us, Mum and Dad tootled along, and we all most certainly worried about Gran.

"Well, I should probably go and see if a tidal wave has taken out our bathroom, either that or the kids will have drowned Chris."

"Give them a big kiss and a squidge from me."

"Will do, and call me if you think of anything to get for Luke, otherwise it's going to be money, and I don't know how much more shelf room he has for those bloody Pop things he collects!" I laughed.

"Okay. You can call Mum and check what's happening this weekend then."

"Yep, I'll have a word. Night, night Em."

"Love you, bye."

There are some nights when I get home from work when I just know that I will get a ton of work done. This was one of those nights where you get home, and you just think 'fuck it'. It'll all still be there tomorrow (you just don't remind yourself that there'll also be tomorrow's work piled on top of today's as well).

After I spoke with Charlotte I gave my brother a ring, I realised as we ended our phone call that I hadn't spoken with him in some weeks. The occasional text to check in, but not a proper conversation. Anyway, when he finally picked up, he asked if he could call me back because he was in the middle of an online Final Fantasy game with some friends! What the hell twenty-year old boys were doing playing online games and not out drinking and partying I could never figure out. For a split second I considered asking about it, then I thought better of trying to work out the debatable logic behind the choices made by a young man not long out of his teens.

I was now lying in the bath. It had ended up feeling like quite an exhausting day and I needed to cleanse it all away to have any hope of sleeping peacefully. I had lost track of time until I heard Olivia shout goodnight to me through the bathroom door, which meant it was about half past eight. I hadn't seen Beth since Olivia walked in to say her dad was on the phone, which was about two hours ago. This was now becoming one of those horrid situations where the longer it went on, the more you could dwell on what had happened and the harder it was going to be to move past it. I hated it when that happened.

I was becoming quite prune like, so I got out of the bath and put my pyjamas on. It was only a few moments later that Beth appeared upstairs and stood in the doorway of our bedroom.

"Can I come in?" she asked.

"Why on Earth are you asking me that? It's your bedroom too."

"Well, you've done all you possibly could to avoid me all night, I presumed you didn't want me anywhere near you."

"Don't be ridiculous. You had a phone call, I had a phone call, and I wanted a bath. It's as simple as that. What did Adam have to say? Is Sarah on board with the trip?" Beth nodded, "good, so that's all sorted then. I presume there's an educational aspect to the whole thing and it's not just about taking selfies with Mickey Mouse?" she laughed, and I felt the ice beginning to thaw.

"Yeah, they're going into museums and stuff the day they get there, Disneyland is the second day and then they travel back overnight, she'll be one tired grumpy girl when they get home."

"She'll be buzzing. Although, probably not as buzzing as I would be if it were me going," Beth laughed again and sat beside me on the bed.

"I am sorry. I didn't mean to make you feel like you don't matter. You do, of course you do."

"I know. Just not where parenting decisions need to be made."

"That's a bit harsh."

"Well, it's how I feel. You seem to forget that out of the four of us I'm the only one who isn't actually a parent. So I try my best, Beth. I really do," she sighed and put her arm around me. I don't like to talk about this sort of stuff because it makes me think about a conversation that I need to have with Beth that I don't want to. Purely because I do not know what the outcome of it would be and that scares me.

Sarah, Adam's fiancée, has two children, Max, fourteen and Daisy, twelve. They both live full time with the two of them and I know that Olivia gets on well with them. I liked that she now had a brother and a sister she could share secrets and laughter with, just like I had had growing up. When Beth and I first got together the subject of children never came up, and now I found myself in a 'if it's not broken don't fix it' sort of situation. Everything was so perfect in our lives, and I had no desire to turn things upside down with my feelings of longing to become a mother.

Beth is forty years old, and I turned thirty-two a couple of months ago. Beth had done the early morning get ups, the middle of the night feeds, the screaming baby that you can't figure out how to soothe, the potty training, teaching the do's and don'ts, rights and wrongs. I couldn't imagine that she would want to go through all that again. So how on earth was I supposed to tell her that right now all I could think about was experiencing all of those things for myself?

The rest of my week went by just like any other really. Don't get me wrong, no two days were ever alike – that was impossible working with five and six year olds every day, but there was no great catastrophe or major incident, and there was usually something that kept me awake over the weekend. However, at 3:15pm on Friday afternoon, I saw my class out of the door and turned back around to peace and quiet, and the joyful presence of two days to recharge before doing it all over again.

The 'secret' plans to visit Luke had been abolished as when I finally did manage to get hold of him for a real conversation, he said he knew all about it because Gran told him when he rang her to see how she was after the whole banana incident. He did very openly ask her if she had felt any effects from smoking the banana skin before her face almost went up in flames, and I won't repeat the response that he was given as quite frankly nobody should ever have to read that many expletives in one sentence.

So, Luke said that he would come down and visit all of us instead, as he hadn't been down since Christmas, and he couldn't be arsed to tidy his flat up or tell his mates to behave. His exact words were 'if you bring Gran up here then smoking banana skins with my mates around will be the least of your worries'. I was not prepared to take that risk with a woman of her age.

Everyone knew that Luke was coming down to visit apart from Mum. Nobody had had the heart to tell her that he had found out about our impending visit, and it had all gone tits up. I wasn't aware of this until she called me today asking if I thought she should pack a bathing suit for the weekend. Quite what she planned on doing with that in March, I don't know, but at that point I realised my sister had chickened out of telling her. So, it fell to me to explain the new plan. After she spent twenty minutes sobbing down the phone that her surprises never work and someone always ruins them (usually Gran), I managed to console her by suggesting we still do a surprise party of sorts and have everyone at home when he arrived. She liked this, and when I spoke to Charlotte about ten minutes after, Mum had already told her everything and of course the surprise party had then been her idea.

When I got home, I jumped in the shower right away as we had all been strictly instructed to be at Mum's for six o'clock at the very latest. Which was code for 'you need to come and help set up the buffet so don't you dare arrive as late as six'. Beth doesn't work Fridays, so she had picked Olivia up from school and taken her to visit her parents, which was the norm for the weekends we had her. It wasn't that I didn't want to go or that they didn't want to see me (although they understandably took a while to warm to the idea of Beth and I), it was just a nice opportunity for them to get together, especially if I was stuck at work.

By the time I was ready to leave there was still no sign of them and I was getting a little worried. I tried Beth's mobile and there was no answer, I tried Olivia's and I heard it ringing from her bedroom. This was not good. It was just after five o'clock and if I didn't hot foot it to my mum's within the next ten minutes, I would most likely have the door slammed in my face for being 'late'. I was about to leave a note saying I had had to leave without them when I heard the front door open. I dashed into the hallway expecting some big drama or traumatic story but was greeted by two smiling faces.

"Hey Babe," Beth kissed my cheek and I stood still, very much baffled by her casual tone. Was I in some sort of parallel universe?

"Beth, where have you been?" She stared at me for a minute and Olivia ran off upstairs, presumably and hopefully to get changed.

"At my mum and dads, you knew where we were."

"Yes, I am aware of that, but why are you so late?" She looked at her watch, as if I were not capable of working out the time and telling her she was late for myself.

"You said we were leaving for your mum and dad's at six."

"No, I said we had to be there no later than six, and that she would want a hand setting out food and stuff."

"Oh," I wasn't quite sure what I was supposed to do with an 'oh', it didn't exactly make me feel all warm and snuggly inside.

"We're going to have to go in separate cars. I need to leave now, you and Liv will have to follow."

"Oh, okay." She had a look that I knew well. She was now annoyed with my sense of urgency and the audacity of my wanting to arrive at Mum's alone. "Give us ten minutes and we could be ready though."

"No, it's not fair to rush Olivia, she said she wanted her hair doing."

"By you, not me, and you're leaving. So she can't have her hair done can she," it wasn't a question, it was a statement and I prickled at it instantly. Beth had a way sometimes of causing waves of guilt to ripple through my body, even when I had done nothing wrong. It was my turn to look at my watch now. Without another word I went up to Olivia's bedroom and French plaited her hair for her. We all left at the same time and arrived at my mum's at 6:11pm.

The house was in complete and utter chaos. Charlotte was on the phone to what I believed to be a take-away restaurant ordering pizzas, Gran was standing over her (which is hard for a woman presumably in her late eighties to mid-nineties who shrinks at least a centimetre a day, but trust me, she had a way of standing over us all when she needed to). My niece and nephew were running around trying to catch the cat, my dad was sitting reading the newspaper and my mum was crying in the kitchen. All in all, a typical Friday night in the Taylor house.

Olivia joined Amy and Charlie in a bid to stop them running through the house like Usain Bolt at the Olympics, Beth made polite conversation with my dad, and I went to see what was wrong with Mum.

"Ruined! It's all ruined! And it's all her fault!" she pointed at Gran. I didn't really need the visual clue; I could have guessed who was getting the blame.

"Mum, what's happened?"

"I didn't have time to get any food because your gran decided to go for a 'power walk' with her friend from Zumba, only they got lost!"

"I can hear you, you know!" Gran walked in and sat with us, "REMEMBER NO FECKIN PEPPERONI OR JALAPENOS, I'LL BE SHITTING THEM OUT FOR WEEKS," the shouting was directed at Charlotte on the phone. "It's not my fault my KYG lost its signal, how was I feckin' supposed to know it could do that."

"You mean GPS?"

"Same feckin' thing! Have you seen this blister?" Gran lifted her leg, surprisingly easily, and flashed a big as yet un-popped blister on the back of her foot.

"Jesus, Gran, where were you walking? Up Everest?"

"Don't give her any sympathy! She ruins everything!" Mum started crying again and I suddenly had a nauseating vision of my future. One day I would be sat in my kitchen crying and blaming my mum for everything always going wrong. It was just the natural order of life. Kill me now.

"I had to put a feckin' sanitary towel round my foot to shield the pain, it was genius; I'm sending the idea to that Lion's Den lot."

"Dragon's Den, Gran, and I really don't think anyone will buy a sanitary towel to be used as a plaster."

"Well if it wasn't for that then I'd have probably lost my foot, but does your mother care? Does she feck!" at this point I was envisioning a full-scale war breaking out across the kitchen table, but Charlotte walked in with her rational 'mum' head on and took much needed control of the situation.

"Right, the pizzas are ordered, I think we ended up with almost one of everything on the bloody menu to accommodate everyone's ridiculously picky pallets, Chris is bringing the cake, he'll be here any minute, Mum you need to go and sort your grandchildren out as they've dressed the cat up as Spiderman, Gran go and sit down in the living room and put your feet up, and Emily pour me a bloody vodka!" everybody instantly set about doing what they had been asked to do, nobody argued with Charlotte The Mum. She was very good, but then I watched her knock back what I can only guess was about a triple measure of vodka, and I suddenly realised where she got her fuel.

A short while later I wandered through the house and the picture before me now was the polar opposite to what we had arrived to. Dad was reading Charlie a story about a monster that liked to eat snot, Mum was French plaiting Amy's hair because she had seen Olivia's and wanted hers to look the same, and Beth was talking to Gran about her adventures walking the outback. She was very good at making a gentle stroll through the woodland sound like she had fought crocodiles and kangaroos, any minute now I was expecting her to use the word 'strewth'.

"So, I've got to ask, why did you even have a sanitary towel in your bag anyway?" Beth asked a somewhat intriguing question, Dad sunk further into his chair and held Charlie close, as if he was protecting him from this sordid world of women.

"I'd ran out of them thingy-me-jigs to catch your wee, you know, when you get your dribbles, I just can't keep it all in me bladder like I used to, Beth. So, I went to the loo at the park before we set off for the walk, and I got one out of them machines on the wall. Cost me a feckin' fortune, robbing bastards, but you can't put a price on your limbs, so you can't. Without it, I'd have probably lost the whole foot," Beth smirked, and I couldn't help but smile myself, not before catching my mum's eye roll, and just in the nick of time there was a knock on the door.

My dad shot out of his seat almost catapulting Charlie across the room and rushed to the door. I think he was looking for an additional male ally in his very female dominated world.

"There's my boy!" Luke was home and my mum rushed second to the door, by the time I got there my mum and dad had an arm each, and Charlie and Amy each had a leg. Luke was the normal one, the one piece of normality that our entire family could cling onto.

"Hey, sis," I smiled at him and managed to beat the groupies away so I could give him a big hug myself, then Charlotte arrived beside us and got in on the action. There was a bond between the three of us that was stronger than anything else I knew in the world, if there was one thing I would be forever grateful to my parents for it was not making me an only child.

"How was the trip?" we ushered Luke into the living room, and he sat next to Gran who planted a big sloppy kiss on his cheek. Everyone else crowded around him as if he were some sort of messiah.

"It was fine, I wasn't expecting you all to be here, it's an awesome surprise," I looked at my mum and a moment of horror flashed over her eyes. Out of nowhere, she stood up, went out of the room, came back in holding up a 'welcome home' banner she had clearly had Amy and Charlie help her with as it read: 'welcum hoam Look' and shouted 'surprise!' It wasn't your traditional surprise party entrance, but it made Mum feel better and so that was good enough for us.

Thankfully the rest of the evening passed us by without any further incident. Gran was on her best behaviour, and to be honest seemed somewhat subdued (I half wondered if my dad had slipped her something in her gin, he'd been very uncomfortable when she asked Luke if he had ever ridden 'bare back', to be quite honest I was more horrified that she knew what the term meant rather than the fact she had said it).

Charlotte and Chris left with the kids at around nine, way past their bedtime after being totally revved up by their favourite uncle. I carried Charlie out to the car asleep in my arms, he didn't even stir as I fastened him safely into his seat. I smiled to myself and looked across to the front door where Charlotte and Chris (carrying Amy in his arms) were heading out towards us. Everyone else followed out to the car and we said our goodbyes.

Mum had offered to cook Sunday dinner for us all (Mother's Day) and despite our protestations she was adamant. So, we would all see each other again before Luke had to go back to university, and my mum had had the chance to spend Saturday showing him off to the neighbours and her friends at Salsa. (Yes, my mum did Salsa, think about the gene pool she has come from and her love for a stage and an audience should not come as a surprise).

I gave Luke a big squeeze before we left, I was really happy to see him, and it felt good having everyone together. I was also very glad to be leaving as some of his old school friends were texting him, now they knew he was back in town, trying to get him to meet them in a bar to go clubbing. Luke had never been a 'clubber'. He was a gamer. Having said that, he enjoyed a good social life and so would be keen to catch up with his friends whilst he was down. Mum was trying her best to make it seem like the worst idea he could ever possibly have, but as we pulled away and Luke gave Mum a hug and a kiss on the cheek, I was pretty sure she was losing this argument.

We got home and I poured myself a glass of wine. I loved my family but as anyone who was being honest about their relatives would testify, handling your whole family sober was a big ask. The wine hit the spot and as Beth bellowed up the stairs for Olivia to get herself into bed, I curled up in the armchair and watched the beginnings of a down pour patter against the windows.

"I'm exhausted!" Beth flopped into the chair opposite and flicked the table lamp on. I screwed my eyes up and felt frustrated that the peace and darkness had been interrupted. "I didn't know where to look when your mum offered up Sunday lunch. A slightly longer break before doing all of that again would have been nice! We having a pyjama day tomorrow to make up for it?"

"What do you mean 'a break'? A break from what? Why do you want a pyjama day?"

"I just meant it's all a bit full on isn't it, you know I love them, but I do love weekends when we just get to potter around by ourselves. We've got Liv *and* your lot to contend with now."

"I wasn't aware that my family and your daughter were something that needed 'contending' with. They're not cattle that need herding into order."

"It can feel like it though!" she laughed, and I felt myself starting to get irritated. "Come on Babe, you've got to admit, a night like that would wear out the most patient of people."

"I can't say I have ever given thought to my family as being 'wearisome'," I stood up.

"Where are you going? You haven't finished your wine."

"I'm going to bed. Like you said, it's been an exhausting night." I left my words hanging and went upstairs to bed, firmly keeping my eyes closed when Beth joined me minutes later.

Chapter 4

The next morning it seemed to be that it had rained continuously through the night. Huge puddles left their imprint on the roads and pavements, and guttering was overflowing causing a cascade of water down the street. Beth was up and having breakfast before I had even stirred. I joined her in the kitchen and poured myself a coffee. I wasn't a coffee drinker as a rule, but I had struggled to sleep and already knew I was going to need caffeine to get through the day. Beth looked up at me and frowned.

"Coffee? You were very restless last night."

"Sorry, I know. I couldn't sleep. I don't know why," I replayed the conversation about my family before I had walked away from Beth last night, and then I slurped my coffee and burnt my tongue, "shit that was hot."

"It's supposed to be hot, and don't slurp," I rolled my eyes and sat down as I looked at the clock on the wall.

"What time are we expecting Liv to surface?" Beth made a sound somewhat akin to 'ppfftt' which I translated to mean 'who knows'. "I need to pop out with her when she's up and ready."

"Why?"

"Why do you think, I've been a mixture of equal parts forgetful and busy, so there are things I need to take care of," I said the last few words slowly, knowing full well that Beth knew what I was referring to.

"You don't need to do anything."

"Can we please not have this conversation every year for the rest of our lives? Tomorrow is Mother's Day, every year that we have been together I have taken Olivia to get something for you for Mother's Day. Things are no different this year, nor will they be next year, and I dare say a number of years after that," Beth pulled a face and yawned.

"If you're going out does that mean I can go back to bed?"

"I did wonder why you were up so early."

"Someone kept me awake tossing and turning, so I gave up trying to lie in," she winked, and I stuck my tongue out at her, "I don't want to go back to bed anyway, it's no fun when you're on your own," she grinned, and her eyes twinkled as she rested her gaze on me.

How could she look at me in that way as I sat in my Miss Piggy pyjamas with my hair sticking out at degrees no angle measurer could ever make sense of, with mascara under my eyes and not forgetting of course the morning breath? She moved closer to me and slid one hand around my waist and the other around my back and up to the base of my neck. A shiver of anticipation ran through my whole body as she leaned in and kissed me softly on the lips. I moved my own hands around her as she kissed me again and pulled me close. As things began to heat up, we both pulled away at the exact same time and looked at each other, then at the kitchen door. Quickly releasing our hold on one another, Olivia walked in yawning and slumped on a dining room chair.

We had quickly developed a sixth sense for when Olivia was about to enter a room and to stop any overt displays of affection. For me it was because no child wants to see their parents making public displays of affection. For Beth it was because we were two women. I wasn't making any presumptions with that, we had actually discussed it, and despite being in a relationship with a woman, Beth didn't want to thrust a lifestyle in her daughter's face that may make her 'uncomfortable'. I'd given up arguing that one out very quickly.

"What's for breakfast?" Olivia asked. I looked at Beth and she sighed, momentarily resting her head on my shoulder.

"Whatever you want, I don't know what's in the cupboards," Beth answered the question and I looked at the still half-asleep Olivia (it was more like three quarters asleep to be honest).

"I'll make us an omelette," I knew that might do the trick and Olivia lifted her head up, suddenly seeming much more alert.

"Omelette? With cheese? And ham? And peppers?" she queried. I smiled.

"With whatever you want."

"Flippin' heck, I don't get this VIP treatment on weekends when we're on our own, when have you ever made me an omelette?" Beth chuntered.

"I can do you one now?"

"No point now, I've just had a bowl of muesli."

"You had a yoghurt on it."

"Ooo, yeah, I forgot that a yoghurt was the equivalent of the working man's champagne breakfast."

"Oh, ha, ha, don't be such a baby."

"Hello?" Olivia waved, "omelette, I'm a growing girl and need feeding up," I laughed and set about making breakfast. I got chatting to Olivia about Luke's party/gathering/reunion last night and Beth left us to it. I had thought she was joking, but it seemed she really didn't want an omelette. I could only presume that she was taking herself back to bed after all.

Once Olivia and I had full bellies and enough energy to tackle the high street on a Saturday afternoon, we headed out into town. I had no idea what we were going to get for Beth, so we started with the card shops – that was the easy bit! As Olivia read through at least a dozen cards looking for the right one her eyes were drawn to a section that housed the 'you're like a mum to me' cards.

"Who are they for?"

"What?" I desperately needed to play this down.

"These ones here, how can you be 'like' a mum?" Jesus, it was getting worse. "You're either someone's mum or you're not."

"Well, sometimes some children or even adults lose their mum, and their dad might remarry or find a new partner and then she would be 'like a mum', she wouldn't be their real mum but she would do the same sort of things that a mum does – feed you, clothe you, clean up after you, give you lots of hugs and kisses," she laughed at this point and came over all embarrassed.

"Only babies get hugs and kisses off their mums, not big kids."

"Big kids like who?"

"Well Mum doesn't hug and kiss me," I paused for a second and the realisation of this truth hit me so hard I almost felt winded. "So, when Dad marries Sarah, will I have to get her one of these cards?"

"Well, I don't know, would you like to?" she shrugged at me.

"I think it should just stay as it is now."

"What do you do now?"

"Max and Daisy just put my name in their card," wow. So, all of the adults/carers/parents/people who helped to raise Olivia into this very sensible and mature young girl were recognised for playing their part in her life. Well, most of them were anyway. We moved down the stacks of cards and she finally picked one, "this one will do."

"Okay," I took it from her and headed towards the tills. Olivia waited beside me until we were served and the woman behind the counter smiled, and then she gave a little chuckle.

"You're not the first ones to come in so that you can choose a card and Mum can pay for it!" she chuckled again, and Olivia laughed.

"She's not my mum," her words tore through my heart, "but she's like a mum," and off she skipped to wait outside whilst I paid.

In the end Olivia chose a box of her mum's favourite chocolates and a new pair of slippers. She contemplated a photograph frame to put a picture of the two of them in, but she quite rightly pointed out that there weren't many photographs of just her and Beth together, which I made a mental note to rectify at some point.

When we got home Beth was watching TV, so I made us all a cup of tea and sat down at the kitchen table to kick my laptop up. If I was going to spend Sunday at my mum's, then I needed some time for schoolwork today. Beth walked into the kitchen to bring her mug in and looked at me, then she looked at the folders and papers around the table and gave me a familiar look of 'so much for a restful weekend'. I didn't respond to her, and she walked straight back out. I tried so hard to free as many of our weekends up as possible, but sometimes it was just unavoidable. I can assure you that the teaching profession is definitely one for which the phrase 'not enough hours in the day' applies to.

That night, after Olivia had gone to bed, we sat together with a glass of wine and the subject of Olivia's birthday came up.

"Any suggestions? I know that whatever I end up getting her, Adam will do one better anyway, he always does." Ever the pessimist.

"Don't be like that, we just need to think of something that will stand out more than anything else, something that can stand up on its own two or perhaps four feet…"

"Such as what? We've only got a few weeks or so, I can't believe I've been so disorganised," okay here we go, it was now or never. My mission to get Olivia a puppy was about to commence.

"Well, I do have one suggestion."

"Go on."

"What about a pet?" ease her in gently rather than just dive right in with 'puppy'. Pet was more generic and left things open for negotiation.

"A pet?"

"Yeah, you know – something she can look after, feed, play with…"

"Well, you know I'm allergic to cats," yes, I was aware of the allergy to cats. I grew up with cats my whole life and living with Beth was the only point in time I had not owned one.

"I didn't say a cat. I said a pet. Could be anything…"

"I've got it!" hallelujah! This was only ever going to work when it was her own idea. "A goldfish," I looked at her and although I'm sure I responded in adequate time, it felt like hours passed whilst I processed the word 'goldfish'.

"What is she going to do to take care of a goldfish?"

"Loads of stuff! Clean the fish tank, feed it, maybe we could get two, so they keep each other company, she'll love it. She could even keep them in her room, although we might forget to feed them when she's not here, so maybe we should keep them in the dining room or something," I couldn't listen to anymore. How had this happened?! One minute I'm gently planting the seed of a pet, preparing the ground for introducing a puppy, and the next I know we've got two goldfish living in the dining room! Good grief. I had failed miserably on this one, Olivia would be gutted.

The rest of the evening passed with Beth on her iPad looking into what you need to set up a fish tank, by the time we went up to bed, she had ordered the majority of the required supplies from Amazon and seemed rather chuffed with herself. My concern was the track record I held with looking after goldfish. I had had several as a child, and even as a teenager, but they never seemed to live very long. One even jumped out of the bowl and committed suicide – on my birthday! I used to talk to her as if she were my therapist (I say her, I've no idea how you know whether a fish is male or female, all I know is I felt a lot better talking to a female fish about conflicting issues over my sexuality than I would have if it had been a male one). I think it was perhaps my therapy sessions with the fish that sent her over the edge. Literally. Hopefully Olivia would have more luck.

Chapter 5

Mother's Day.

Olivia got up early with me and we made Beth breakfast in bed to take up with her gifts and card. She loved the presents and the card, and breakfast went down very well. We didn't really have time to hang about as we had to call in on Beth's parents, Penny and Brian, before going to my mum's for dinner. We had been strictly informed to arrive by 2 o'clock at the very latest, so we needed to get moving.

I was doing very well handling this day of celebration for mothers up and down the country, sometimes I pretended that it was more of a birthday celebration than that of having given birth. The Queen has two birthdays, so I built a world where Beth has two birthdays and that makes everything seem a little less blue. It is easier to spend the day pretending it is her birthday than remembering her, and all the other mothers, are being thanked and celebrated for taking such wonderful care of their children. I didn't want thanking for being a mum, I just wanted the privilege of the title.

Beth's parents were nice enough people, I had no issue with them whatsoever, and as I mentioned earlier, they had been exceptionally understanding of what Beth and I had 'done' to their family. Under the circumstances, they could have refused to have anything to do with me (or her to be fair, they were very angry and disappointed with Beth in the beginning). So, as we piled into the car to complete the fifteen minute drive to their home, I felt very lucky that the three of us were able to go together as a family.

We entered the house to the sound of bickering, which wasn't unusual, but you would have thought that at least for Mother's Day they could have reigned it in.

"Morning," I had to break the tension in the air, I don't think they had even noticed us walk in.

"Happy Mother's Day," Beth kissed Penny's cheek and handed over a card and a gift bag.

"Thank you, is this my toffee?" Penny laughed. The predictability of recurring gifts was something that I hated, but if it fits the bill and brings a smile to the recipient's face then who was I to argue?

"Can I get you a drink? Pop, juice, tea?" Beth's dad, Brian, kissed my cheek with his offer of a beverage and I smiled. His hearing wasn't what it used to be, but I thought he was pretty awesome, and he had a great sense of humour.

"Tea would be lovely thank you," I replied, and Beth nodded in agreement. Olivia had an orange juice and we all settled down on the sofas. Penny opened her gift, which was of course the requested toffee, as well as a voucher to go and get her nails done with her regular beautician. It entailed manicure and pedicure, which made my toes curl, in fact they curled up so tightly that no beautician would ever be able to get her hands on my toe nails. Feet should be covered at all times, it's pushing it to think it's okay to expose them just because they have a lick of nail polish on them. They're just ugly necessities. Apart from baby feet. Baby feet were just so unbelievably gorgeous and smooshy Yes, I have a made up word for the affect baby feet have on me. They're smooshy.

Beth was an only child, but when she was five years old, she had an aunt who passed away and her cousin, who was eight, came to live with Beth and her parents. There were many conflicting issues over this matter, Beth has felt for a long time that her cousin, Julie, was the daughter that her parents wished they had had. It was utter nonsense, but if ever there was someone who was going to earn a 'you're like a mum to me' card today, then it was Penny.

She and Brian raised Julie as a daughter and from what I know of the situation, she was that lovely polite, well-mannered and successful woman who any mother would be proud of. So, much of our morning consisted of listening to how busy Julie was and that she wasn't able to make it home for Mother's Day as she had a big case to prepare for (she was a solicitor and lived about an hour or so away in Northampton where she had studied for her degree – the degree was paid for by Julie's inheritance. Beth's parents had been unable to send Beth to university, another sticky topic of conversation).

We stayed for a couple of hours, and I apologised that we couldn't stay any longer as Beth sat already in the car with the engine running. My family had not really had many opportunities to get together with Beth's family, so there were rarely occasions when the two would mix. This wasn't something I liked, but Beth was adamant that this was just the way it had to be. It was probably because of Gran. I of course love her dearly, but she's got enough personality to share out with at least a dozen other people. I got into the car and Beth never said a word as we pulled off the drive and Olivia and I waved goodbye. I don't quite know why, but I had a bad feeling about how the rest of today was going to pan out.

Upon arriving at the Taylor household, Amy and Charlie were drawing pictures with chalk on the driveway and Dad was in the garage. I walked over and he half waved, half nodded at me.

"Hi, Dad, where is everyone?"

"Inside. With your mother," it was an unusually brusque greeting for my dad. I frowned but knew better than to try and probe him for more information. So, I went inside and followed the sound of voices (and crying) to the kitchen.

It was here that I discovered Charlotte, sitting with my mum and Gran at the dining table. I half expected to hear them uttering the words 'when shall we three meet again', but the presence of tears made it clear I should not make what was clearly an upsetting incident into an opportunity for literary references to Shakespeare. Gran was pouring whiskey, never a good sign. She knocked one back when everyone else was looking away and then poured herself another. I rolled my eyes and saw this as the right time to make my presence known.

"Hello," I tentatively said, "everything okay?" they all looked up at the same time and I had to do a double take as I almost thought my sister had been replaced by a scary clown with black mascara running down her face. "Crikey, Charlotte, have all of the mirrors broken in your house?" nobody smiled, I sensed that this was a little more serious than I had expected.

"He's gone, Emily, he's just… gone… left me… packed a bag… eeeeeeeiiiiiiiissssssnnnnnnnn and his lucky socks," a large portion of what she was saying turned into screeches that only cats and dogs could probably hear, between screeches there was a sniff or a sob. Then more screeching. After a beat I was able to deduce that Chris had left her.

If there was ever a shock to the system, then this was as big as they came. They were supposed to be the solid couple who I was striving to be like, I had always been so envious of how easy everything had come to Charlotte; boys, marriage, babies, and now look at us. I sat down on the spare chair and Gran poured a fourth whiskey. I should point out that we were drinking this whiskey out of my mum's best tea-cups, and that the whiskey actually belonged to my dad, and if he could see what she was doing then he would not be shy about letting us know for the fiftieth time that despite my gran's claims, the Irish did not invent whiskey, nor is she a descendant of the original John Jameson.

Luke arrived a few minutes after my fifth whiskey with a bottle of milk. He looked at the half empty whiskey bottle and shook his head with a smile.

"Well, I can see my rushing out to get milk for the tea was worth the energy."

"Your sister's husband has left her, Luke, for feck's sake have a heart and get yourself a tea-cup," Gran motioned to the emergency dining chairs that were folded and stacked in the cupboard under the stairs. Luke did as he was told and poured himself a whiskey just as my dad walked in with Beth and the kids.

"What the bloody hell is going on in here?!" everyone looked at Dad. He never raised his voice. He never swore. This was about as serious as things got for him. He looked at Luke and I realised that this put him primarily in the frame of guilt and Dad shook his head in disappointment. He picked up the whiskey bottle, took Luke's teacup and left the room again. I looked at Beth and she had a raised eyebrow over the scene before her. The kids started fussing trying to make themselves drinks and Gran started chuckling to herself.

"You took one for the team there, Luke, proud of you," she raised her glass, my mum did the same (totally arse-holed) and they clinked mid-air before knocking another one back. Happy Mother's Day!

The day disappeared at some speed. By dinner time Charlotte was trying to imagine what *she* had done wrong to make Chris leave her. Dad and Luke had taken the kids out for a McDonalds, it was the first time since Dad could remember that the males in his car outnumbered the females. He had forgiven Luke for the whiskey incident and had started to give Gran an extra watchful eye, he wasn't stupid, if he genuinely believed that Luke was the whiskey thief, he knew that he wouldn't have been acting alone.

So, we sat with mugs of gin and tonic (which I don't even like can I just add, it's vile, but we had run out of vodka, which I had made a big drama of until it became clear that I didn't really give a shit what the drink was so long as it was at least 12% alcoholic).

"Maybe Chris has gone to get me something nice for Mother's Day."

"You're not his mum," I hiccupped.

"From the kids you eejit," Charlotte morphed into a diluted version of Gran when she was drunk. Everyone was an eejit when she had had a few drinks.

"For feck's sake Charlotte, I love you my darlin', but wake up and smell the pot noodle. He's obviously gone off with another woman," we all stopped and looked at Gran. She was an alarmingly observant woman, when most of the time we presumed she wasn't really aware of what was going on.

Upon hearing the words 'another woman', Charlotte turned back into a woman who could only be heard by animals. As Mother's Days go, this was going to be up there with one of the worst of them.

We stayed at Mum and Dads through to the evening, but rather than a full Sunday roast dinner, we ended up with cheese on toast. The kids had beans with theirs, but Mum couldn't stretch to another tin, so the grown-ups had to go without, even though, as Gran pointed out, the kids had already had a McDonalds as Charlie wheeled his happy meal toy over her wrinkly knuckles. She had also ran out of tomato sauce, so there was nothing to add a little extra flavour, and I was pretty sure that the reason Mum spread so much butter over my two slices of toast was to disguise the fact that she had also ran out of cheese.

The kids were so well behaved, Amy and Charlie had clearly picked up on their mother's blood shot, tear stained eyes and constant nose blowing, but Olivia did her best to keep them entertained. I couldn't help but wonder how much Olivia had picked up on regarding what had happened, and I was then pained by guilt over the fact that she had watched this happen to her parents, she had lived it. So, she knew exactly what it was that Amy and Charlie needed to survive it.

Beth ran me a bath when we finally got home. Quite unexpected, but as I sat down on the bed and actually let myself respond to the day's events, her arms pulling me close were the only thing that could stop my sobs. Tears that rolled down my face at the thought of my sister, my happy, confident, brilliant baby sister, sat at home with two small children whose lives would never be the same again.

"They'll be okay you know," I paused for a minute to think about whether I had said my thoughts out loud, but it wasn't that. Beth just knew me well enough to know that I would be going out of my mind worrying about Charlotte.

"I hope so, she's never had to do this alone," I sniffed.

"Do what?"

"Life. Be a mum, have a job, run a house, Chris has always been there. I can't even remember life before Chris."

"I know, it will be hard for everyone, but Charlotte will be fine because she has all of you, the kids will be fine because kids are, look at Liv," I nodded. I knew that we had been so lucky with Olivia. She was amazing, I prayed that Amy and Charlie would cope as well as she did.

I sat up, wiped my eyes dry and took a deep breath. I would be fine now I had got that out of my system. Now I could be strong for Charlotte, Amy and Charlie.

Chapter 6

I woke up Monday morning with a headache and feeling like the Princess from Princess and the Pea. I had barely slept a wink and the thought of going and teaching for the day just seemed incomprehensible. I had received a call from Charlotte at 3:28am, mostly just sobs and sniffs, with an occasional question of 'why?', 'what did I do that made him not love me anymore?', 'did he never want to have kids?', 'should I have done more for him?' – The usual questions that any woman in her shoes would be asking. What I didn't have though were the answers. I wished so much that I did, but honestly, all I wanted to do was find Chris and chop his nuts off.

I arrived at work and went straight to the coffee machine in the staff kitchen. When I say kitchen, I mean what used to be a storage cupboard and now runs a one in one out policy in order to use the sink, access the fridge or make yourself a hot drink. I rarely ventured in there, too likely to bump into someone and have to make conversation, and quite frankly I couldn't be arsed with the effort on a day that I wasn't slightly hungover, never mind when I was.

As I hid back in my own classroom, I tried to turn thoughts to the day ahead. My job was a most welcome distraction from the weekend I had had. Beth had been great and was at her most supportive, which must have been hard for her under the circumstances. I was very aware of the old wounds this could potentially open for her.

I was just about to pick up today's lesson plans when my phone buzzed in my pocket. It was Charlotte.

"Hello?"

"Em, he rang me."

"Chris?"

"Yes, he wants to meet for dinner tonight, could you please have the kids for me? I'd ask Mum but I know she'd just sit and look at them and cry all night at the thought of her poor abandoned daughter and fatherless grandchildren, and Gran would just try and ply them with drink."

"Of course I'll have them. Do you want me to pick them up from school?"

"No, that's okay. I can do that, I'll give them an early tea and then bring them over. Chris said to meet him at the house at about six, so can I drop them off around half five?"

"Yeah, that's no problem."

"Thank you so much," I could hear the optimistic hope in Charlotte's voice, and I was so nervous for her.

"Did he say why he wants to meet with you?"

"No. He just said we need to talk. What do you think it could be? Jesus, Em, all I can think is he's coming home. It's been one feckin' night and all I want is for him to come home."

"I know honey; just don't go into it with any expectations, okay? Promise me?"

"Okay. Thanks Em, love you."

"Love you too, see you later," she hung up the phone and I could see her now and knew how her day would pan out.

She wasn't at work (she was an estate agent and did very well for herself selling properties in the part of town that Gran referred to as where the 'la dee, feck dee da' people lived. Basically, they earned enough money to buy houses that were of six figures in price, which is nothing unreasonable I hear you say, but the first digit never began with anything smaller than a four, so you get the picture). Charlotte would spend the day tidying the house, making it spotless. She would drop Charlie off at nursery after lunch and the afternoon would be dedicated to making herself look her absolute best. Hair, make-up, outfit – the works. All for a man who had walked out on his wife and kids on Mother's Day, with no explanation or indication he would return. My heart ached for Charlotte and the kids, I would be saying a lot of prayers for them today, and I just hoped that someone would be listening to them.

When the hustle and bustle of the day began and I was surrounded by my class, it was easier than I thought to face the day and allow school to distract me from the worry I felt inside. I was confronted with a child arriving at my door in a wheelchair at half past eight in the morning, which was something I had never had to deal with before! He had kicked a door over the weekend and broken his toe, but as his brain and mouth were in perfect working order, he was wheeled in to join his friends. I can't deny I enjoyed doing a few wheelies and speeding across the playground with him pretending we were on a fairground ride at break time.

At the end of the day, I was seeing the children out to their parents and was greeted by Luke at the door.

"What on earth are you doing here?" he kissed my cheek and the children giggled, "he's my brother, you silly bananas," they laughed again, and Luke stepped aside whilst the children made their way out. Once all but one of them had gone we stepped back inside the classroom, the remaining child obviously still with me – I didn't just abandon her on the playground or send her off to hitch-hike her way home.

"Happy birthday Baby Brother," I gave him a hug and he sat down.

"Thanks, and thanks for the card and money."

"You're welcome. So, to what do I owe this pleasure on your birthday of all days? Surely there are warlocks and quests that need completing? Or dare I say bars calling your name for entertainment until the early hours?"

"Ha! Don't mock the world of gaming, Emily. Some of the lads called, but I didn't really fancy it. You want some company with the kids tonight?"

"Turning down gaming, alcohol AND offering to help with babysitting? Are you having a very early midlife crisis?" he pulled a 'whatever' face and I laughed. "I thought you were going back to Sunderland today anyway?"

"Yeah, I couldn't be bothered. I'm only missing independent studies, I can catch up with it later in the week."

"Is the key word in that not the 'studies' part? So, when do you intend on going back?"

"Bloody hell, you sound like Mum," Luke groaned, and I gave him a playful jab in the arm.

"My dad says my mummy sounds like her mum. He says it when she shouts at him to clean the mud up off his football boots and to not leave his socks and pants on the bathroom floor. Mummy just stares at him, and he says she looks like an angry squirrel and then she says if it wasn't for this angry squirrel he wouldn't be able to afford the money to buy his football boots and pay his subs every week anyway, so then Dad says something in a different language and tidies his stuff up," Luke and I turned to the little girl sitting a few feet away as she stared up innocently at us, casually swinging her legs as she perched on the table. She was one step away from asking if we wanted a shot of tequila and cheesy chips before getting a taxi home.

"Your dad speaks a different language? That's pretty cool, what language is it?" Luke's enquiry made it blatantly obvious that he didn't listen to these little anecdotes on a daily basis. He was genuinely interested in what this little girl had to say to him. It was a pity he was more interested in languages now than when he had studied one himself at school.

"I don't know what language it is, but he uses the words bastard and shit a lot, and Mummy says I am not to use those words because they're like a different language that children can't understand. So, I don't," Luke stifled a laugh and looked at me. I shrugged my shoulders. Same shit, different day. Looks like I'm multi-lingual too.

"So can I come and lend a hand or not?" Luke shifted his awkwardness away from the tiny stranger before him to kids that he was actually related to.

"Of course!" I laughed, "You don't have to ask, you're welcome any time. How did you know I'd got the kids anyway?"

"Mum. Apparently she called round to see Charlotte and let herself in. Charlotte was giving herself a bikini wax in the bathroom and was wearing a bra with nipple holes in when Mum found her. Needless to say, Mum has been praying for most of the afternoon for her daughter's soul and the sanity of her grandchildren." I laughed and we both turned to the child in my class still with us.

"What's a bikini wax?" she asked...

Luke came home with me, and we walked through the door to an empty house. This probably meant that Beth was food shopping. When she was AWOL, she usually reappeared with bags from the local supermarket. I had let her know that the kids were coming over, so maybe she was out buying snacks and sweets. I shoved some chips and some sort of chicken in bread crumbs type thing in the oven and opened a tin of spaghetti hoops.

"Wow, Em, you didn't fall from the same cookery tree as most of the Taylor women did you," it wasn't a question and it earned Luke a second jab in the arm.

"You don't have to eat it, I could just make you sit on a chair and watch me eat."

"I suppose it's better than going hungry," he eyed up the empty boxes and put the kettle on, "won't Beth be eating with us?"

"Yeah, I'll save her some," Luke processed my answer and then frowned.

"Is that all the chips you've got?"

"Luke!"

"Okay! I get it, shut up or go hungry. I'm only here to be able to play board games without it being weirdly childish. I've bought Frustration and the Game of Life!" I picked up the two game boxes and laughed.

"These are from when we were kids."

"Yep. I fetched them out of the loft at home. Although the dice from Monopoly is in the Frustration box because the dome in the middle still doesn't work from when you threw it at the wall when all of your pieces got sent back to the start."

"Everyone was ganging up on me and purposefully landing on my spaces!"

"Have you tried rolling a number 'on purpose' in a Frustration dome? Why the bloody hell do you think it takes so long for all the pieces to come out in the first place, that bastard elusive '6'. So much power. Nobody was ganging up on you."

"That's beside the point. Anyway, you were all mocking me and taking the piss. I was only a kid."

"You were twenty-five, Em."

"Bugger off! No I wasn't!"

"You just tell yourself whatever you need to. But you're explaining to the kids why the dome doesn't work."

"Whatever," this time Luke gave me a jab in the arm, but he then ran as far away and as fast as he could. Well, to the other side of the room. "You'll be squealing like a girl next, make the feckin' tea," he grinned and obviously, did as he was told.

When Charlotte arrived to drop Charlie and Amy off it was exactly as I had feared. She walked down the drive like Bambi, staggering in a pair of heels that I had no clue how she had managed to drive in. Her dress was showing more cleavage than a woman openly breastfeeding her baby and her hair was loose around her face, full of bouncy curls. She looked amazing, but I had hoped and prayed she wouldn't get lost in thinking that this was the night for things to be made right between her and Chris. I just had a horrid feeling in my gut, and I couldn't shake it.

Luke told me I was being paranoid and not to worry so much. He also used the words "she's a grown woman and she knows what she's doing". What my foolish brother didn't realise was she was a grown woman with a broken heart. And those are the most reckless kind. Full of irrational thoughts and emotions. I wished I could go with her, but that was a ridiculous idea. I just had to trust she would be okay. It was going to be a long night.

Beth had indeed been shopping, but there were no goodies for the kids, just boring household things and some stuff for school. Yawn. We played Frustration (Beth watched as for those of you who are unfamiliar with the game, Frustration is a game for four players). I didn't win, Charlie did, he had a lot of help from Luke, and it had pretty much turned into a game of girls versus boys. Amy sulked for about twenty minutes until Luke offered to make everyone hot chocolate and marshmallows. We didn't have any marshmallows, so it turned into hot chocolate and Haribo sweets (which were in the shape of spiders and cobwebs, leftovers from Halloween), which was an interesting combination that the kids found most amusing.

I watched them play with Luke as he rolled around the carpet giving piggy back rides and having tickle battles. He was a natural with kids, he always had been, he didn't run away from babies and toddlers like most boys. He had doted on Amy and Charlie from the second they were born and had always showered them with hugs and kisses.

I went to wash up the mugs from the hot chocolate and Amy followed me into the kitchen.

"Auntie Em?"

"Yes, sweet pea?"

"Where has Daddy gone?" my hands stopped dead in the bowl of hot water, I hoped the fact they were submerged meant my reaction went unnoticed.

"He's at home with Mummy right now, sweetie."

"Why did Mummy dress up for him tonight? I know she thinks that I don't know why we're here, but I do. I know Daddy is there. Is he there to come home? Are they making up? Jack Tipson in my class at school says that when grown-ups fight, they have to make up with each other and that they have to do it on their own in a special grown up way that's a secret. He said he hears his Mummy and Daddy making up in bed at night sometimes if he wakes up because he's wet the bed. Are Mummy and Daddy making up now? Is that why we're here?" I smiled at my beautiful innocent niece and dried my hands, then we moved to the dining table, and I sat her on my lap.

"Sometimes grown-ups do things or say things and they don't really think about what it will make other grown-ups feel, sometimes we upset each other and do silly things before thinking it through."

"That's silly, Miss Forest says you should always think about other people before you say or do something that might upset them."

"And Miss Forest is absolutely right. It's just that grown-ups are sometimes forgetful, and they don't remember to think before they speak and then it's too late. They've upset the other grown-up and then they have to talk about things to decide how to make them better."

"So are Mummy and Daddy talking about things so that they'll be better than they were before?" I paused and didn't know how deep I should take my line of enquiry. I didn't want to pry into my sister's personal life, but then I didn't want her alone dealing with a situation that I could be helping with.

"What do you mean sweetie? What was it like before?" Amy gave me a look that said she didn't know if she was supposed to talk about it, but I think her own worries over what was happening to her life overtook any warning to keep quiet about things she had seen or heard.

"Mummy and Daddy were shouting a lot. Daddy lost his job," this was new information. Chris had worked for a landscape gardening company and had been with them pretty much since he left school, he trained with them and had thought it was a job for life. Evidently not. "Mummy kept telling him he had to get a new one or we wouldn't be able to live in our house anymore. Daddy was grumpy and started to go out all the time, but he never told Mummy where he was going. Miss Forest says you should never go anywhere without telling a grown-up where you are going first. But then Daddy came home one day, and we went to McDonalds for dinner because he had got a new job, Mummy was excited and then he said he was working at 'B Three'," B Three was a club in town. I say a club. I mean a shit hole of an establishment owned by three sleazy brothers, hence B (brothers) Three. It was regularly raided for drugs and was known for having women solicit themselves inside. It was a vile place, and I couldn't quite believe that Chris would lower himself, no matter how desperate for a job.

"Did Mummy and Daddy argue over Daddy's new job?" Amy nodded and then threw her arms around my neck.

"Can we stay here with you? I don't want to hear Mummy and Daddy argue again," I gave her a tight squeeze and kissed her head.

"My darling little Amy, you can stay with me any time that you want, but I think tonight your mummy would like lots and lots of cuddles from you and Charlie. Do you think you can do that?"

"Will she be sad because of Daddy? Daddy makes Mummy cry," I sighed and didn't really know how to respond to that one without making Chris sounds like the disappointing let-down he was proving to be.

"Sometimes we make the people that we love the most cry. I bet you sometimes make Charlie cry don't you?" she nodded.

"Sometimes I want to play with his toys and then if I need to go to the toilet, I hide them until I come back. He doesn't like that."

"See! But you love him don't you?" Amy thought about this carefully for a few seconds and nodded.

"He gives me his peas and carrots when Mummy isn't looking. I love peas and carrots. And I give Charlie my tomatoes, Miss Forest says we make a good team," she smiled to herself and looked up at me. "I don't like it when Mummy cries, will she stop if Daddy comes back?"

"I think that with you and Charlie there to look after each other and make everything better, Mummy will stop crying. And I tell you what, sometimes grown-ups cry because they're happy. So, if you see Mummy cry over the next few weeks then I bet it'll be because she is soooooo happy that she has you and your brother, because she loves you both so very much."

"Will Daddy come back?"

"I don't know sweetie, but they both love you and that's what you need to remember," I gave her another kiss and a hug and then she jumped off my knee.

"I'm going to go and see if I can put my hair bobble in Charlie's hair. Sometimes he lets me do pigtails!" she dashed off into the living room and I took a deep breath as I wiped a stray tear from my eye. Just then Beth walked in and kissed me softly.

"You were brilliant with her," she kissed me again and then put the kettle on. Luckily the sound of the boiling water helped to mask the sound of the small cries I let out as tears slipped slowly down my face.

At nine o'clock I got a text from Charlotte asking if I could bring the kids home as she had had too much wine. Crap. There was no mention over whether she was alone or not and I didn't ask. I just quickly replied to say I would bring them straight away. They had both fallen fast asleep on the sofa and I was tempted to say they could have stayed the night, but I meant what I said to Amy earlier – she and her brother were the key to bringing a smile to their mum's face, I wasn't going to take that away from her.

I carried Charlie out and fastened him into the car, Amy had woken momentarily and managed to walk out herself, but as soon as she was in her seat, she was fast off again. I stood watching them both for a few seconds and smiled. I wanted this so much. To look at little faces that my body had so cleverly grown and know that I was doing a good job looking after them and teaching them about life. I wanted this more than anything in the world.

"Have you told her yet?" I turned around to see Luke standing behind me. Had I been talking out loud?

"Told who, what?" I asked and Luke paused before answering.

"Have you told Beth that you want a baby?" my breath caught in my throat and I almost gasped that he had been able to see into my head like that.

"Why on earth would you say that?" I tried to brush it off but the fact he had even brought the subject up and my totally 'gave it all away' reaction meant that he knew he had hit a nerve.

"My dear, dear Emily, you know you're my favourite sister," we both laughed, "so don't pretend that I don't know you better than you know yourself. When Charlotte used to steal your clothes and make-up and bring boys back into your bedroom, who was there for you when you needed a masculine saviour?" I laughed and Luke feigned being hurt. With a role of my eyes (just like Mum) I fed my baby brother's ego.

"My dear, dear Luke, you know you're my favourite brother," he laughed and jabbed me in the arm, "you do know me incredibly well, I'll give you that, but what you just asked me stays between you, me, the moon and the stars. Okay?" he looked at me and I saw a glimmer of sadness flash across his eyes.

"You can't pretend, Em. It's not being honest with Beth or yourself. I can't believe Charlotte hasn't had this conversation with you, seeing you with Amy and Charlie."

"It's different, they're her children, so all she sees when she looks at them is how much she loves them and what they mean to her, nobody else comes into the equation. When someone else shows love and affection towards your child it's just a pat on the back or a 'well done', affirmation that they brought a beautiful and perfect little person into the world. That's why Charlotte has never said anything, because she's a parent, and we're not. She sees my love for her children because she made them, not because I want to be able to make my own." I turned to look at Charlie, still fast off, and Luke put his arms around me.

"Well, for what it's worth, you'd be an awesome mum, anyone can see that. Some people were born to nurture and help things to grow, you're one of those people, Em. Don't sacrifice something so important, the right woman wouldn't want you to," I turned to respond to what Luke had just implied but Beth came out and hovered in the doorway. Luke kissed the kids goodbye and went back inside, I did the same and then got into the car with Luke's words rattling around in my head.

When I got to Charlotte's she opened the door in her pyjamas and scooped Charlie out of my arms as Amy managed to somehow walk inside pretty much with her eyes closed. I waited whilst she put them both to bed and then she came back to me as I stood in the kitchen. I had my arms folded as I leaned against the kitchen units, I think I was trying to protect myself from the inevitable.

"Has he gone?" I asked the question and Charlotte nodded.

"I can't do this tonight, Em, thank you so much for having the kids."

"Any time. Do you want me to go?" she nodded. She looked worn out. I gave her a big hug and a kiss, and she saw me to the door. "I'll come round after work tomorrow, okay?" she nodded again, and I was desperate to stay with her. I couldn't though. If he was gone, then this was her trying to get used to that fact. Her husband, the father of her children was never coming home.

I didn't get much sleep that night. I couldn't get Luke's words out of my head. Everyone had always said that there was no question over the match of Beth and I, that we were meant to be, and our love was built to last. You name the cliché, and somebody had at some point in the last four years fired it at us.

I had always believed that and felt it from the tips of my toes to the top of my head, but Luke suggested that he didn't think that anymore. That the 'right woman' wouldn't do anything other than encourage my growing need to have a child of my own. If the right woman wouldn't expect that to change or go away, and it turned out that Beth couldn't support me, Luke was saying that she wasn't the right woman for me. What was I supposed to do with that information? I knew one thing for sure, I was never going to find out staring at the bedroom ceiling, so I looked for answers in the bottom of a big mug of hot chocolate and listened to the rain patter down against the kitchen windows instead.

Chapter 7

The next day passed me by in a complete blur. The only point in which I felt like I was actually living in the moment was when a child in another class was caught trying to pee up the wall. When asked what he was doing, he quite honestly declared he was 'peeing up the wall'. He claimed that he wanted to see what it was like because his dog did it when he took it for a walk with his dad. I managed to deal with the incident without any further attention being drawn to him, but whenever anyone passed my classroom door for the rest of the day, all you heard was little bits of conversation such as: "like a dog?", "up the wall?" and "at least he wasn't barking." Lucy stuck her head in the door laughing at the end of the day.

"I've just told his mum," pee up the wall boy was in her class, "she was mortified, but the best bit was when she asked him what he was thinking, and he then announced that he'd watched his dad do it outside their house one night when he came home from the pub drunk!" Lucy continued to laugh and when I gave her a half-hearted laugh back, she parked herself on a chair in the classroom. "So, you've been quiet today. Everything okay?"

I sighed. "Not really," I replied.

"Anything I can do to help?" I shook my head and continued to pack up my things. I was eager to get to Charlotte's house and make sure she was okay. "Well, you know where I am if you need anything," she gave my shoulder a squeeze and left. I picked up my bags and headed out.

As I unlocked the car and got inside a call came through on the Bluetooth as I pulled out of the school car park.

"Emily?"

"Tom?"

"Oh God, Kate!

"Tom! Is everything okay?"

"Yeah, I mean – I think so, I'm at the hospital, we think Kate's gone into labour."

"Oh wow! That's so exciting! Do you need anything?"

"The last nine months back, would be good, it's all happened so fast! I'm a little nervous, Em. Any chance you can get here?" I held my breath for a second and I looked at the clock.

Charlotte would be picking up Amy up from school, Charlie always made them stop at the park behind the school field for at least half an hour after they had collected her. That gave me maybe an hour. The hospital was about fifteen minutes away. I could check in on Kate and Tom and then go to see Charlotte. Easy. I called Beth to fill her in on what was happening, she wasn't entirely pleased with my dropping everything to go to the hospital, as this meant I would be later arriving at Charlotte's and later home. This could be a big no-no sometimes, Beth liked to be my first thought when it came to how I spent every spare moment of my time, but I wasn't about to abandon my friends or my sister when they all needed me. I had a plan, and I was going to stick to it.

When I arrived at the hospital, Tom was pacing the floor with his mobile phone attached to his ear. The look of relief on his face when I walked towards him was as if I had just paid his mortgage off. He gave me a big hug, one of those hugs that you give to someone but really the hug is entirely for your own benefit. I smiled when he finally let me free, and we sat down on the chairs in the waiting area. It was at this point I noticed he still had his phone up to his ear, but he hadn't spoken a word. I nodded towards it, and he rolled his eyes before lowering it slightly.

"It's my bloody mother. Just because she had four kids and is already a grandma to three boys, she thinks that she can talk me through the labour. Honest to God Em, I've almost passed out twice from her describing the delivery, and what the bloody hell is an afterbirth?!" I couldn't help a small stifled laugh as I took the phone from him. Clearing my throat, I addressed the situation.

"Hello, this is Nurse Florence, I'm afraid I have had to remove the mobile phone from your son as the use of mobile phones and any other technological devices is strictly prohibited on the maternity ward. I'm sure he will update you when there is any news. Thank you, goodbye," I hung up the phone and gave it back to Tom. He grinned from ear to ear.

"I bloody love you," he gave me another squeeze and then an actual nurse approached the two of us.

"Mr. Richards?" we both stood up and Tom nodded nervously, "your wife is asking for you."

"Can I see her?" the nurse looked at me and smiled.

"Are you family?"

"Yes, she is," Tom answered before I had even registered the question. The nurse, or I suppose I should say midwife, led us down a corridor and we turned into a room on the right where Kate was wearing a hole in the floor.

"Em!" she waddled and gave me a hug and then continued pacing.

"How are you doing sweetie?" she looked at me as if I was asking whether she had got wet in the rain.

"I swear if this baby doesn't show soon, I am going home, and it can just live up there until it's ready to get married and have kids of its own!" I looked over to Tom and he blew out a very big sigh.

"How long have you guys been here?"

"Her waters broke just after midnight, we came straight to the hospital, but they sent us home after examining her and being here a couple of hours. We came back at eight o'clock because the contractions were only a couple of minutes apart, but they keep saying she's only four centimetres diluted," I laughed and rubbed Kate's back as she doubled over at the edge of the bed with another contraction.

"I think you mean dilated, Tom."

"Yeah, that's the one. Sorry. It's been a long day," Kate looked up and threw literal daggers at him with her eyes.

"Oh, I'm sorry honey, are you tired? Do you want to get your head down for an hour whilst I try and push YOUR child out of MY VAGINA?! The size compatibility of which is non-existent and completely incomprehensible!" I looked at Tom and I could see how exhausted he was, they both were.

"Tom, why don't you go and get you and me a cup of tea, I'll stay with Kate."

"Are... are you sure?"

"Absolutely, go on," he didn't even look at Kate, I think he was afraid of what might be said if he made eye contact. He bolted through the door, and I helped Kate lie down on the bed. "Is there anything I can do sweetie?"

"Have this baby for me?" I smiled.

"I would if I could, believe me," Kate looked up at me and realisation washed over her face. She finally saw what I had been trying to hide from her for the last nine months. Shit.

I was busted, I could see it in her eyes, and I could see how stupid she felt that she hadn't figured it out sooner. As she started to speak another contraction stopped her and she growled out through the pain.

"Oh God I need to push this thing out of me right now!" I gave her hand a squeeze just as the midwife came back in. "Please, I need to push, I need to get it out," the midwife laughed a friendly and supportive little chuckle and slapped on some medical gloves.

"Let's have a little look at you then, shall we?" Kate had an examination and very quickly the midwife was pushing the buzzer up by Kate's head on the bed.

"Is everything okay?"

"Yes dear, you were right, baby is ready to say hello!" I looked at Kate and she burst into tears.

"Where's Tom gone? I need Tom!" Kate's words didn't actually come out that clear, I managed to translate the howled vowel and consonant sounds to decipher that she was asking for her husband. Quite right as she was about to give birth to their first child. I kissed her hand and told her I would go and find him.

As I ran down the corridor frantically trying to remember which direction the tea machine had been in, I crashed into Tom and his two cups of tea as he was heading back towards the delivery room.

"Oh God, Tom I'm so sorry, are you okay?" he had tears in his eyes, and I knew he was trying to remain manly and in control. "The baby's coming, you need to get in there," he looked at me and suddenly the third degree burns across his chest were the last thing on his mind as he raced back in Kate's direction. I followed at a more casual speed and took a seat in the waiting room, nervously awaiting the news of baby Richards's safe arrival.

It was quite a surreal experience, sitting and waiting for a baby to be born. I hadn't been at the hospital for Amy and Charlie's births but had visited soon after in both cases. As my nerves started to get the better of me now, I soon realised that it wasn't just anxiousness for Kate, it was my longing to be on the other side of the waiting. To be the one that had a waiting room full of people on tenterhooks to hear that my baby had arrived safely. And I couldn't help but let the niggle grow that that day may never come.

I could hear babies letting out their confused first cries, thrust into the world with no idea what was in store for them or why they were no longer safely tucked up inside their mummies. An involuntary hand moved to my own belly as I considered for a moment how it would feel to have a little life starting inside there, those first flutters that I had only ever experienced from the outside.

My hand suddenly felt wet, and I looked down before realising I was crying. Wiping the tears away, I took a deep breath and gave myself a quiet talking to. I wasn't here to feel sorry for myself, I was here to support Kate and Tom, my own potentially life-changing needs could wait.

"It's a girl!!!" Tom shot out of the delivery room door with his arms in the air, "I'm a daddy!! 8lb 8oz! Christ… Em… I'm a father…" I jumped up and threw my arms around him.

"Congratulations!" I kissed his cheek and as we parted, he had a little tear rolling down his face.

"She's beautiful, Em, she's just lying there on Kate, like the best magic trick ever, one second she wasn't there and the next she was."

"Abracadabra?" he looked at me and a smile spread further across his face than I knew was humanly possible.

"Yeah, abracadabra. Come on, come and meet her," I smiled through a happy little laugh, and we walked together back to Kate.

Tom opened the door and there she was. My best friend and her beautiful daughter staring up into her mummy's eyes. I cried instantly and walked over to them, Kate looked euphoric, as she beamed at me before holding out her little girl towards my arms. I took her gently and stood for a second not knowing what to do. The only way I could describe the feeling I had was like being star-struck. Like meeting your all time idol, the hero of your childhood or the person you always looked up to and wanted to be. And not quite knowing what to say or what to do because it didn't feel quite real, and the next morning you wake up and you think did that really happen? I was star-struck by this tiny bundle of life in my hands, because she represented my beautiful dream.

Chapter 8

When I pulled up outside Charlotte's house it was almost seven o'clock. My evening was not running on time and my schedule was completely out of the window. I had called Beth and filled her in on baby Richards arrival (there was no name yet), and luckily her joy and words of happiness were able to overcome any feeling of resentment that I was not yet home. She did ask if I was coming straight home from the hospital, and I said that I was still going to call in on Charlotte first. The line went quiet before a little sigh could be heard on Beth's end and I knew she didn't understand my need to check in on her. In the same way that I didn't understand why she couldn't accept I needed to make sure that my sister was okay, nor why she didn't want me to make sure Charlotte was okay for her own peace of mind and not just mine.

We stayed on the line for probably another ten seconds in that silence, which felt more like ten minutes, and then I announced I had pulled up outside of Charlotte's house. Beth said bye, I said I loved her, and she was the first to hang up. I didn't have the space in my head right now to worry about any of that. I would deal with it when I got home.

Amy opened the front door and jumped up into my arms. I could hear Charlie crying upstairs and I could see a shadow move across the kitchen down the hallway.

"Hey sweet pea, where's Mummy?"

"She's in the kitchen, she said she can't stand listening to Charlie crying. He wants Daddy and she said Daddy is never coming home," Amy wiped away a tear as it slid down her face, clearly not the first as I glimpsed her blotchy cheeks. She buried her head in my shoulder, "she said he doesn't love any of us and we won't ever see him ever, ever again. Is that true Auntie Em? Has Daddy gone forever?" I put Amy down and closed the front door behind me. Taking her hand, we went upstairs, and I found Charlie stood in his bedroom wearing nothing but a pair of wet pants and a face covered in tears and snot. He was a lost and confused little boy, and this visit was going to take longer than I thought.

Forty-five minutes later Luke arrived, and Mum and Gran followed in mum's car. I opened the front door and ushered them into the living room. Amy and Charlie were now showered and in their pyjamas, watching Frozen in Mummy's bed with the big telly. Mum was frantically looking around for Charlotte, and Luke sat down.

"How bad is she?" he asked.

"If I didn't know any better, I'd say she was behaving as if Chris had died. Maybe it would be better if he had."

"Emily! Don't speak like that! I did not raise you to wish people dead," even when faced with a family crisis my mother couldn't hear anyone spoken badly of. She probably would have been a character witness for Hitler given half the chance.

"No, Jane. You just raised your children to marry their childhood sweetheart when they found themselves in 'trouble' and you couldn't bear the thought of them tainting the good 'Taylor' name!" everyone turned and looked at Gran.

Nobody had noticed that she didn't come into the room right away, and she now entered with an arm guiding Charlotte to join us, sharing this revelation as she did so. I looked at my mum, she had turned a pale grey in her complexion and was sitting on the chair nearest the window.

"What on earth are you talking about?" I asked, "Amy is only five, Charlotte didn't have children until she and Chris had been married for nearly six years, Gran you must be confusing them with someone else."

"I'm confusing nothing. Look at your mother. She knows. She knows all about her darling son-in-law, what sort of man he really was! I'm not standing here and pretending that he was some feckin' saint who Charlotte and those beautiful children are at a loss for not having around. Good riddance! Everyone knows it! The dirty bastard," I was more confused than ever, and I caught Luke's eye as he shrugged his shoulders and sighed. Without speaking he nodded his head up and made his exit. He was going to check on the kids. Luke didn't like conflict and as much as he was wholly committed to being there for us all and helping in any way he could, he would do just fine by hearing all of this when it wasn't being screamed and slung about in accusatory tones.

I sat down and practically pulled Gran beside me, Charlotte stayed standing on the other side of the room.

"Will someone please explain what is going on?" I looked from Mum to Gran and then back again. Silence had never seemed so loud. The light from the street lamps was casting an orange tint over Mum's face and she had never seemed so alien to me.

"I was pregnant," I looked at Charlotte, her voice making me jump as it suddenly filled the room. "When I was sixteen. I was pregnant. Mum said the right thing to do was for us to get married. So, we did. Right away. It was at the registry office, only Mum and Dad came, and Chris's dad, his mum refused to come. She's still an ignorant bitch even after all these years. We didn't tell anyone about the wedding or the pregnancy straight away. And then I miscarried," tears streamed silently down Charlotte's face as she continued to relive this part of her life that for all I knew I may as well have been watching an episode of Eastenders for any knowledge I had of the story. "We decided to stay together and stay married, we loved each other. But Chris was too young for that sort of commitment. He had oats to sew. And boy did he sew them. But then we turned eighteen and decided we were grown up enough to do things properly, so he proposed, and we did it all the way it should have been done in the first place. But the thing is, there were other women over the years. And Gran's anger, her frustration is that Mum knew. Mum knew what Chris was doing and she didn't tell me. She didn't stop me from making a life with him, from having his children only for him to go and break all of our hearts. She just watched it all play out, like an episode of Coronation Street." Another soap opera reference, the Taylor women clearly needed to get out more.

I looked at my mum and she just stayed with her back to the room, staring out of the window. Gran was sat with her lips pursed in an 'I told you so, but you all thought I was talking shite' kind of way. Charlotte didn't move or say anything more. She just stood there, broken.

"So," I began to speak and the break in the silence made even me jump, "have you known about his behaviour all along?" I looked to Charlotte. "I mean, Chris left you, you didn't throw him out because of his extra-marital affairs. What happened?" Charlotte looked back at me, and I could see in her eyes she was replaying something in her mind, the moment she knew that her husband was not the man that he had promised to be.

"When Chris was late coming over to Mum and Dad's for Luke's birthday. He was with one of them then, "one of them? Jesus Christ. My mother made the sign of the cross and dropped her head. She might have known what Chris was like, but I couldn't see how she could possibly have known his every little move with these women, it just didn't make sense. "I called him to see where he was, and *she* answered his phone."

"The feckin' dirty whore, she knew exactly what she was doing answering that call, I'll have her up against the dried fruit when I see her in Tesco, she doesn't mess with the women in this family and not find herself choking to death on some dried coconut and raisins!" in any other circumstance Gran would have had me in stitches with this outburst. But on this occasion, I couldn't even muster a smile. In fact, all I could think was I wanted to be there when Gran bumped into this woman so I could help ram the coconut and raisins down her throat myself.

"So, I confronted Chris about the woman who was answering his phone, and he admitted it straight away. I'll give the man his dues, he never tries to bluff his way out of anything, just tells the truth without a second thought for the damage he is causing. He of course said it was a one off and that he wouldn't do it again, all the usual bollocks. And like the desperate and pathetic woman that I am, I believed him, to keep my family together, I believed him. But then Mother's Day happened, and I woke up to breakfast in bed from the kids, which he had clearly helped them to make, and the three of us sat in bed, watching TV, eating boiled egg and toasty soldiers. By the time I got downstairs ready to go out, he was long gone," Charlotte sat down, it was a half fall really, she must have been feeling those emotions that she felt that day, all over again.

"Charlotte, I'm so sorry..." I moved and sat beside her.

"I don't need you to be sorry. You all know the rest. It isn't Mum's fault. Not really," we both looked at our mother who seemed to have halved in size as she sat across the room from us. She still couldn't turn and face anybody. Even with Charlotte defending her. Sort of.

Gran stood up and walked over to Mum, Charlotte and I looked at one another and then back at the two women who had been such a big influence on the adults we had become ourselves. As for what happened next, well, nobody saw that coming. Gran looked over at us, gave us a small smile, a nod of approval, and either a wink or a nervous twitch. The next thing we knew her hand was in the air and swiftly swiped across Mum's face. Charlotte and I stood up as if we had just seen a huge spider scurry across the room and Mum turned to face us all, finally standing up with her hand on her cheek. And Gran? She was laughing.

"Jesus, Gran."

"Jesus had nothing to do with that, it was all the devil's work!" ah! Mum had a voice after all.

"Well, look at you, feeling all sorry for yourself." Gran had the bit between her teeth and there was no stopping her now, nobody would dare. "Has your husband left you? No! More fool him. Has your husband been sleeping with other women? No! Not unless you believe that rumour about him and Brenda Hawcroft in 1971, although technically you weren't married then, just courting, so he was fair game. And you've been no saint yourself Jane Evelyn Colleen Taylor nee Byrne! What about that yoke at the bingo when you were only two weeks married? Don't you think that I didn't see you sneak out when I shouted 'house' to meet him behind Betty's Blowhouse! You were gone for twenty-six minutes, I know that because we were timing Brenda Hawcroft's mam to see how long it took her to drink a pint of Guinness, one feckin' pint and she was still going at it when you got back. Couldn't stand the taste she said, I was Irish royalty around these parts back then and she had the nerve to speak to me like that, I showed her and downed my pint in less than 10 seconds. But you, you were nowhere to be seen! Looking very sheepish when you got back. Dropped wee Emily in the toilet so she did when she was just a week old! Blamed it on slipping through the towel! I made sure you were christened after that so I knew God would look after you where your eejit mother would fail!"

"Gran! Seriously!" I stood between them now, three generations of women, and the youngest standing before them learning by example. Yeah, right! I was suddenly aware of a strange unfamiliar noise. Mum and Gran heard it too and the three of us looked around the room trying to figure out where it was coming from. And there it was. Charlotte. She was laughing. Her laughter grew until it turned into the hysterical 'I can't breathe but this is too funny to not keep laughing and crying about until I have snot dripping from my nose' kind of laugh. Then Mum started laughing, she crossed the room and threw her arms around Charlotte and the two of them stood wildly cackling. Naturally, so as not to make them feel awkward or silly, Gran and I took one look at each other and we started laughing too.

I have no idea how much time elapsed with the four of us in this state. To be quite honest I started to get a little bit freaked out that we would never stop, that my body was no longer mine to control, and I would be stuck laughing like this until the day I died, none of us ever being able to tell anyone what the laughter was all about. Our tombstones would read 'at least they went with a smile on their faces'. However, it was Charlotte who slowly regained control of herself and then the rest of us managed to follow her example. But what was wonderful about this whole thing was the four of us smiling at one another. In this gloomy, room lit by nothing but street light, where a family was falling apart.

Actually. No. There was no family falling apart, because that's not what Taylor's do. We stick together. There isn't a 'fall apart' bone in any of our bodies. Our family crest ought to have 'what doesn't kill you makes you stronger' scribed onto it, that works well for us.

Mum went into the kitchen once her smile had worn off. She was back to serious Jane Taylor. Mother of three, respected member of the community. But we would always have tonight, it was a night that brought us all closer than ever and the night that my grown-up mum was slapped across the face by my not so grown up gran.

Gran went into the hallway to take a call from her dealer. Her words not mine. I looked at Charlotte and took a small step to give her a big squeeze. She grabbed hold tightly and then jolted us apart.

"Oh God, the kids, I've broken my kids."

"No, no you haven't. They're fine. Go up and see them," she kissed my cheek and ran off upstairs, I went into the kitchen to help Mum make tea and tried to blank out the words: "no I said ribbed, for feck's sake, he doesn't like them if they're not ribbed, and don't be giving us any of that cherry flavoured shite, I can't eat cherries since I choked on a Mr Kipling Bakewell tart at Dave Dixon's wake." Some things a granddaughter should never have to hear.

I walked into the kitchen to see Mum pouring a shot of whiskey in everyone's tea.

"Mum!" she jumped half a mile in the air.

"You're going to judge me? Really? After all of that 'sharing' of information? I'd be drinking the whole fecking bottle if I was at home," I smiled and picked up one of the mugs of tea. I took a sip and coughed/choked.

"Jesus! I've got to drive home!"

"You'll not be anywhere near the limit, so long as you only drink about half the mug. Any more than that and you could be at risk," she sounded awfully knowledgeable on this subject, and I didn't think I wanted to know anymore. Not tonight. One Taylor revelation at a time would suit me just fine. I looked at Mum as she stood before me sipping her whiskey with a shot of tea, and a question arose in my mind that I couldn't shake.

"Mum, can I ask you something?"

"Well after tonight I don't think there's really anything you could ask me that would make things any worse."

"Did you really drop me down the toilet when I was a baby?" my mum shot a fast, sharp look that made me feel like she could turn me to stone. She took a big gulp of whiskey tea and nodded.

"Now we're never to speak of this again. And for heaven's sake don't tell your father." I wasn't sure how surprised I was to hear that Dad didn't know about his eldest daughter's first encounter with having her head down the toilet. It certainly wasn't the scenario he would usually associate with it, more so some sixteen years later when his first born first encountered vodka. But I knew better than to pursue the subject any further, so I just finished my whiskey tea and followed her back into the living room. Gran was still on the phone, and I managed to blank out all of her conversation apart from the words: "no we don't need any replacements, he thought one got stuck last time but we just hadn't noticed it fall on the floor," I did not want to know what she was referring to.

I drove Luke back to Mum and Dad's, Mum, Gran and Charlotte had decided to stop putting tea into their whiskey. I had taken their car keys and given them to Luke, Dad would have to go over and check they were all sober, and alive, in the morning. The kids were okay. I went up to say goodbye to them and Amy was smiling from ear to ear, Charlie was jumping up and down on the bed in his pants. No pyjamas. Evidently, he just enjoyed wearing less around the house.

It was after midnight when I walked through the door. I was bone-tired, my body suddenly seemed to realise how worn out it was as it slumped against the door and begged me to stop making it move around. I closed my eyes for a second and sighed, I had no idea what day it was, what I should be doing, whether I was supposed to go to bed or make coffee and get ready to go to work. It was like those strange twilight days between Christmas and New Year where nobody ever knows what day of the week it is or whether they should be lying in bed with a hangover or dragging their over indulged and liver poisoned bodies into work.

I was pretty sure I was safe with the going to bed option and hauled myself upstairs. Beth was in bed, so I did what everyone in a relationship does and tried to be quiet, but the quieter you try to be the louder everything seems. A dripping tap becomes Niagara Falls, brushing your teeth turns into a pneumatic drill (I had an electric toothbrush), and the sound of the duvet being lifted is like a flock of pigeons taking off around Trafalgar Square. So my attempts at being quiet were not entirely successful, but I managed to slip into bed beside Beth who made a small shuffle as she turned to face me.

"You're late."

"I know. Can't talk, need sleep."

"Have you been drinking?"

"I had a large whiskey in a small tea, Mum's fault."

"Your mum? I thought you were at Charlotte's?"

"I was. It's a long story, can we talk about it in the morning?" I heard Beth's silent glare and could sense her resentment.

"It's always a long story when it comes to your family."

"This is true. But you always knew what you were getting yourself into. Us Taylor women!"

"I was worried you know, when it started to get late."

"I was at my sister's, I wasn't abducted by aliens."

"You didn't even text to tell me what was happening. I mean, shit, Em, I've been going out of my mind."

"You've been asleep in bed."

"Do I look like I've been asleep?!"

"Don't yell at me! Jesus, Beth. Calm down."

"Don't tell me to calm down. I'll calm down when you actually decide to put me first."

"I'm not doing this now. We either put this evening behind us or I'm going to sleep in the spare room. Your call," silence. Another shuffle as she turned her back to me and I let sleep finally take hold. I would deal with Beth in the morning. Something to look forward to.

Chapter 9

I decided to play it as if the 'argument' the night before had never happened. I filled Beth in on the shocking revelations of the previous night and whilst she listened attentively, she was not allowing herself to become 'involved', she was good at that. Good at being objective and not letting her emotions get the better of her. I know that a part of her was thinking it was just the crazy Irish Taylor women. And she was right. But she was silly enough to have fallen in love with one of them.

We arrived at work and parted ways to go and get ready for the day ahead. I had a meeting with the headteacher and our school improvement officer today, so I had made a little bit more of an effort with my appearance. All this meant really was I had slapped a little extra make-up on, and I was wearing a skirt and a pair of heels, which also meant I knew Beth watched as I walked away down the corridor. I turned as I took the step up through my classroom door and caught her eye as she moved to continue walking. I smiled and the corners of her mouth turned up in a way that I was pretty sure meant I was in all sorts of trouble when we got home. The good kind.

The day went by without any major mishap. I was showing our visitor around school when a boy in my class ran over to us outside the library.

"Miss Taylor! I wee'd my trousers so I'm wearing shorts now!" I smiled and we both laughed a little before the boy went on his journey back to the classroom. We continued on our tour and then we had to sit in the head's office whilst we looked at data and analysis of children's progress in learning.

By the time the day was over I was ready for a drink. A big one. We had Olivia with us tonight, but that was okay, she could distract my head from work and everything else that we had going on by telling us about what she had been up to. The world of a nine-year-old was so much more pleasant and endurable than the grown-up world. Although we had already seen hints of teenage hormones starting to rear their ugly head, there wasn't a bad or ungrateful bone in Olivia's body.

I had a take away for dinner kind of head on my shoulders as I walked down the corridor to see if Beth was ready to leave, and as I approached the door thinking about whether I wanted my sweet and sour chicken in balls or not I heard footsteps behind me.

"Miss Taylor? Can I have a quick word?" It was a parent. Great.

"Of course, everything okay?"

"Well, I just wondered if you could help me with something. It's my Hermione," (yes, she said Hermione), "she won't let me get her dressed in the morning. She's been getting worse and worse, and she just stands there screaming if I try and help her, she just won't do it. I think I'm going to take her to the doctors. We practised so much over the summer holidays, getting ready for school, changing into her PE kit from her uniform and back again, she had it all sorted and was brilliant at it," I could believe every word.

This parent was somewhat militant and unfortunately had an older child who I taught some years ago, there were comparisons going on here that I never thought possible. I had seen a change in Hermione in class, but had gone no further than trying to suggest to Mum to ease off on the pressure she was putting her five year-old under.

"Well..." here we go, my best and most sympathetically friendly teacher voice was ready for action, "I'll have another little chat with her and see if there's anything bothering her or that she is keeping to herself. As I said the other day, she has been a little quiet and other staff members have noticed this too, perhaps just try and make things at home as fun as you can and ease off a little bit with reading and homework, just so she is having a break from all the learning, then I'm sure we'll see her back to her old self."

"Mm, I'm sure you're right," she was humouring me, "I'll see how she goes over the next week or two," she wouldn't, she'll be on the phone to the doctors as soon as she gets out of my ear shot, "I just don't know what's got into her," try your overbearing and pushy mother syndrome.

"Well, if there's anything else that we can do to help then please do pop in and we'll see where we might need to go next."

"Okay, thank you very much for your help."

"No problem, that's what we're here for," I smiled and started to walk away. I hoped she was done. I paused with bated breath. Yes, she was done.

I stepped into the classroom to find Olivia dancing around to music on YouTube through the computer and Beth was nowhere to be seen.

"Hey, Liv," she stopped dancing and gave me a big smile.

"Hi, Em, I don't know where Mum is, she wasn't here when I got here."

"Okay, she can't have gone far, get your stuff together and we can go home," I stepped back out of the classroom and directly onto someone's foot. It was Beth. "Oops, sorry."

"It's fine," she said as she winced in pain and grabbed for the nearest chair. "I have two feet, it's fine if one is broken."

"I didn't stand on it that hard, don't be a baby."

"Ha! Says the woman who cries over papercuts."

"Papercuts are the work of the devil. God taught us to endure suffering through famine and poverty, the devil thought, sod that, here's a papercut to make you weep like a baby."

"You're spending too much time with your gran," we both smiled and after a moment or two of recuperation, we were finally ready to go home.

I decided to go with balls in the end. It was a good choice as it meant that Olivia could share with me, I was never going to eat as many as they send, and we ordered an extra pot of sweet and sour sauce. Olivia filled us in on the latest happenings in her life and we watched some rubbish quiz show on the TV whilst we ate. We then approached the subject of my family developments and explained to Olivia that Charlotte's husband had gone away and probably wouldn't be back.

She responded to this simply as if I had told her it had started to rain outside. She asked if Amy and Charlie were okay, I said that they were and that we would go and visit them at the weekend, which she liked. She asked if she could draw a picture for them and disappeared off to her bedroom.

I cleared up the plates from dinner and poured a second glass of wine. It might have only been a Wednesday night, but I was ready for the weekend about two days ago. I stood at the sink looking down the garden, wondering what I could do to brighten it up a bit. I wasn't a gardener by any standard, but I liked bright colours, and I liked to put bedding plants in, no matter the season, to stop the garden looking like a cemetery. There were currently too many dead things for my liking. Dead plants, baron tree branches – buds of blossom not quite ready to burst. It had to be time to visit a garden centre and sort out this sorry state of affairs.

It was at that exact moment, the moment I called out Beth's name and waited for her to join me in the garden discussion, that I pictured very different things out there to brighten it up. A little swing set. A small toddler sized slide, a play house. Maybe even a little scooter or bike.

"Babe?" I jumped out of my head and back into the room, "you okay? You were miles away."

"Mm? Yeah, I'm fine. Just thinking about the garden. It's looking a bit drab, fancy a garden centre visit this weekend?"

"Yeah, we can do, might be a bit early though for new plants," I carried on talking about the ideas I had and the colours I liked best in a flower. Beth came and slid her arms around my waist from behind to look out of the window from over my shoulder.

"I didn't like those ones we put in last year," I continued, "too many oranges and reds, I like yellows, pinks and purples. We'll have to have a look at what they've got," I had been so busy talking about flowers and steering my head away from the direction it had very briefly taken, that I had not noticed Beth's hands start to slip down my waist and towards the tops of my thighs. As I realised what she was doing I smiled to myself and turned to face her.

"I'd rather talk about your skirt, and your heels, and how sexy you looked today," she had a twinkle in her eye that could have lit up the darkest sky.

"Is that right?"

"Mm hmm, I kept thinking about you and replaying your strut down the corridor this morning..."

"I don't strut..."

"You did in my head, I think you should strut off upstairs right now..."

"It's only just gone six o'clock! And what about Olivia?"

"I do hope you're not trying to spoil my fun. Otherwise, you know I'll just have to punish you," this time I grinned and placed my hands on the sink behind me to stop myself falling over.

"Oh really?"

"Mm hmm," she leaned down and kissed my neck, which sent sparks flying around to all sorts of places. She stepped back and smiled at me. "Later," my legs went weak, and I couldn't believe the power of that one word. I gave myself a moment before leaving the kitchen to let my legs regain their ability to keep me upright.

Olivia reappeared about an hour later and showed us the pictures she had drawn. She had spent a long time over one in particular that she explained was of the first time that we went out together as a family. Beth, Olivia and me. She said that she knew on that day that her mum was happy and better because she had me now, and her dad was better because he had Sarah. She said she hoped that Charlotte would find someone like me, and that Chris would find someone like Sarah, then everyone would be happy. I gave her a big squeeze and told her I was sure that Amy and Charlie would love the pictures. She then happily skipped off to bed and left us to the rest of our evening. I turned to Beth, and she was staring at me with that same sparkle she had had earlier, but with a level of intensity that made my heart race.

"What's wrong?"

"I just. I just love you. I have told you for a long time now that you saved me, you saved me from a life that wasn't right for me and that was making me unhappy, making me a bad wife, a terrible mother... but what I never really think about is how you saved Olivia too. She was growing up in a very miserable and tense house that was never really open to much laughter or happiness, and now look at her. She loves you, her life is happy, and you made that happen, by falling in love with not just me, but with her too," she leaned across the sofa and kissed me, and I managed to reciprocate the kiss without crumbling into a thousand heart broken pieces. Yes, I loved Olivia dearly, but she would never belong to me in the same way she belonged to Beth. How could she not see that?

Chapter 10

The next day after work, we went to visit Kate. I had been desperate to go and see how she and baby Richards were settling at home and had raided the local Baby's R Us (although to be honest I'd been stock piling gifts as soon as I found out she was pregnant. I had a bad habit of doing that, any excuse to buy a baby grow, a cute little two-piece, or little booties, I was a retailer's dream when it came to baby products). In addition to the teddy bear with a pink bow and a summer dress with 'I'm blooming cute' that Olivia had picked out, I also added a pack of 5 bibs (educational of course – days of the week, although it didn't sit comfortably that Saturday and Sunday were missing. Was the multi-million pound baby product market suggesting that we starve babies at the weekend?) Our gifts were finished off with a beautiful pink dress and matching frilly pants and tights, and a pack of 3 baby grows with various Disney characters on.

Beth had rolled her eyes when she saw the mountain of gifts that I dropped onto the table to wrap up. Luckily, she and I were yet to be acquainted when Amy was born, I had had a major issue with knowing when to stop when it came to the arrival of my beloved niece. If there had ever been a need for an intervention and some sort of baby merchandise buyers anonymous, then I was perfect for such a group. Hi, my name is Emily and I'm addicted to buying baby clothes.

When we pulled up outside Kate and Tom's house, I got out first and Olivia helped me get the gifts out of the boot of the car.

"Jeez, Em, you're like a kid on Christmas morning!" I was halfway down the drive way and turned round to smile at Beth.

"I'm excited! There's a baby!"

"Yeah, come on Mum, babies are well cute! I can't wait to have a baby," Olivia skipped off and knocked on the door. I caught Beth's eye as she swallowed hard and balanced herself momentarily against the car door. I laughed and rolled my eyes.

"Come on Grandma," I winked and turned back around just as Tom appeared to greet us.

We all piled inside to find Kate and a sleeping baby in its Moses basket. Kate had her hand casually resting on the side of the basket as she was sat curled up on the end of the sofa, showing that she was relaxed enough to know her baby was safe out of her eyesight, but that she would be there the second she woke. I sat beside her and gave her a big squeeze, Olivia sat on the floor by the basket and Beth gave Kate a kiss on the cheek before sitting down on the sofa opposite us.

"Oh Kate, I'm so proud of you, she is beautiful," Kate was glowing.

"I know, I can't believe I made her. It's the most surreal thing. Like, from Tom and me, here she is, this little person, a bit of me and a bit of him, all mushed up together."

"Go easy on the biology there, there's a minor in the room," Beth nodded towards Olivia, and we laughed. Olivia was too busy peering over the side of the baby basket to notice she'd missed anything.

"Technically, there are two minors in the room, does the youngest of these minors have a name yet?" I asked. Tom walked in to the room and I could hear the kettle boiling in the kitchen, he had got his routine of open the door, greet the guests, show them to the baby and put the kettle on down to a T. He looked at Kate and I honestly don't think I've ever seen so much love in one person's eyes, until he shifted his gaze to his daughter and then somehow the love only grew. He smiled and then looked back at Kate.

"I know you're waiting for me to say it's okay, and you're daft because you don't need to, you can tell them," he said.

"But we haven't told our parents the name we've picked yet, and your mum has only just left," agonised Kate.

"Yeah, and don't I know it, I've got way more grey hairs than I had before she got here!" Tom ran his hands through his hair for dramatic effect.

"Come on people!" I intervened with my impatience. "As thrilling as it is to know the latest grey hair count upon Tom's head, what have you decided to call her? Because as a member of the teaching profession, I can assure you that sending her to school as 'Baby Richards' will mean she endures endless levels of ridicule throughout her education."

Kate smiled at me and stood up. She lifted out 'Baby Richards', who only gave the smallest of murmurs to indicate that she was even aware she had been moved, and then Kate placed her gently in my arms.

"Auntie Emily, meet Amelia Grace Richards," Kate sat back down, and I looked at the little life in my arms, and then I burst into tears. "Oh Em! You daft thing, you're such a big softy!" Kate laughed and I looked her square in the eyes as tears rolled down my cheeks. Through the blur of my vision, I could see it again. That same look she had given me in the hospital just before Amelia had been born. She knew, she could finally see what I had spent so long desperately trying to keep to myself, trying to convince myself that I was okay, that my life was exactly as I wanted it to be. It was easy to do that when you only had yourself to convince. Only had the voice inside your own head trying to convince you otherwise, but then Luke had seen it too. The same thing that Kate could see now, that I was desperate for the next baby I held in my arms to be my own.

I somehow managed to compose myself and blamed it all on how happy I was for Kate and her growing family, that I was overwhelmed by how much it meant to see her with all she had ever dreamed of, and a part of that was true. I couldn't bring myself to look at Beth until I had managed to take some deep breaths and calm myself down. A small part of me was thinking 'for fuck's sake Emily, get a grip of yourself', and it was that rational head that allowed me to close my eyes just for a second and think of all the wonderful things that Beth, Olivia and I had done, and all of the amazing things to come. A split second that was a window into my future, I was okay and just an overly emotional, sensitive eejit. And I did it. I convinced everyone I was okay. Everyone except Kate.

Tom was very good at socialising. Not in a bad way, he had never been one for going out and getting drunk with the lads and until he had met Kate, he had never really experienced women. But as we sat in his home now, with so many unsaid things hanging over us, he did an amazing job at keeping it all together. I was sure that Kate and I were the only ones in the room who were aware of the desperate need to talk alone, to speak of what I had shielded her from throughout the happy time she spent as a pregnant woman. Every now and again she caught my eye, and if I wasn't looking at her then I was convinced I could feel her gaze burning into the back of my head. So had it not been for Tom and how excellent he was at keeping the small talk flowing, how well he got on with Beth and how much he loved chatting to Olivia, then the whole visit would have blown up in my face as soon as I let myself get so upset.

We sat chatting with Kate and Tom for about an hour, it was time for dinner though, and I knew Olivia would start to get grumpy, Beth too actually, so that meant time to make our exit. I carried our empty mugs out to the kitchen and rinsed them before leaving them on the side for washing. I turned to re-join everyone in the living room just as Kate appeared in the doorway. She looked at me with a seriousness that I wasn't sure I had ever seen before, then she stepped into the kitchen and shut the door behind her.

"Beth has Amelia, so she won't disturb us. I encouraged one last cuddle before you all go."

"Ooo, let me go and take a picture," I tried my best to sound light-hearted and jovial, smiling as I moved towards Kate and out of the door. But she didn't move an inch. She just held my gaze with *that* look. I should have known better than to think I was getting away from her before an inquisition.

"Oh Em, how long have you felt like this?" I had two choices. Play dumb, or just accept the predestined conversation she was going to force me to have.

"Felt what?" I played dumb. I know. Now even I wanted to roll my eyes at me.

"Don't do that, don't pretend that I haven't figured it out. All this time, I knew. I knew there was something that wasn't right, something you were doing a bloody good job at keeping from me. And now I know, now I can see, and I feel like the biggest and blindest idiot for not realising it before," she paused and I looked at her, feeling tears burn the back of my eyes but trying desperately not to let them out.

"Please, please Kate, don't make me talk about this," it wasn't the time or the place. Not with Beth and Olivia in the next room. I could admit she had marked my card, but I couldn't have it out with her now.

"We need to talk about it, you need to talk about it."

"I can't…"

"Of course you can, you don't have to hide anything from me, you don't have to try and be brave or protect anyone from the truth, from what you're feeling, for all of the things you have been thinking for goodness knows how long, wanting something that conventionally can't be yours doesn't mean that it can't still be yours…"

"Yes it does! Yes I do have to hide it!" I interrupted and lost my cool. I didn't shout, but I raised my voice in a way I was uncomfortable with. I didn't want to fight with Kate. I looked at her and this time she was the one that couldn't prevent tears from escaping.

"Em, I'm so…"

"Please don't say you're sorry. Please. You have nothing to apologise for. I can't talk about this with you whilst my family are sitting ten feet away."

"But you want a baby. You want to have a baby and become a mother, I can see it written all over your face," I lowered my head and took a deep breath.

"I need to go, I'll call you," I kissed her cheek and she grabbed me as I tried to walk away. She pulled me into the biggest hug you could ever imagine, and I hugged her back. I knew though, that just like Tom's hug when he was anxiously waiting to become a dad, this hug was for Kate.

The drive home was quiet, and I tried to be as normal as possible, but in truth, I was feeling a little bit exposed and in need of protecting myself. I had held myself together throughout Kate's entire pregnancy, but now it was over, and her baby was here, instead of it being resolved, I was worried that for me it was all only just beginning. We drove home via the local chip shop and had a 'dinner on your lap' tea. Beth did most of the cooking, it wasn't an area of life I had ever had much interest in. I was a microwave dinner or chicken dippers with a bit of salad and a few chips, kind of girl before Beth introduced me to ingredients and making things from scratch. I didn't mind eating it, but I had no desire to start learning how to make it.

After dinner we watched the usual rubbish on TV, I marked some writing from work and downloaded some resources for lessons the following day. Olivia was babbling on and on about baby Amelia and I was managing to drown most of it out. There was no question that I was going to love this new little life with all my heart, but I couldn't allow myself to think about it, it was just bringing back that look in Kate's eye, and now that she knew and Luke had seen it too, I didn't like how 'out of my hands' this was all becoming. It had started off as just an innocent thought in my own head and I had managed to keep it there for all this time. Suddenly I faced everyone finding out and my world turning on its head. I couldn't let that happen.

Once Olivia had gone to bed, I turned to look at Beth as she lay sleeping at the other end of the sofa. She fell asleep like this most nights and despite sometimes wishing we were doing something more exciting with our time rather than being sat at home, I found the sight incredibly endearing, and my heart fluttered. Maybe my fears were all in vain and she saw the same things that I did, that a baby we could raise together would complete our family. Perhaps she could see the two of us changing nappies, doing late night bottle feeds playing peek-a-boo and pulling silly faces. Teaching a tiny human being together that love conquers all. We were living proof of that.

I was the reason that this woman walked out on her husband and split her family apart. She chose me, despite the risk and the danger of losing everyone and everything in her life as she knew it. She chose me. She loves me. Loves me more than anything. If she doesn't want a baby, then only a fool would consider throwing everything we have away. And for what? The small possibility of even being able to have a child? Of becoming a mother? Was that what I wanted? Would I throw it all away for that chance? I picked up my phone and flicked through the photographs I had taken of Amelia this afternoon. Yes. For that chance. Yes, I would.

Chapter 11

As Fridays go, this one was pretty non-descript. The last day of the week usually had everyone on pins, the anticipation of two whole days without school, and that was just the staff. Kids tended to save their best exhibitions of 'bad' behaviour for the end of the week, just when you thought it was safe to relax a little in preparation for the weekend. But today, no major incidents, no playground tussles or classroom disputes to resolve.

I called Charlotte at lunch time, and she sounded unusually chipper all things considered. She invited Beth, Olivia and I round for lunch tomorrow and said she had asked Mum and Dad to come with Gran too. Their invite had been in person, and she was trying to explain the look on our father's face as he looked up from the newspaper; first his eyes had lit up at the thought of something being supplied for his lunch that didn't come out of a tin, and then when he heard that Gran was invited too, he slunk back down into his chair and hid behind the paper. I could picture the scene. Deep down, Dad loved Gran. Deep, deep, deep down. Whatever depth the Titanic lay at the bottom of the ocean. Maybe that deep down.

Although my day had been a little 'quiet' as far as work was concerned, my phone hadn't stopped buzzing in my pocket. Kate was not letting go of me and was insisting we meet up over the weekend. After seeing the children out at the end of the day I retrieved seven text messages and five missed calls. You could be forgiven for forgetting she had just given birth, as she seemed to have made that second to her fixation on the growing complications in my own life. I had to see her, I couldn't live like this. If nothing else, I had to get her to swear that whatever she thought she had seen or knew stayed between us. I wasn't ready to discuss any of this with Beth.

I was just about to call her when Beth walked into my classroom.

"I've just been handed a party invitation from Liv," she rolled her eyes and sat down on the corner of a table.

"Wow, she's turning 10 and she's already organising her own birthday parties?" I joked. "At least she's inviting you though, that's good of her," I laughed.

"No, she has been invited to a party but it's all the way out at Cannock Chase, they're going to do the junior 'Go Ape' on Sunday morning and then for some crappy food somewhere after."

"Sounds fun."

"I just wish she would tell me about these things sooner. She's had this for three weeks, she said she told Adam but what bloody use is that when she's not with him this weekend."

"She's just forgotten, it's not the end of the world. So, what's the plan?"

"Well, it's going to be full of kids from here, so it'll be easier if I take her and you use the day for work or something," as much as I knew that Beth was trying to be helpful and supportive with her suggestion, I already knew exactly where I would be spending my Sunday after this sudden turn of events.

"I don't particularly fancy being 'Miss Taylor'd' all day, so yes, I'll find something to occupy myself here and you go. You're friends with the other mums anyway, you never know you might actually enjoy yourself!"

"Ha! Yeah, surrounded by hyped up 9 and 10 year olds. There's 15 of them going!"

"Jeez, that's going to cost a fortune!"

"I know. Olivia had better not get any bloody ideas about her own birthday celebrations! It's not like it's a milestone or anything," I nodded in agreement and Beth stood up. "Are you ready to go?" I nodded again. "I'll grab my stuff, and my disorganised daughter, and then we can get out of here," she smiled as she turned and left the room.

I picked up my phone and sent Kate a text:

> I'll come to yours Sunday morning. Not sure what time yet, is that okay? XX

I waited a matter of seconds before the response came:

Of course. Doesn't matter what time. See you then. Lylaaf. K xxx

Lylaaf stood for 'love you lots as a friend', it had been something we came up with as a joke so she could tell me she loved me without me thinking she was chatting me up (which of course I would never think). She put it at the end of all of her text messages now, but this one gave me a level of comfort I hadn't been aware I needed. I had been sure I was the one in control of all this, but I was swiftly losing my grasp. So to read her words and know that no matter what happened Kate would always be there and love me, gave me the courage to face whatever came of our talk with a level of bravery akin to a mouse running from a hungry cat. That was better than having no courage at all right?

Saturday morning disappeared in the blink of an eye and before any of us knew it, we were sitting around the dinner table at Charlotte's house. Me, Beth, Olivia, Mum, Dad, Gran, Charlotte, Amy and Charlie. Oh, and the Colonel. Lunch was sponsored by Kentucky Fried Chicken and boy was it finger lickin' good.

My dad looked horrified as big pieces of greasy chicken got plopped onto his dinner plate with chips and little packets of salt. He was supposed to salt them himself? With a packet not much bigger than a postage stamp? He looked utterly bewildered by the whole thing. Mum wasn't faring much better. Everyone under the age of fifty was doing just fine with their chicken pieces, coleslaw, baked beans and chips.

Gran, however, was having no such technical difficulties with her food. She was gnawing chicken off a bone as if she hadn't eaten in about a month. It was hard not to watch, but it didn't exactly bring upon much of an appetite as grease and bits of chicken skin stuck to her slightly furry upper lip and chin. I looked around and saw that Dad was watching Gran with his jaw open. She clocked him and he jumped.

"What the devil is wrong with you?" I sensed the uncomfortableness grow inside Dad and could see he needed rescuing.

"Gran, do you have any wipes over there? I'm getting in a bit of a mess with my beans," she flew her eyes from Dad to me and back again at least half a dozen times, it made me feel queasy. My stomach was churning as it was from watching her eat like a coyote enjoying a kill on an excursion in the wild by David Attenborough. A couple of wipes found their way across the table to me, and Gran settled back into her chicken. I snuck a look at Dad, and he was keeping his head down slowly shuffling chips into his mouth, unsalted. He didn't touch a single piece of his chicken. It didn't really matter though. The coyote finished it.

After lunch the kids disappeared off upstairs and we all settled with a cup of tea in the living room. Polite conversation went on all round, Beth told everyone about visiting Amelia and we flashed some pictures around.

"She looks Chinese."

"Gran! Don't be ridiculous!"

"She looks feckin' Chinese! Look at those eyes."

"They're closed."

"They're feckin' Chinese. Mind you, that Chinese man who delivers around us puts the sweet in my sour! If you know what I mean," Gran licked her lips and laughed, Charlotte and Beth snorted their cups of tea, and I watched my parents pretend they couldn't hear anything that was being said.

"Gran you've met Tom, he isn't Chinese."

"Who says he's the father?"

"Gran! Seriously! You shouldn't go around saying things like that," I looked at her and she was still laughing. Then she looked at me and she stopped.

"I was only joking, you daft eejit, come on now," I took a deep breath and watched as I can only describe Gran as 'squirming'. I don't think I've ever seen her squirm before. "She's a grand yoke, break the hearts of them all when she's grown-up she will," Gran was genuinely worried she had upset me, and I felt guilty now for making a thing of it.

"Let's call Luke!" Charlotte intervened and grabbed her laptop so we could Skype our little brother. Perfect distraction tool and the best opportunity ever for Mum to steal the limelight to talk to her baby.

I went upstairs to check on the kids and they were all playing in Amy's bedroom. Charlie was zooming cars around the floor pretending to run over Amy's little woodland animal families, and Amy and Liv were playing with dolls, dressing them and feeding them with pretend bottles. Everything seemed to be ticking along nicely so I turned to go and say hi to Luke (if I could get a word in edgeways), but I stopped as I heard Amy start to ask Liv some very tricky questions, and I don't mean algebraic equations.

"Livvy, where is your Daddy?"

"He's at his home."

"Is that your home?"

"Sometimes my home is with my dad and sometimes my home is with Mum and Emily. My dad lives with Sarah and Daisy and Max too."

"So, your dad has two families? He has you and he has Sarah?" Olivia thought about this one for a minute and smiled.

"Yes. Dad has two families. Just like I do. I have loads of families. I have all of you, I have Nana and Grandpop Walker," Beth's Mum and Dad, "I have Dad and Sarah, and Max and Daisy, and Sarah's mum and dad, Max and Daisy call them Grandmother and Grandfather," both girls laughed.

"That sounds silly," Amy put her hand to her mouth and laughed a little more.

"It's okay Amy, we are the lucky children."

"But my Daddy has gone, and he doesn't want to live with us anymore. I don't know where my Daddy is. What if I need him?"

"But he still loves you, and he will still spend time with you, and you'll be able to have sleep overs at his new house. And if he meets someone like my dad met Sarah, then you will get loads more people to play with and you get loads more presents at Christmas," Amy stopped for a second and I could see she was preparing her next question.

"Will Santa still come even though my dad isn't here to put the milk and cookies out? And a carrot for Rudolph?" I peered a little closer through the crack in the door and watched as

Olivia mulled this one over and then smiled. I won't lie, a small part of me was terrified that in her beautiful honesty she was about to shatter another area of Amy and Charlie's lives, but the curiosity in me allowed it to play out.

"Santa has so many cookies and so much milk from all the other boys and girls that he won't even mind if he doesn't have any at your house. And Rudolph has to fly a long way, he doesn't want Santa eating all those cookies and getting really fat and too heavy to carry in the sky!" Olivia stood up and pretended to puff her body and blew her cheeks out. She gave a 'ho, ho, ho,' and jiggled her pretend fat belly up and down.

I beamed from ear to ear at what I saw and turned to leave my beautiful niece and nephew in the very safe hands of their older cousin.

As I turned, I bumped into a figure behind me.

"Christ Gran, you scared me to death."

"Don't exaggerate, Taylor women don't feckin' exaggerate," she winked at me and then she held my hand. "You do know that you shape that girl's little personality, don't you? You're just as much of a mammy as Beth. You've made her the caring yoke in there that's helping two confused little children work out what the feck is happening in their lives." She gave my hand a squeeze before continuing, "you're not yourself Emily, and I'd say you've not been yourself for around about nine months now... Follow your heart and choose your own path. Be proud of yourself. I am," she kissed my cheek and turned towards the bathroom.

I had no idea where that had all come from or where *she* had come from. She was like a bloody ninja. How long had she been listening to the kids talking? What exactly was it she had seen change in me and why the hell did it have to have been for that ominous 'nine months'? Nothing was ever straight forward with gran. She was at times an enigma, and I loved her for it. She pulled her knickers out of her arse as she closed the bathroom door behind her, and I stifled a small laugh before heading back downstairs.

Chapter 12

Beth and Olivia left the house at nine o'clock on Sunday morning. I followed them out about ten minutes later and made my way to Kate and Tom's. My stomach was doing back flips the whole way there and I took a lot of deep breaths trying to figure out where we would even begin once I walked through the door. How do you start a conversation based on a subject you've spent almost a year trying to hide? Something that you were trying to stop yourself dwelling upon and you were desperate to simply move past. How do you pour all of that out when you never wanted anyone to know just in case it culminated in your life crashing down around you?

I knocked softly on the door, I didn't want to disturb Amelia, and Kate opened it with a big smile. I stepped inside, turned around to look at her, broke down in tears and sobbed into her arms. That's how you start a conversation with someone about your biggest secret. You allow the relief that it doesn't need to be a secret anymore to wash over you, the relief that someone is going to say it's okay to feel this way, that it's perfectly normal. I was tired. Tired of pretending that this didn't matter. Hiding it for so long hadn't made it easier for me to live my life, it had made my life unbearable to live.

Kate made us both a cup of tea and we sat down in the living room, a sleeping Amelia none the wiser of my arrival. My eyes felt puffy already and we hadn't even skimmed the surface.

"I'm so sorry Emily."

"What in the world are you sorry for?"

"For not realising. For being so excited about my pregnancy and being selfish enough to force you to live through it every step of the way."

"No, don't apologise for that. Don't ever think that I haven't loved awaiting your baby's arrival. The scans, the midwife appointments, hearing the heartbeat, feeling the kicks, laughing about silly names and shopping for baby clothes and nappies has been an absolute pleasure. Doing things like that with you has almost made me feel what it would be like to be an expectant mother myself, all that preparation before the baby arrives. I got to share that with you and Tom, and if that's all I ever get then I will be forever grateful to you for letting me become a part of your new family," I stopped talking and took a deep breath to steady my voice. Kate wiped away a stray tear and looked at Amelia.

"I just... I look at her. My daughter, it still feels weird saying that, and I know how much I love her. She's been here five minutes and I would die for her. I feel a love for her that is bigger than I could ever try and put into words," Kate had kept her eyes on Amelia as she spoke, and now she turned to look at me. "But it breaks my heart, Em. It breaks my heart to think that what I'm feeling, these wonderful, scary, exciting, terrifying feelings might not be something that you get to experience." She wiped more tears away and I realised that I had begun to cry again too.

"I have such a full life though, Kate. I feel guilty for wanting any more than I already have. Life is good, I'm loved by my family and friends, I have a job I adore, I'm healthy, there are people in the world with so much less than me, and they don't complain. I have no right to expect my lot in life to give me any more than it already has."

"But, Em, no woman should have to give up the chance of being a mother. It's the one thing that as a woman our bodies were made to do, we were given the ability to have children and raise them in our own individual messed up ways. To repeat the mistakes of our own mothers and make some brand-new ones along the way. To show another human, a person that you made, that they are the most important thing in the world to you. I feel all of that and it's only been a matter of days that I've been a mother."

"I don't think that feeling comes just by having a child of your own. I think when a woman knows she wants to become a mother, the longer those feelings sit in a residual state, the stronger they get. And the power of the love you feel for a new-born baby, is just as strong as the knowledge that you want to give that love but can't."

"Em, there is no feeling in the world like that of when a midwife places your child into your arms, the feel of their skin on yours, knowing that they are a part of you, you made them and now you have to raise them and protect them."

"I'm not saying that my desire to become a mother is a stronger feeling than the love you have for your daughter, I'm just saying that the emotions that it brings out are more powerful than someone who is already a mother could possibly try and understand. Just as I can't truly know how you're feeling with your baby girl safely by your side, you can't possibly know how it feels to know that that's all you want in the world, but you can't have it."

"You don't know that you can't have it. There are ways, things that can be done."

"You make it sound so romantic," we both managed a small laugh. Actually, not a laugh at all, more of a sigh with a hint of a chuckle.

There was a level of sadness in the room that buried Kate and I. The noise and expected sounds from two women who were crying were nowhere to be heard. The room had fallen silent, yet tears rolled down my face at a rate I had never experienced before. Talking about this so openly and honestly was taking things to their worst. I wasn't trying to pretend that I was happy with the path that my life was currently on, which meant I wasn't even able to fool myself anymore. It would seem that real sadness was when even tears daren't break the silence.

Amelia woke during the silence of sadness. She didn't cry, but she made her presence known and so Kate stood and lifted her out of the basket. Kate asked me if I minded her feeding, and I rolled my eyes to show it was a silly question. We continued to sit in silence, the sounds of a content and hungry baby enjoying lunch being all we tuned into as the minutes ticked by.

After feeding, I was handed Amelia whilst Kate tidied up and went to the bathroom. Amelia's eyes were wide open, she hadn't really opened her eyes when we all visited the other afternoon. She looked at me as if she had heard every word I said and wanted to understand more. Her little brow furrowed slightly as she tried shifting her head to get a different angle on me, as if looking at me from a slightly different perspective would make things all the clearer. I smiled to myself and could almost hear the thoughts in her little head, and I wished that just tilting your head to one side or the other could make things easier for grown-ups to understand too.

Kate came back into the living room and settled beside us. She looked wonderful, but she also looked tired. Motherhood was natural to her, and I had always known it would be, but she wasn't invincible, and I could see she had probably been missing out on some very valuable sleep.

"Does Beth have any idea?" Kate's question almost made me jump. For a few seconds I had allowed my mind to fool me into thinking I was just here to visit my friend and her new baby.

"No."

"You haven't spoken to her about it at all?"

"No. It's not exactly a conversation to just casually bring up over dinner one night."

"I realise that. But you've been together for almost four years, has it never come up?"

"Four years ago I hadn't ever really thought about whether I would be a mother one day or not. It wasn't something that I ever felt I needed to make an absolute decision on. Like I had all the time in the world and if I wanted it one day, I'd have it."

"I don't mean this to sound as blunt as I know it'll come out, but you might have found you were missing a vital ingredient for it to 'just happen one day'." We both laughed with a slightly higher level of conviction this time, "surely if Beth knew how you were feeling she wouldn't just expect you to change and switch off your feelings."

"Just because I've decided that I want to have a child doesn't mean that she should be expected to automatically turn around and say okay let's do it. She already comments on her age and that her bones creak more than they did five years ago."

"But if you don't even talk to her then how will you know? Your love for each other has grown into something so big and important in your lives, you're both bound to have your own ideas about where your relationship has been and where it will go. And Liv would love it, look how she cooed over Amelia, she'd be a brilliant big sister." Kate nodded at her own statement, and I smiled back at her. I knew Olivia would love having a baby to help take care of and would take on big sister duties with pride. But what about how it would make Beth feel?

"I can't do it to her, Kate."

"Do what? You don't know what you're doing yet. You don't know what she'll say."

"I know I don't want to lose her, I know I love her. She's the woman I'm supposed to be with."

"The woman you are supposed to be with wouldn't make you miserable by taking away your chance to be a mother. Trust me Em, I'm less than a week into parenthood and I would help anyone to know the joy and love that brings to your life. If I was into women and I was with you, there is no way I would stop you from being a mum. You've always been brilliant with kids, everyone always thought you'd have kids, and to be honest, I don't think anyone thinks that's changed. I mean, I had always presumed that eventually that's what you guys would do, that it was the next logical step in your relationship."

"I suppose that's what people do when they're in love."

"Exactly. So neither of you have a penis, so what? Same sex couples have babies every day."

"Really? Every day?"

"Okay, maybe not every day I don't have statistics or a survey analysis or anything. But it happens."

"Traditionally people get married and have babies, but my life is far from 'traditional'. I made my choice, I have Beth, Olivia and the most beautiful family and friends. I can't risk losing all of that. When we first got together and went through all that shit as people started to find out, I promised her that I would always be there for her. I promised."

"My darling Emily, you promised to stay in a relationship that was less than a year old, you didn't say you'd give her a kidney."

"What does that mean?"

"It means people change. We all change, and a promise you made three or four years ago doesn't necessarily still stand, not when it comes to love and the complications of relationships."

"If she said no, no to a baby, I would have to leave her to allow that to happen for myself. I can't leave her, Kate, I can't walk away, and I can't lose Olivia."

"You don't know that you would have to do that."

"But I have worked my arse off to make sure she doesn't suspect anything about how I feel. I pretend that every advert on the television for baby milk or characters in TV shows that have babies don't make my heart sob inside. I try to be jovial about people at work who've had babies and bring them in, and I make the right noises and point out things to Beth in shops, cute little outfits and babies in pushchairs to make sure she knows 'I'm okay with this' and 'I'm okay with these women thrusting their happiness at being a mother in my face', when I'm really, really not," I was getting upset and Kate took Amelia, who had fallen asleep in my arms. She kissed her softly and placed her back in her basket. Then she sat down and pulled me into a hug. This hug was for me.

I stopped crying but Kate kept me in her arms, rocking me ever so slightly. I don't know how long I sat there like this with her, but I started to smile, and I gave her a quick squeeze before sitting up. I took a deep breath and looked at the time. We'd been at this for almost four hours.

"I should go."

"You don't have to leave yet," she squeezed my hand.

"I know, but I should," I stood up and she followed me as I made my way to the front door.

"If you need anything, Em, anything at all, please call me. Or just turn up, anytime, night or day, just come in. We can even get you a key!"

"Bloody hell, Kate. I think Tom would have something to say about that!"

"Tom does as he's told. Besides, the key will come in handy when you're on babysitting duties," she winked at me, and I laughed.

"Anytime," I leaned in and kissed her cheek. "Thank you for today."

"For what? I don't feel that we actually achieved anything."

"No, we did. Despite my apprehension over it, I know I have to talk to Beth. I just don't know where to start."

"It's the right thing to do, Em."

"I know," Kate gave my arm one last hug, and I opened the door.

As I walked out to my car the cool spring air wrapped me in its arms and for the first time this year, I could sense that winter was over. I sat in the car for a minute and watched a blackbird hop along the pavement and then take off into the sky. I was a little envious as I watched it fly away from or towards whatever it wanted, and as I thought about spring arriving and summer close behind, a sense of warmth rose within me.

I don't know whether it was just talking with Kate or if I was having some kind of 'epiphany', but I was beginning to see things a lot clearer than I had for a while. If I wanted to have a chance to lead the life that I desired and have the things I craved, then I had to be just as brave as that little blackbird. I had to fly towards it and grab hold of it before it was too late.

I drove straight home and got my school work done, it was rare to have the chance to blast some music out on the iPod and knuckle down to some paperwork on a Sunday. By the time Beth and Olivia got home it was almost five o'clock and I had managed to find time to dance around to my favourite Steps and S Club 7 tunes as well as deal with a big pile of marking that I had been pretty sure would come back to work with me unmarked on Monday morning.

Beth and Olivia had eaten whilst they were out, so it was a microwaved jacket potato with cheese and beans for tea for me. I sat in the living room to eat and listened whilst the two of them shared their day. They talked non-stop about how high the ropes were and that the mums who were there ended up going on the adult course. Apparently the birthday girl's mum wouldn't go up because she was afraid of heights, but most of the others did and it caused great amusement for the kids. Olivia was clearly still buzzing from the experience and began demonstrating her amazing balancing and climbing abilities by building an assault course out of the sofa cushions.

I watched her and laughed as Beth left the room claiming she didn't know if she was more worried about the cushions getting damaged or Olivia injuring herself. It was at that point that I decided I could wait two more weeks. In two weeks, Olivia would have had her birthday and if I could make sure that she had the best birthday ever then I could finally open up to Beth. I would once and for all share my deepest longing with her and our life will then be able to move forwards, in whatever direction that may take.

Chapter 13

As the days passed, I felt an enormous sense of relief just knowing that I was going to bring everything out in the open with Beth. It didn't matter that I hadn't been completely honest with her yet, it was having made the decision that I would be, that I was finally going to tell her I wanted a baby.

Olivia was getting more and more excited for her upcoming birthday. She made a countdown chart and had it pinned to the wall in her bedroom, every day she would run downstairs telling us how many days were left. I had been unsuccessful in tempting Beth to rethink the goldfish, so I had been working on Olivia instead, making her think about having a pet that might not be as interactive but would be a lot easier to take care of. I'm not sure if I was doing a great job of convincing her but I was giving it my best shot.

Charlotte and the kids were doing remarkably well. She was doing extra days at work and asking Mum to do a lot more regarding picking up Amy and Charlie from school and nursery. I was surprised by that, but glad she was getting on with life and making decisions that were best for her and the kids. We hadn't heard from Chris since the night he went round to the house, and I babysat with Luke. To be honest I was glad that he hadn't hung around so that Charlotte could get her head straight. I know the kids missed him, but between us we were doing our best to keep them distracted.

Gran had taken them out the other afternoon after school, she had picked them up with Mum. Mum was cooking what she called a 'proper' dinner because she presumed that Charlotte would have been too tired to cook a healthy meal. Gran had decided that it would be a great idea to teach the kids about the 'real' world, so they helped her to sell some of her 'goods'. Gran was thrilled because it turned out people were willing to pay a lot more for things when a cute little smile came along with it, Mum however was less than amused and has banned Gran from leaving the house with anybody who is not old enough to leave the house alone.

The day before Olivia's birthday we were sat at the dinner table talking about nothing in particular. Olivia would wake up on her birthday with us and then this weekend she was due to be with her dad. It all worked perfectly as I had checked the weather and was taking Beth out for a picnic, so that we could 'talk'. It was all set, and I was ready to lay all my cards on the table, and I had a really good feeling about it too. Things at home had been great and Beth seemed very chilled out and happy with life. Some people may see that as a 'don't rock the boat' kind of situation, but I saw it more as an opportunity to grab life and make it what I wanted.

"What time can I get up tomorrow?" Olivia flicked her eyes from me to Beth and back again, her head didn't move an inch.

"Hmm, well, I'd say just a normal school morning. Get up, get dressed and out the door," Beth teased.

"But if we don't get up earlier, I won't have time to open my presents and I'm at Dad's this weekend, so I won't get my presents from you until Monday!"

This was clearly a huge injustice to Olivia, and I smiled at her.

"Your mum is joking, we will be up at whatever time you would like to get up."

"Woah, I didn't agree to that!"

"Don't be mean, what time do you want to get up Liv?"

"Hmm. Well, I'm thinking I'll need about an extra hour..."

"Trust me you won't!" Beth scoffed and I shot her a glance that said 'humour your daughter'. Beth knew not to argue with that look. "Fine. We'll set an alarm for six, I'm not getting up any earlier than that!"

"That's okay, I will make sure I am outside your bedroom door to knock at six am promptly," Olivia smiled and excused herself from the table. I was fairly certain that she was going to go and get ready for bed, and we wouldn't see her now until morning. I laughed and Beth rolled her eyes at me.

"She's bonkers," Beth joked.

"She's brilliant," I said. Beth looked at me and we held each other's eyes for a moment. In that instant I briefly felt as if she knew. But it passed and she stood up and started to clear the table.

Once we were certain that Olivia was tucked up asleep in bed, we set about constructing the most intricate fish tank you have ever seen. There was not a gadget that Beth hadn't purchased to ensure clean water, the best filter, multi-coloured stones, the top recommended goldfish food and enough plastic seaweed and decorative pieces to fill acres of sand at the bottom of the sea. Then of course came the goldfish, which we had left amusing itself in the bag he/she had come from the pet shop in, resting in a mixing bowl out of the cupboard. It looked happy enough as it swished about, we had only got one in the end and decided we would take Olivia to buy a friend for it that she could choose herself.

At six am on the dot, there was a tap on our bedroom door, and I rolled over and nudged Beth. Olivia might have been turning ten, which arguably was a step closer to no toys and games, but more clothes, make up and money, however I'm sure she got more excited about her birthday every year. I loved it and I planned on encouraging as much excitement about birthdays each year as possible.

As Beth and I opened the bedroom door, Olivia stood before us fully dressed, ready for school. Hair scraped back into a ponytail and I'm fairly certain she had probably also had breakfast and brushed her teeth by now too. I smiled at her and she beamed back.

"It's six o'clock! I waited just like you said, and I made you both a cup of tea."

"You've been downstairs?"

"Yes. But I didn't go in the living room. Just the kitchen," Olivia continued to smile widely, and I laughed.

"Happy birthday Liv," I gave her a squeeze and the three of us made our way down stairs. I was both excited and terrified to see her reaction to the goldfish. We opened the living room door to reveal strategically placed gifts and cards, with the fish tank placed on the coffee table in the centre of the room, an extension lead to the wall behind the TV ensuring that no algae developed overnight (Beth's words not mine). We missed the first expression to cross Olivia's face, but as she rushed squealing to the fish tank and then jumped up and down screaming 'it's just like Nemo!' I was fairly confident that maybe the goldfish hadn't been such a bad idea after all.

Once Olivia had opened up all of her cards and presents it was almost quarter to seven, Beth went for a shower and I sat with a bowl of cereal as Olivia wondered if she had got time to build the Lego set that my mum and dad had bought her, listen to the CDs that Luke had bought or act out a wedding with the new Barbie doll from Charlotte. She had also had some new clothes, books, some more Lego and some money from Beth's parents. But it was 'Nemo' that kept her attention for the rest of the morning until we all left the house for school.

We were given strict instructions that 'Nemo' was to be moved into her bedroom so she could look after him properly. Credit where credit was due, the goldfish had gone down better than I could ever have imagined, and I was chuffed to bits that Olivia was so delighted by it. All of my fear of disappointment had been wasted energy, and this just added to my euphoric state that everything was going to work out just as I wanted.

When we arrived at school, Olivia appeared behind me in the classroom and hushed me into the corner.

"I just wanted to say that it's okay," she rather cryptically announced.

"What's okay?"

"It's okay that Mum didn't want a puppy or a kitten." Ah. Now I understood. "I know you tried to get her to think of it herself, but I just wanted to tell you I'm not upset or disappointed, I love my fish, and it's better that it was a pet who will be okay when I'm at Dad's. A dog or a cat would have missed me too much and that would make me feel sad. Nemo will be okay until I see him on Monday," she gave me a big hug and I was yet again completely floored at the maturity and kind heart inside this little girl, "thank you for an awesome present." I kissed the top of her head and she skipped out of the classroom.

Friday went by in the blink of an eye, and it was the traditional early dart out of the door for most of us. I met Beth at the car, and we drove home talking about Olivia and how happy she had been with her birthday presents.

"You don't think she was disappointed then?" Beth nervously posed the question and I had to stop myself smiling as I recalled the conversation I had with Olivia this morning.

"Not at all, she was thrilled, and she's so excited to go and get some friends for little Nemo," I reassured her.

"I just had a panic that she would have preferred a bloody puppy or kitten or something. Can you imagine?! Nightmare!" I managed to fake a small laugh and the rest of the drive home was a silent one.

Saturday morning my brain woke up before my eyes were prepared to open. It was as I snuggled into the duvet and pillows that I registered what I could hear. Rain. My perfect plan for a beautiful picnic and lovely romantic day together was now pouring down the windowpanes with very persistent force. Absolutely frigging typical. I kept my eyes closed and tried to think of a plan B. I could still do this, simple. An indoor picnic. In fact, the more I thought about it the more it made sense. In the event of my chosen topic of conversation not going well today, the privacy of our own home could be a better suited location after all.

I rolled over in bed and reached out for Beth, but she wasn't there. It was then I managed to hear the sound of the shower fighting for its waterfall to be heard over the rain. I got out of bed and pulled my dressing gown tightly round me. It was cold and dark, and I had to make Beth feel warm and light today.

We pottered around the house for a little while, emptying the dishwasher, doing some housework. We managed to transfer Nemo from the living room to Olivia's bedroom without slopping too much water around. He swished around a bit more than he probably would have had he been left to his own devices, but he looked settled enough as we cleared a space on top of the chest of drawers. By lunch time my stomach was doing backflips and the thought of actually eating made me feel rather sick. Nevertheless, I disappeared downstairs whilst Beth was on the phone to her mum and quickly set about transforming our dining room into an indoor picnic venue.

When she came down stairs, Beth stopped in the doorway and smiled widely.

"What's all this in aid of?" she asked and came to sit beside me on the floor.

"Just wanted us to have a nice weekend, and a little lunch date. Despite the bloody weather!"

"It didn't forecast rain for today I don't think," no shit Sherlock I thought. I poured us both a small glass of wine, and we clinked before tucking into pasta, salad, tortilla chips and dips, and little bowls of trifle for pudding.

We talked, we laughed, we drank a bottle of wine between us, and it was perfect. I had fetched in our big beanbag seats from the garage, and we were sat snuggled beside each other. This was it.

"Beth. Can I talk to you about something?"

"Mm? Sure," I could tell she had hit a wall made of a full belly, a few glasses of wine and a warm cosy room.

"It's just something that I've been thinking about for a while now, and I wanted to talk to you and see what you thought."

"Well now you've got my interest peaked, what is it? Is something wrong?"

"No, nothing's wrong. It's just, I love you, you do know that don't you?"

"Of course I do."

"And I love our life and everything we have, and Olivia, and it's just everything I thought I ever wanted."

"Everything you *thought* you ever wanted?" she was questioning my choice of words, so I turned to look at her and I reached out to her hand. Here I go.

"I want a baby," I blurted. Beth stared. Not at me, it seemed, but almost through me. For some time. "Beth? Did… did you hear what I said?" She took her hand away from mine and my heart felt like it was going to burst through my chest. I was sweating and suddenly the comfortable and cosy picnic area became stifling, and I felt as if I couldn't breathe. "Beth, please say something," she looked at me and took a deep, slow breath, her eyes were wide and clearly in a state of total shock.

"I... umm... well, I... I don't know what to say... I mean, I had no idea... how... how long have you felt like this?"

"A while," I said. Honestly, I had no answer to that question. I had maintained a 'never say never' attitude about having children, but it was my relationship with Beth that had made me want to expand our family. Perhaps the idea had lay dormant in my mind until I had found the person I wanted to have children with.

"How long is a while? A week? A month? A year?"

"I don't know, maybe a year," Beth stood up and started pacing, "maybe not that long, I don't know, Beth, you're scaring me, talk to me please." I stood up and positioned myself in front of her to stop the pacing.

"I'm just... I'm a little shocked... I mean, you say that Olivia and I are all you ever wanted, but then you throw this in and I just, I didn't see it coming."

"I know it must feel like it's come completely out of the blue, I do, and for you I can see how it would feel that way, but for me... for me this has been something I've held onto and tried to keep from you for so long because I was so afraid of how you would react."

"Afraid? Because I'm such a scary person?"

"No, I didn't mean that. Okay, not afraid, but anxious. I don't want things to change between us..."

"You don't want things to change? But you want a baby? That's about the biggest change you could throw at a relationship, Emily."

"I know, I just mean I don't want to lose you, I want us to do this together. I want us to have a baby. Our baby."

"I hate to break it to you, but you must have skipped a few biology classes at school, we can't have *our* baby," Beth closed her eyes, and I could feel her slipping from me.

"Please, let's just talk…"

"I can't talk… I need to, I need to go, I need some air…"

"But it's raining, Beth please," I wasn't too big to beg and as I moved to take her hand, something pinged in her pocket. She moved quickly to avoid my touch and pulled out her phone. With a scoff of disbelief, she looked at me and then showed me the screen.

"It's Olivia, her dad got her a puppy for her birthday," and with that she turned on her heels and left. She just left me standing there in the dining room and I had no idea what I was supposed to do next.

Chapter 14

I had no clue where Beth had gone or what she was going to do or say when (dare I say if?) she came home. She didn't really do much in the way of socialising or confiding in friends, so I didn't know who she would even seek out to talk to about any of this. It was still raining, and I had tried calling her, but she wasn't answering her phone. I just went into auto-pilot, I tidied up the picnic and felt sad when I looked into the dining room back in its everyday state, as if the last few hours had never happened. Is that what I should be hoping for? That she could rewind the clock and pretend the whole conversation had never happened?

By the time it started to get dark I was beginning to panic, but I didn't know who to call. Beth liked to keep our private life just that – private. But I couldn't handle situations like this alone, I needed to talk to someone. As I sat listening to the ringing tone dial out on Kate's phone I started to get upset. It was one of those self-pitying cries, because I felt alone and abandoned and for all intents and purposes, I had just killed my relationship and any kind of future with the woman I loved.

Sitting in the dark, watching the rain water cascade from flooded drains down the street, I wondered if Beth had maybe gone to see Kate. Or my mum? No. She would know that I would never in a million years have spoken to my mum about this. Charlotte yes, but not Mum. Mum would have been crocheting blankets and picking out baby names for months if I had told her about how I felt.

I was remembering Luke's words to me about being a mother and that it wasn't something that anyone should be told they can or cannot do. And that was coming from a man. If a woman wanted to have a child, then that was literally her God given right. Maybe Beth *was* with Kate, which would explain why Kate didn't answer her phone. Although a new-born baby was also a very good possibility to explain that she was busy with something else.

I needed to hear somebody's voice to quiet down all of the other voices I could hear inside my head. The voices that argued amongst themselves over whether I should even have said anything to Beth in the first place. I had done the right thing; ultimately, I knew that much at least. I couldn't have gone on the way that we were, I needed to be honest, and we owed it to each other to make sure we were both getting what we wanted from our relationship.

As I sat in my own little world, imagining Beth lying in a ditch somewhere, there was a knock on the door. Oh God. Was that the police? Coming to find me and tell me that there had been an accident? I walked to the door and tentatively reached out to open it. Standing on the other side was Kate with a sleeping Amelia snuggled into her car seat. I ushered them in out of the rain and couldn't believe I hadn't noticed the car pull up on the front. Kate took one look at me and I shook my head, desperately trying not to cry.

"Fuck. You told her. I take it that it didn't go well?" I shook my head and shrugged my shoulders. "Where is she?"

"She left."

"She's left? Left you?"

"No. Well, I don't know. I don't think so. She just, I told her, and she left. I don't know where she is."

"Shit, Em. So, she wasn't all that keen on the idea then?"

"I don't know," I half laughed but it was full of exasperation and frustration and any other 'tion' word I could think of. "I told her I wanted a baby, and she didn't say anything. She made a comment about it meaning that she and Olivia are not enough for me, and then she said she needed some air and off she went. Of course matters were not helped when Olivia sent her a photograph of a puppy that her dad has bought her for her birthday."

"What? Oh for God's sake, what did you guys get for her?" I didn't answer straight away. It somehow felt like an anti-climax.

"A goldfish," there was a pause whilst the word 'goldfish' hung in the air for a minute and then we both laughed.

"Well, I'll hang around for a little bit. When I found your missed call, I knew something must have happened, I wasn't sure if you would still go ahead and tell her today though, with the crappy weather."

"Trust me, I am beginning to wish I hadn't."

"Don't say that, you've done it now. Now comes the exciting bit," Kate smiled at me, and I looked at her puzzled. "Well, whatever happens now, you've told her you want a baby. So, whether she sticks around or not you're going to be a mum, Em. It's what you've been waiting for, now it can happen," right on cue Amelia started murmuring, so Kate went through to the living room to take her out of her car-seat and de-layer her of her coat and cardigan. (I had made a joke of the fact every time I saw her, Amelia was wearing a cardigan knitted by either Kate's mum or Tom's mum, she had responded with a slightly angry frown and eye roll announcing that the two of them had knitted so much that she was having to change Amelia several times a day just to allow each cardigan to get an airing, a quick photograph and job done).

I thought for a second though. I hadn't actually processed that part of my day, but Kate was right. I'd done it, I had told Beth I wanted a baby and now whatever happened, whatever decision she came to about it, I was free to go through with it. No more hiding how I felt, no more pretending that everything was just as I had always wanted it to be. I could have a baby. A small smile managed to form at the edges of my mouth, but it was soon wiped out by the knowledge that it was looking increasingly like I would have to do this alone. I just prayed that wherever Beth was she was thinking and realising that she wanted this just as much as I did.

Kate and I had a cup of tea and she finished off a packet of biscuits whilst I cooed over Amelia. She said it was rare she got to drink a cup of tea that was still hot and enjoy biscuits to go with it because babies always have other ideas about what Mummy should be doing. I sat with Amelia on my lap, pulling daft faces and making silly noises. She looked a mixture of enchanted and baffled by what I was saying to her but ultimately, I hoped she could see the love in my eyes.

Kate and Amelia left just after eight o'clock. As I shut the door behind them, I looked around my home and felt a sudden need to wrap my arms around myself. What if I was going to have to do this alone? What if I ended up as a single mother and had to figure out parenting without somebody by my side during night feeds and potty training and the first day at school? Wow. I hadn't really thought about what it would mean if Beth wasn't prepared to do this with me. Could I even do it alone? Was I capable? As I stepped back into the kitchen to respond to my rumbling tummy, I mulled those thoughts over.

I see a lot of families and children at work who just can't cope. I didn't want to become one of those mothers. A statistic. I dropped a couple of pop-tarts into the toaster and waited for them to pop. When they did the sound was synchronised with a knock at the front door. I heard it open, and my stomach flipped. I wasn't sure if it was down to nerves or just relief that Beth was home. (I also wondered if it was just my stomach showing excitement at the popping of the pop-tarts.)

"Emily? Are you home?" it was my mum.

"Ah Jane, will you not be such a gom now. The feckin' door was unlocked, of course she's home," Gran.

I heard footsteps approach and they both appeared in the doorway, it struck me how alike they looked side-by-side like that. Would my future child think that of me and my mum one day?

"Hi, Mum, Gran. Tea?"

"Grand idea, I'll have me one them popping hearts as well now Emily."

"Here, have mine," I didn't have it in me right now to correct Gran with the name of my very unhealthy snack, I just handed her the plate and put the kettle on as they both sat themselves at the breakfast bar. "To what do I owe the pleasure? Is everything okay?"

"Yes, everything is fine," Mum nodded, "your father is entertaining some men from the angling society, and I felt a little in the way so thought I'd come and see how your week was. Your gran was staggering back from lunch at the pub, so I put her in the car before she ended up in the middle of the road."

"I had a date," Gran spat through chocolate pop-tart crumbs. "It was a real craic; he was a true gentleman."

"He paid for everything then?" I asked.

"No, he asked if I preferred being on top or on bottom," Mum rolled her eyes and shuffled uncomfortably in her chair, I smiled at Gran, and she winked at me. "The answer was on top," she whispered.

"Where's Beth?" Mum was using her best diversionary tactics.

"Umm, she just popped out."

"Had a fight?"

"No!" I scowled at Gran, but she looked at me knowingly.

"Emily Yvonne Taylor, I think you forget how well I know you. All those years babysitting when you were a tiny little poppet, I was there when you first crawled, walked, fell over, spoke, threw up, sang, cried – there was nothing I wasn't there to see, I know you inside out and back to front, that's what Grans do. Now, what's happened with Beth?"

"Oh Gran..." I started to speak, and they both had their eyes glued to me. It was then that we all heard the front door open and this time it was Beth.

She walked into the kitchen and found the three of us sat around like the witches in Macbeth. To her it must have looked very much like I had requested their presence because she had walked away. I wanted to tell her that wasn't true, I wanted her to know I hadn't called them or spoken to them about any of it. That it was still ours to sort a way through, nobody else needed to get involved. She looked at me and I had no idea what she was thinking.

"Nancy, Jane, sorry I didn't know you were coming over."

"Ah, sure it was all one of them spur of the minute things," Gran spoke and then she stood up. "Come on now Jane, let's leave the young yokes to it."

"No, it's fine. Actually, it's quite good that you're both here. There's something that I need to do, and I think you should both be here whilst I do it," shit. What was she going to do? Was she leaving and she knew I would need them with me whilst she packed her stuff up? I felt sick.

"Umm, well, we don't want to be in the way, no we'll go," Mum was feeling as anxious as I was, I'm not sure what she thought she was about to witness.

Beth came and stood in front of me, and my breath caught in my throat.

"Emily, the time that we have spent together has been the best years of my life, I love you and I want to be with you forever. You make me happier than I knew it was possible to feel, you're funny, beautiful, smart and I am so proud that I get to call you mine, and so lucky that you want me by your side and in your life," she paused, and I think I was still holding my breath, "Emily," she got down on one knee, oh God. "I want you to be my wife," she pulled a small box out of her pocket and opened it up to show me what was glistening inside. "Emily, will you marry me?"

Everything stopped. Even the air itself in the room around us seemed to freeze and stay perfectly still. I looked at the ring and I looked at Beth. She needed an answer to her question, but I had yet to receive an answer to mine. I could feel Mum and Gran's eyes burrowing into me, neither of them knowing quite what to do with themselves or whether they should be saying or doing anything at this precise moment. It was like we were in an unspoken agreement to perform the mannequin challenge. In a matter of seconds, I processed a thousand different thoughts, and I had no idea what the right thing was to do. I looked into Beth's eyes, and I knew she wanted this, she loved me, and I had no doubt she always would. But did she want a baby with me?

The silence was broken by a noise coming from Gran. She flushed and then gave a nervous laugh.

"I had beans with lunch, the feckin' things get me every time," she laughed a little and Mum put her hand over her eyes in despair. Beth looked back at me and stood up. I'd left it too long, she needed an answer, and I hadn't given one.

She leaned in close and whispered to me.

"If we're going to raise a baby, then let's do it properly, marry me," I leaned back and stared at her. Did she mean it? Oh shite. Did she really mean it?

"Do you mean..."

"I mean, I want us to be a proper family. Marry me," she said with light hearted exasperation. I laughed and pulled her into my arms.

"Yes. Yes of course I'll marry you!"

"Oh Emily! My first born is *finally* going to be a bride!" Mum was ecstatic, so much so she got up and kissed Gran on the cheek before coming over and giving Beth and I a big squeeze. "I need to ring your father, he's been saving for this day since the moment we knew you were conceived! He was so sure his first child would be a girl and he wanted to give her a wedding fit for a queen!" Mum rummaged in her handbag and pulled out her phone, then disappeared into the living room to call Dad. She said she didn't like the sound of her voice when she was on the phone and so she never rang anybody if there was someone else in the room. I have tried explaining that your voice only sounds different when you hear it play back yourself, not just because you're on the phone, but she didn't understand.

Beth slipped the engagement ring onto my finger and kissed me. I still felt a little confused about what had happened, this was not how I had thought this day would end. She gave me another hug and then said she had got some of Aldi's finest Prosecco in the boot of the car to celebrate. Gran came over towards me and lifted up my hand.

"There a rock in there somewhere?"

"Gran!" I looked down. "I think so," Gran laughed at me and then patted my hand between the two of hers.

"You're sure about this now Emily?"

"Yes! Of course I am, why wouldn't I be?"

"Something has changed between the two of you, and I might be old but I'm not an eejit, something bad happened today and you were just about to tell us when Beth got home."

"Gran you're being paranoid, everything is fine. Everything is perfect! I'm getting married!" I laughed and she smiled at me.

"Yes, that's what usually happens next," I pulled her into a hug and held on tight.

"I promise you Gran, I believe with all my heart that everything is going to be just as it is meant to be," I pulled back and kissed her cheek just as Beth walked back in with the Prosecco. "Let's drink!"

Mum came back into the kitchen and was almost giddy. She announced that Dad was thrilled and didn't want to miss out on any celebrating, so he was on his way as we spoke. I had never seen Mum so animated and happy, I did wonder if she was feeling a sense of relief. One of her daughters had been married for years, had two children, and it had all fallen down around her. Her eldest child had ended up on a slightly less conventional path in life but was now able to offer her all of those same things. Her chance to be mother of the bride again, her chance to become a grandmother again. All of these things I wanted for her just as much as I wanted them for me.

Gran's words rattled around my head about how much she had been there when I was a baby and growing up. You forget those things, those moments that your grandparents or aunts and uncles, cousins, extended family all shared with you as a child. If Beth had made a different decision today, then at least I now knew that there was never any need to fear being a single mother. No fear of doing it all alone. Because Taylor women didn't let each other do anything alone. Although at some points in my life boundaries of some description would have been nice. Healthy.

The evening progressed at a rate that knocked me for six. Dad arrived, and whilst Mum was correct about his excitement, Dad hadn't cancelled his angling meeting, he had brought it with him. Once they were settled with drinks around the dining room table to continue through the agenda, Charlotte and the kids arrived. Apparently, Mum had called her straight after Dad. I was so glad that I had been able to share this joyous news with my family myself. Ha!

Drink flowed, toasts were made and well wishes were passed on by everyone. However, one part of the evening that I could have done without was catching Gran with one of the men from the angling club enjoying their own little party in the bathroom. It was the same man who had taken her for lunch apparently. He had not long lost, and was grieving for, his wife. Gran was handing out sexual favours as therapy sessions.

Beth sat with Mum for a while, and it wasn't until I approached that I realised they were talking wedding details. Christ! We'd been engaged all of two hours! I looked around at the people who were with us, celebrating our happy news, or celebrating another successful fishing season (they did make a toast to us in 'any other business'.) I looked at the time and wondered if it was too late to call Kate. It had dawned on me she was the only person who I really cared about knowing outside of the people here tonight, and I had a bursting urge to tell her. It was coming up for ten thirty, was that too late?

Charlotte left with the kids, Charlie fast off in her arms and Amy bouncing around by her legs full of sugar from Gran's sweets, at least I was pretty sure they were just sweets... Once I had seen them out and left Dad saying good bye to his angling club (apart from Gran's new friend, who she had asked to stay because she saw him as family now too) I slipped away upstairs to call Kate. I was pretty sure that no matter what time it was, she would be thrilled to hear that everything had worked out.

"Hello?"

"Kate? Did I wake you?"

"No, I've just put Amelia down. What's wrong? Is Beth still not home?"

"No, I mean, yes she's home."

"Oh good, have you guys talked things through then? What did she say? Is she on board with the two of you having a baby?"

"Kate. She asked me to marry her. We're engaged!" the other end of the phone stayed silent. It stayed silent for a little bit longer than I would have liked it to. "Kate? Are you still there?"

"Yes! Mm, yes, I'm here. Wow, umm, congratulations. So, I guess that means she said yes as well, right? I mean, you ask for a baby, she walks out, she asks you to marry her, you say yes. So, that must mean she wants a baby too?"

"Of course!" I answered.

"So how did she propose? I mean, did you talk about things first and then decide you wanted to get married?"

"Well, not exactly. She came home, Mum and Gran were here, still are incidentally, and she did a little speech, got down on one knee and asked me to marry her."

"It sounds lovely, Em. It really does. But, how did she get to proposing from storming out of the house at the suggestion the two of you have a baby?"

"I don't know that I'd say she stormed out..."

"Emily! You were worried sick, she didn't exactly skip out of the front door singing Do, Re, Mi! She walked out on you."

"To think! She did some thinking and then she reached the same place that I was at."

"In a remarkably short space of time. I'm sorry, Emily, it just seems a bit false."

"How can you say her feelings are false? She proposed!"

"To you! To stake her claim on you, I'm just not sure that I would be able to accept so freely that she had legitimate reasons to propose. I'm not saying she doesn't love you, but there have been times when it comes across like she wants to possess you rather than share life with you."

Was Kate right? What the hell had happened today? Beth came home and distracted from having a conversation regarding having a baby by asking me to marry her. Why would she do that? Why didn't she come home so we could talk things through before bringing marriage into the equation? I mean, okay, traditionally you would hope to marry before becoming parents. But we were far from a traditional couple. I needed to talk to her.

"Em? Are you okay?" Kate was still on the line, and I'd almost forgotten she was there.

"Yes. I'm here, I'm okay."

"I can hear the thoughts and questions in your head through the phone. Talk to her Em. If she really wants a baby and you're going to get married and live happily ever after, then I couldn't be more thrilled for you. But you need to know what was meant by her impromptu proposal. Why today? Are you sure that she really wants a baby and isn't just saying what you want to hear? It's almost as if she thinks putting a ring on your finger is some form of entrapment. You need to ask her why she proposed today, Emily."

"I know. You're right, I will."

"Okay, I should go and get some sleep. Talk soon. Love you."

"Love you too, night."

"Night, night," Kate hung up the phone and I sat on the edge of the bed not quite sure what to do next.

"Em! Em are you up there? It's Luke, he wants to talk to you!" Beth's voice wrapped itself around me as if it were a lasso to bring me back to her world downstairs. I stood up and went to talk to Luke. He knew too, he knew what was going on in my head. What would he make of all this?

It turned out his male intuition only went so far. But then he didn't know I'd told Beth I wanted a baby. He was so happy for me and said he would come down and visit as soon as he could. I told him to concentrate on his studies and not to get carried away, but he was already telling me he could be our honorary best man and would he be able to make a speech. My heart melted for my baby brother, and I hoped and prayed that I could give him what he wanted.

It was almost midnight by the time we saw the last people out, which of course were my parents and Gran. Gran was newly single again, as it turned out her new man's wife wasn't dead, she had just been away visiting her sister for a few days and he had genuinely thought he had lost her somewhere. An easy mistake to make. If you're ninety and don't know what day it is.

Beth and I went up to bed and I knew I wouldn't sleep at all unless I knew why she had done this today. She was talking non-stop about her discussions with my mum: who we would have as bridesmaids, what we would wear, who Beth would ask to give her away, who we would ask to make speeches, what the colour scheme would be... it went on and on. And yet all I could find myself thinking was, are we going to have a baby? At the end of all of this, was the goal that we would be raising a child together?

"Beth, where did you go this afternoon?"

"Well, you may have not noticed, but there's an engagement ring on your finger. I kind of had to go and buy that before I could ask you to be my wife," she laughed.

"But you were gone for so long."

"I wanted to make sure I got the right one!" she exclaimed.

"Why didn't you let me know you were okay? I was worried."

"Babe, I was fine. I was planning for our future. I was making sure that I never lost you."

"So, what about what I told you I wanted?"

"I thought you wanted the same thing I wanted. To get married."

"I do, of course I do. But I asked you if we could have a baby. And you just walked away. You left and I had no idea what was going on in your head. Evidently you were hearing wedding bells."

"Em, if you don't want to marry me then we just call the whole thing off," she snapped, and I took a beat to figure out how to handle this.

"That's not what I'm saying."

"Well what are you saying? Because it sounds like you're not so sure about this anymore."

"You're putting words into my mouth, do you not see what I'm trying to say to you? I want a baby Beth. I want to be a mother. I want us to do it together. Is that what you want? Is that why you proposed today? To tie a pretty bow around our future family? I need to know," I watched as she fiddled with a corner of the duvet, and I waited for her to give me an answer. I didn't know why it was taking her so long to respond.

"I wouldn't have asked you to marry me if I didn't want the same things that you did. For us to be happy, to make sure that Olivia is happy, that we are a family and look after each other."

"You're avoiding my question."

"I'm not avoiding it. I just... I don't know. Okay? There's my answer. I don't know."

"You don't know if you want a baby?"

"Yes, yes I don't know. And I was scared that if I said that to you, you'd walk away. That it wouldn't be enough to keep you by my side and for us to carry on together, just as we are."

"You ask a person to marry you when you know them and want to share every part of the rest of your lives together, but it sounds like you don't know me at all. I would never rush you into a decision, if you need time then you need time."

"You totally blindsided me Emily, I don't know what you expect from me. I did what I thought was right."

"Beth if you need time to think about something you don't just ask someone to marry you to buy some time."

"I know, I panicked. But I do want to marry you."

"I know, and I would love to be your wife. But I can't not be a mum. I need to do this, I need to have a child of my own. It's not something I have a choice in, my heart, my body, my soul – they're all dictating to me that this is something I have to do. I feel as if every life I have ever lived and every life I'm yet to live, if you believe in all that past lives stuff, involves me having a baby. It's what I'm meant to do."

"You make it sound like you're one of those 'women were put on the Earth to procreate' bullshitters. Next you'll be telling me you want to be a stay at home mum and bake cakes, knit cardigans and send me out to work to keep food on the table and a roof over our head. No career for Emily anymore, she's a mother."

"You're twisting this out of context." I retorted.

"And you're making me feel like I'm being forced to decide on this right away. You tell me I can have time, but you don't sound like you're actually prepared to give me any. Your decision is made, you'd just throw us away. That hurts." She was getting upset. She did this sometimes. Cry, imply I didn't love her as much as she loved me. That she only wanted me to be happy and it hurt her that I could ever possibly think otherwise. "I need to think about what you're asking of me."

"How long?" I had to keep a strong resolve.

"I don't know. Just give me a chance to think about what this means. I've had a baby, I've lived the raising a child part of my life."

"Olivia is ten, she's hardly living in a three-bed semi with a husband, two kids and dog."

"Well she's got the dog!" ah, I wondered how long until we would cover the puppy topic and her 'woe is me I failed my daughter on her birthday' speech. "I mean let's face it, I can't even get my own daughter's birthday present right, so how would I fair with a child that wasn't even mine?"

"But it would be yours, you would be a parent just as much as I was."

"How can you possibly think that? It would be nothing to do with me."

"So is Olivia nothing to do with me?"

"Well she isn't enough to make you feel like you're already a mother, so you obviously don't think she's anything to do with you."

"Don't do that. Do not imply that I don't love every last tiny hair on her head. I adore her."

"And I don't I know it. I should have seen this coming a mile off. You spend more time with her than you do with me when she's here."

"She's a child! She is supposed to have adults with her!"

"And she's getting closer to an age where she won't rely on adults so much anymore."

"So you *are* saying no?"

"No, that's not what I'm saying. I'm saying give me time," she lay down and sighed, "I've got to say, I've imagined proposing to you a million times, this is not how I had pictured the day we got engaged would end," she turned off her bedside light and left me sitting in the darkness.

Chapter 15

The next morning there was a great big, enormous elephant in the room. That elephant shall be named 'baby Taylor'. Beth and I barely spoke and if we did it was mundane things that we just said to keep a show of politeness between us. How had we let this become who we were? Why did she have to propose instead of talk things through with me? Everyone had been so excited last night, although Gran's all-seeing eye seemed to be very tuned in to what was going on before I had even realised myself.

I asked Beth if she would like to go for a walk and she just shook her head. I tried to be as normal as possible, but it was hard, she never made these things easy because she would just let things swallow her up and eventually, she'd be sat wallowing in either self-pity or regret. I wasn't sure what was going to happen. How much time was I supposed to give her to think about this? I had sat twizzling the engagement ring around my finger when I got up this morning. Do I take it off? Do I wait until we talk again before I do anything? One thing that she had been spot on about was how the day we got engaged was supposed to end. I had played the same day out in my mind a thousand times, and never did it result in us not able to speak to one another.

Just after lunch there was a knock at the door and I was absolutely dreading it being Mum with an arm full of wedding magazines, but as I opened it, I was greeted by a slobbery lick to my foot and the biggest smile on Olivia's face I think I had ever seen.

"Hi Emily, I wanted you and Mum to meet Margot, she's my new puppy!" Olivia tried to hold onto the lead as long as she could, but Margot had other ideas and snaffled her freedom to roam around the house within seconds.

"Still learning to hold on tight to the lead?" I asked, Olivia laughed.

"Dad said it would be okay to come over," I looked down the drive and sure enough there he was. He waved and I waved back.

"You don't have to stand outside. Would you like to come in?" I called down to him. I wasn't quite sure what I was doing but it seemed like the right thing to do. He made his way up the drive and smiled.

"Thanks. Liv was desperate for you both to meet Margot, is it okay that we came?"

"Of course it is, come in," Olivia was already inside, and Adam and I found her with Margot on her knee next to Beth on the sofa. "Can I get you a drink?"

"No, I'm fine thank you."

"Can Margot have a bowl of water please?"

"Of course she can," I went into the kitchen and Margot followed, so of course behind the both of us was Olivia. "So what breed of dog is she?"

"She's a labradoodle, she's amazing!" I laughed and watched as they sat on the floor and tussled with each other. A beautiful ten-year-old little girl and her blonde playmate. "Dad said she will feel like my best friend one day, but she already is. She slept on my bed Friday and Saturday! Sarah doesn't really want her upstairs, but Dad sneaked her up to me," she giggled.

"She's gorgeous," I leaned down and gave Margot a fuss, she lapped it up and licked and nibbled at my fingers. "She will be a very good and loyal friend to you I'm sure."

"Would I sometimes be able to bring her here? What if she gets sad when I'm not at home with her?"

"I'm sure your mum and I would love to have Margot come and stay with us."

"Awesome! I knew you wouldn't mind," she gave me a big hug and ran into the living room, Margot following and me bringing up the rear with a bowl of water. I placed it down on the floor and was greeted by Adam with a 'congratulations'.

"Excuse me?"

"Beth just told me your news."

"What news Mum?" Adam and I looked at Olivia and then at Beth. She looked very sheepish, and I knew exactly why. We had agreed not to tell anyone else about the engagement until we knew where we were at with what we both wanted, and also preferably once we were actually on speaking terms with one another.

"Well, Emily and I are going to get married!" Beth just blurted it out and Oliva jumped up and grinned.

"Oh my gosh! I get to be a bridesmaid *twice*!" she jumped up and down and Margot did the same thing beside her. She gave Beth a big hug and then me, and then Adam. I don't quite know why, and I don't think she did either. At that moment Margot left us a little watery treat on the floor, so I went to get a cloth and disinfectant spray to clean it up.

Adam and Olivia shouted goodbye as I hunted around in the cupboard for something to wipe up the mess. I heard the front door close and then Beth appeared in the kitchen doorway.

"I'm sorry."

"Sorry for what? For forgetting that little agreement about not telling anyone we're engaged? Jesus Beth, what happens now?"

"What the hell does that mean?"

"Well if you don't want a baby, there won't be a wedding."

"And what about Olivia, what do you think that will do to her?"

"How dare you! How dare you imply that that would be on me? You did this. You proposed, you wouldn't talk to me about how you felt, you told Adam and Olivia we were engaged.

Don't ever put this on me. You need to figure out what you want and fast. I won't have Olivia or anyone else in our families start planning for a wedding that is never going to happen."

I left that sting hanging between us and decided to go out for some fresh air. Whether I had been too hard or not, I didn't care anymore. This was all driving me crazy, and I needed it to be resolved now. I went for a walk and ended up sitting at the park. My head was a mess, and I didn't know what to do to clear it up.

Was this my fault? Had I unknowingly caused the way this was starting to play out? Maybe Beth was perfectly within her rights to be shocked and angry at the way I was disrupting our relationship. Everything had been perfect. We were happy and even before her proposal, I knew I wanted to spend the rest of my life with her. I've always known that. So, now that I was asking for things to change, perhaps I needed to allow her to be cross with me. For a little while at least.

The word 'perfect' is a dangerous word, when I think about it. Who decides what it even means? Does it even exist? One person's idea of what makes life 'perfect' is surely very unlikely to be the same as another's? Even the happiest of couples, if they are brave enough to admit it to themselves, must want something that they do not currently possess in their life together. Whether it is something as silly as wanting to switch to de-caffeinated teabags, or wanting to have a family pet, or go on more holidays, read more books, go to the theatre, play a sport, it could be anything! If such a couple exists where there is nothing one of them desires that the other has not been willing or able to provide, then please show them to me.

I don't think it was even 'perfection' that I was looking for. The bottom line for me has never changed. I need to be a mother. I need to hold my baby in my arms, and have it wrap its tiny hand around my giant finger, I need to see my baby smile at me when I walk into a room. I had no unrealistic notion that I was going to be the best mum ever. I just knew that if there was any chance of my life meaning something, for me to not wake up one morning and be so completely full of regrets and resentment for a chance that I never took, I had to take it.

As I wandered back through the park, I found myself stood at a crossroads. I'm not speaking metaphorically, I mean an actual crossroads. If I went left, I went home. If I went right, I went to my parents. If I went straight on, I went to Kate's. I looked at the time, I had been gone for just over an hour, and there had been no attempt made by Beth to get in touch and find me. I could go home and sort this out once and for all. Or I could go and sit with Mum and Gran and eat cake and drink some Irish coffee until it all went away. If I went to Kate's I would be told to turn around and be a grown up, to face my life rather than run from it. Decisions, decisions...

I opened the door slowly and stepped inside. I couldn't hear anything, and I didn't know if that's what I had wanted to hear or not. If she wasn't home, then where was she?

"Hi," a voice came from the top of the stairs and startled me.

"Jesus, Beth, you scared me. I didn't think you were here."

"I was in Liv's room. Feeding the fish," silence hung over us like the grim reaper was here with his scythe, both of us waiting to see which of us it would fall upon. I took off my coat and hung it up on the hooks, then I turned and locked the door behind me before properly stepping over the threshold to show that I was home.

Beth remained at the top of the stairs and so I went into the kitchen and put the kettle on. Just because I hadn't got to visit my parents did not mean that I was going to miss out on a medicinal Irish coffee. I shouted out, asking if Beth wanted a hot drink, and she appeared behind me like a bloody meerkat sticking his head up on look-out.

"I think I've aged fifty years in the last few minutes, Beth, make some bloody noise when you enter a room!" she smiled, and I grabbed two mugs out of the cupboard.

"Sorry. I didn't mean to startle you. I want to show you something," she reached out and took my hand and I went with her to the dining room table. I hadn't noticed but it was covered in photographs. They all seemed to be of a pregnant Beth and/or a baby Olivia.

I repositioned a few of them so I could see those hiding beneath, there were so many. Pulling out a chair, I sat down and continued to look through them. I didn't notice the kettle boil, nor did I notice that Beth set about making us both a drink. I hadn't realised that I had apparently lost time somewhere and now had a drink in my hands until Beth sat beside me.

"How come I've never seen these before? I mean, we have one or two photographs of Liv up from when she was a baby, but I had no idea that you had all of these. I just presumed Adam had everything."

"He does have a few, but I made sure that I got the majority of them."

"But then you hid them away."

"I didn't hide them. I just, I didn't want to have reminders everywhere for you, that I had a child."

"The child that lives with us? The child I cook for, clean up after, read stories with, take to the cinema and for days out? That child?" I asked puzzled and Beth sighed.

"What you need to remember, Em, is that I know you. I really know you. Better than I think you even know yourself."

"How can you be so sure? Because I haven't felt like we know each other very well at all just lately."

"How long have you had these feelings about wanting a baby? A few months? A year? Babe, I've known you would want a baby of your own since the very first day I met you. You scream 'Mummy' from your bones, it was always going to come up as something that we needed to talk about. So, I think because I wanted you for myself, and to build our family with Olivia, make her feel safe and happy, I wanted to keep any possible baby triggers out of your way. I had hoped that Olivia would help you to fulfil your Mummy role," Beth paused, and I took in everything she was saying. I had no idea that this was what had been going on, and I didn't really know what to think about it now. "I was just trying to make you feel like Olivia and I are enough for you, enough to make you feel happy and that your life was perfect," there's that word again.

"Beth, this has never been about whether you're enough for me. This is a desire that comes from somewhere deep inside that no woman alive has any control over. You either have this, this, 'calling' for lack of a better word, or you don't. I want to have a baby, not because I'm choosing to, but because my whole entire body is telling me that I have to. I don't think that a woman who feels like that can ever make those sorts of feelings go away. And honestly Beth, I don't think any woman should have to," she reached out at that point and took my hand.

"I know. I don't want to be the woman who takes this away from you. In the last forty-eight hours I have been thinking only of myself and how I could either stop this happening or how I could make it so that you changed your mind. I couldn't bring myself to accept that it was going to happen because I have spent years trying to prevent you from thinking about it."

"So what are you saying?"

"I'm saying, that if having a baby is what is going to make you happy and keep us together as a family, then I'm in," Beth looked at me as she said the words that I had been craving to hear for such a long time and I didn't know whether to laugh, cry, cheer, throw-up or scream. I think the noise that left me as my hand flew up to my mouth in disbelief was a combination of them all.

"Are you... are you sure?" I asked this with great hesitation, not wanting to offer a get out clause, but Beth just smiled at me.

"Yes. Yes I am sure. I am sure that I love you and that I want to spend the rest of my life with you, and that I want to do whatever I can to help you have a baby. *Our* baby," she grabbed my hand again as she said those last two words and it was then that I burst into tears and could hold my emotions in no longer.

This was it. We were going to have a baby!

Chapter 16

The week that followed what was now to be known as 'the worst and best weekend of my life' seemed to last forever. All I wanted was for the weekend to swing back round so that Beth and I could really talk, and so we could talk to Olivia too. I wanted us to be completely honest and open with her about this, I didn't want her at any point to feel like she was being pushed aside or forgotten.

Word of our engagement spread through the school quicker than a fire in a dried up forest. It was happy news, and I understood this, but it was something I felt quite out of control about. I couldn't deny that I was far more excited about the idea of having a baby than I was of getting married, but I could never let Beth see or know that that was how I felt. People congratulated me in the corridors, some of them I wasn't even sure who they were, but I smiled politely, and in my head, I was also responding to these well-wishers with: "I'm going to be a Mummy too!" But obviously I kept those little outbursts to myself.

I wanted to tell Kate, desperately, but she had got Tom's sister staying with them and I didn't want to interrupt their time together as a family. Eve, Tom's sister, hadn't met Amelia yet, so there was no way I could go and get in the way of all of that. I was certain that Kate would not mind, but for now I would wait. I also had reservations about telling Charlotte.

Everyone had been so excited when they came round the night we got engaged, but Charlotte was going through a lot right now and I didn't want to make any of the good things happening in my life make her feel any worse. She was so happy for us about the engagement, but what if this tipped her over? What if she couldn't bear the thought of after her own husband leaving her, her children feeling abandoned by their father, that here I am about to get married and have a child of my own? I knew she would be thrilled at the idea of becoming an auntie, but I had ultimately decided to wait before telling my family about any of the baby stuff until there was something to tell them about.

I had done a little research into the process that Beth and I were about to embark upon. I knew that I needed to have blood tests done at certain points in my cycle to check my progesterone levels, as well as measuring oestrogen, follicle stimulating hormone levels and thyroid stimulating hormone (amongst others). I had booked an appointment with my GP for Friday afternoon, Beth and I were going to go together, we had asked my mum to pick Olivia up from school for us as we were leaving half an hour before the end of the school day. We had told the headteacher (and Mum) that we had an appointment at the bank and that was the only time they could get us in. Friday afternoons were not so bad to escape early so I hadn't thought there would be a problem.

I was both elated and terrified about getting the process started, but it felt like I had been waiting forever to get off the starting block. Nothing stood in our way now. Beth had been wonderful about it all. We spent most evenings looking into sperm donors, if you subscribe to certain websites then you get a full profile, photographs, family history, the works. But as we were planning on letting the good old NHS send us in the direction of a fertility clinic of their choosing, we were sticking with the limited information where all you found out was the level of education, the generic height, weight, hair and eye colour, and a little bit about interests and career.

We did have a lot of fun picturing them in our heads, and we decided to name them after which male celebrity we thought they would most look like. So by the end of the week, we had a brown haired, blue eyed, post graduate who enjoyed reading and going on adrenalin holidays named Hugh Jackman. There was a blonde haired, blue eyed, post graduate who enjoyed the theatre and was just about to apply to do his PHD, we named him Benedict Cumberbatch. We particularly liked the sound of Eddie Redmayne, he had light brown hair, green eyes, was doing a post-graduate degree in Film Making (Concept to Screen), enjoyed reading and was in the middle of writing his own screen-play. Of course, each of these wonderful specimens came with a four figure price tag, but we were not about to jump in and ship baby Redmayne into my uterus without considering any and all options available to us. Although if it was a boy the name Eddie was growing on me somewhat.

As I was packing up my things ready for the weekend and a lovely lunchtime finish to the working week, my phone buzzed across the desk with Kate's name on the screen.

"Hey, are you on lunch?" she asked.

"Yeah, I'm just packing up to leave…" bugger…

"Leave? Did you forget that you have to go back to the classroom after lunch? School is not just for the children, you know, Em, the teachers are supposed to stay too."

"Very funny. I have an appointment this afternoon, so it's an early start to the weekend for me!"

"Ah, I see. Nothing life threatening or criminal to your appointment I hope?"

"No," I laughed, "it's at the bank," I hated lying to Kate, but I didn't want to tell her about our news over the phone. "How's that beautiful baby of yours?" classic change of conversation technique, always does the job.

"Ah, she's still beautiful, although I would say she is louder than she is beautiful."

"You don't mean that."

"Really? How about we see if you feel the same way after a sleep over and she's screaming for milk at 1:00am when you just put her down at 12:52am."

"Wow, you sell motherhood with such ease."

"Yep, I know how to switch on that new mother charm. Speaking of my charm, are you guys free this weekend?"

"Umm, yes, I think so, we have Olivia, but no plans, why?"

"Well, I'm sensing that Tom's sister is getting a little bored of just us and the baby for company. So, I was hoping to do a little nibbles and wine get together. Although I won't get the pleasure of the wine of course."

"It might help Amelia sleep through if you do."

"Ha! Not a bad idea at all! So will you be able to make it over? Tomorrow around six?"

"Sure, I'll ask my mum to come and sit with Olivia for us."

"Great, I shall see you then. Good luck at the bank!"

"Thanks sweetie, bye."

I hung up the phone and Beth appeared in the doorway.

"Hey! You ready to leave?" I asked, excitedly, and she nodded. "Are you okay?"

"Yeah, why?"

"Just checking," I picked up my bags and headed to the door, we walked out together and up the path towards the car park. "This is your last chance to turn and run in the opposite direction," I joked.

"I don't want to run away, I said we were doing this, so we're doing this," she seemed a little on edge. I suppose nerves were to be expected. I was nervous too, but I was excited, and my nerves were mostly down to a fear that Beth was not completely on board with what we were about to do.

I didn't want to question her any further over it, and I wasn't sure if I should have been worried that my gut was giving me warning signs about her level of commitment to this 'project'. I hoped that we just needed to get to the appointment and take it from there. I convinced myself that once we had asked our questions and had some of this process explained to us, we would both feel more confident and happier with moving forward. This was a huge moment for us, and I wanted us to both feel the excitement that was bubbling inside me.

My leg was twitching as we sat in the waiting room. So much so that Beth placed her hand gently on my knee before I even knew what I was doing. I squeezed her hand and we smiled at one another. The sound of the next patient's name being flashed up on the screen above the reception desk was like a sledge hammer bringing down a wall. I jumped up and held Beth's hand all the way to the Doctor's room. We walked in and sat down beside one another, the Doctor smiled and offered her hand out, we each shook it in turn, and I explained to her why we were there.

My research had paid off to a certain degree, but I tried to play down how much I knew and how much I had looked into it without involving Beth. She asked lots of questions, which I took as a good sign, that she was getting involved. I was right about the blood tests, there was one I had to take on day three of my period, and then a whole bunch of other hormone checks in the first week of my cycle, and another on day 21 of my cycle. Fortunately, I could rely on Mother Nature's visit like clockwork, so none of the blood tests would be a problem. Beth and I would also be referred to a counsellor to talk about how we feel about the process, becoming parents and various other elements.

Beth was a little uncomfortable at that thought, she tried to explain that she had a child already and so didn't need to have counselling to talk about the process of entering motherhood. The Doctor explained that this would be very different and that even same sex couples who may already have children but wish for more and need fertility help, would still require the counselling when using donor sperm.

One other thing she made clear to us, upon Beth mentioning her already having a child, was that this would not be funded by the NHS, as we would both already be considered as 'parents'. She didn't mention a sum, and I didn't ask. What would it matter ultimately? I wasn't about to put a price on the whole thing, I honestly couldn't care less. I would find the money somewhere.

We had two options when it came to the actual insemination. There was Intrauterine Insemination (IUI) and In Vitro Insemination (IVF). IUI is when they pick out the best swimmers from a sperm specimen and they insert them into the uterus when ovulation is detected. IVF is the process of removing eggs and fertilizing them in a laboratory, before inserting them back into the uterus in the hope that the embryos take and result in pregnancy. Once I had had the required blood tests and they all came back without any concerns, we would be referred to a fertility clinic.

My head was bamboozled when we walked out of the room. Beth and I looked at one another and took a big breath of air and exhaled heavily. She took my hand and gave it a reassuring squeeze, I leaned in and kissed her softly. It was at that point that we heard a familiar voice, and we were busted on our whereabouts.

"Hello you two!" it was Kate, "I thought you were at the bank this afternoon?"

"Uh, yes, we have been to the bank, and I just came to pick up a prescription," Beth tried her best to cover our tracks, but Kate was not easily fooled.

"Is everything okay with Amelia?" I asked, looking down at the sleeping baby in her car seat.

"Yeah, we were just here for a check-up, she's putting on weight and all is well. So, when I asked you earlier if your appointment was life threatening or criminal, was I on the right lines?"

"No! Not at all!"

"So you're okay? Both of you?" I looked at Beth and she rolled her eyes and sighed. I laughed and turned back to Kate.

"We were here to see the Doctor about getting pregnant," I blurted out. Kate's hand flew up to her mouth and she squealed slightly.

"Oh my God, really? Oh this is the best news ever!" Amelia's car seat got dropped to the floor and Kate flung her arms around the two of us. "So, how does it work, what do you do now? Have you chosen a sperm donor?"

"Slow down! We've had one appointment! It's a process, and we have started it, so now we will continue along it until we get the desired result."

"Oh screw that! You're going to be a Mummy!" she hugged me again and she linked her arm through mine. We started to walk towards the exit and Kate looked back over her shoulder to Beth, "be a gem would you, Beth?" and she nodded towards her sleeping daughter. "It's been a while since you've carried one of those things, it'll be good for you to remember how heavy and awkward they are," she winked, and Beth laughed.

We chatted for a while by the side of the road, and then Amelia woke up so it was time for us to part ways. Kate was so excited, and I was thrilled to have her to share this with.

Beth and I went straight home and my mum was there was Olivia. It wasn't until I walked into the kitchen that I realised Charlotte and the kids were there too. I kissed my mum's cheek and gave Charlotte a hug. Beth went straight through to the kids in the living room.

"Emily!" That was not Beth's happy voice. "What is this?!" we all piled in and stared down at the small ball of fluff climbing over the kids and wagging her tail.

"It's a dog."

"I know it's a dog. What is it doing here?"

"Oh that's probably my fault..." Mum confessed, "I picked up Olivia and she said that Emily had told her she would be able to bring Margot to visit. So we went and collected her on the way home. Adam said he would collect her later. Was that not right?"

"It's fine Mum," I laughed and reached down to give Margot's tummy a scratch. "I did tell Olivia that Margot could visit, I didn't expect her to take me up on it quite so soon, but it's fine. I'll make us some tea," I stood up and the grown-ups went back into the kitchen. Beth was muttering under her breath about dog puddles and shit everywhere, but I managed to tune her out because today nothing could bring me down from the happy cloud I sat on high in the sky.

We arranged our night with Kate and Tom whilst Mum was there, we also ended up convincing Charlotte to come along with us, so we were now dropping Olivia off at Charlotte's house where Mum would be (probably with Gran. She had taken to using Tinder and Mum was her 'wingman' to decide whether she was to swipe left or right). It was quite surreal knowing what I knew about mine and Beth's future, and not be able to talk to the world about it. But we agreed. We would talk to immediate family as soon as my blood tests came back okay. If everything was okay medically then there was no reason to keep it a secret from those closest to us.

Beth and I enjoyed a night curled up on the sofa once everyone had gone. Adam collected Margot and Olivia disappeared upstairs to read to Joy. (The fish had been renamed 'Joy', from the Inside Out movie, which had now replaced Finding Dory as her favourite Disney film.) Beth and I had found the name choice quite amusing as the fish itself could not have looked less joyful if it was floating on the top of the water dead. I had considered talking to Beth about discussing our plans with Olivia sooner rather than later, but I decided against it. When there was something to talk about then we would.

Chapter 17

The following morning, I got a call from Kate in a little bit of a flat spin.

"Oh, Em, this is going to be a disaster!"

"What is? What's wrong?"

"Well, tonight has sort of spiralled into a little bit more than nibbles and wine. It's more of a wetting the head slash making up for all of Eve's birthdays we missed sort of party…"

"Wow, a house party? I understand the wetting the head part, but what's this with Eve's birthdays?"

"Well, it turns out we didn't get her a birthday present in forever, which is what happens when you presume your husband is taking care of his sister's gift, so he suggested we make the little get together tonight a sort of party to make up for the years we have missed, which then snowballed into Eve inviting most of the people she knows still living in the area. Tom then added it would make a great wetting of the head for Amelia, so now I've got somewhere between twenty and thirty people coming to the house tonight and I haven't washed my hair in almost a week, I just keep using dry shampoo, but I ran out this morning so now I need to wash it and I don't have time because I sent Tom to the supermarket to get food and alcohol and so I have to watch Amelia and I just can't do this Emily, it's impossible, the whole thing is just impossible!"

"Kate, breathe. I'll be right there," I had years of practice in recognising when Kate was sending an indirect SOS. She would never outright ask anybody for help, she would just speak somewhat incoherently, rarely pausing for breath until someone came to her aid. Usually me, and then once she was married Tom picked up some shifts too.

"Thank you," she whispered.

"Go and get yourself a cup of tea, help is on the way."

"Okay," another whisper and then the line went dead.

I went to find Beth in the kitchen, she was making brownies with Olivia to take to Charlotte's tonight. They smelt delicious, and I caught them both with spoons going around the mixing bowl as they baked in the oven.

"The idea of baking is to have a product at the end, not just eat the ingredients as you go along."

"We have finished the baking, they're in the oven." Olivia announced with far too much sugar induced sass.

"Mm, I can smell them! Listen, I've just had Kate on the phone, it turns out tonight has turned into a full-blown party and she's sent Tom out for supplies, but is struggling to get herself and the house ready with Amelia in tow, do you mind if I lend her a hand?"

"Sure. We could all go if you can hang on for approximately twelve more minutes? Liv can watch Amelia and we can help Kate."

"Yay! Oh please! Can we?" Olivia started bouncing up and down and I became increasingly concerned over how much brownie mixture she had consumed.

I smiled and closed the small gap between us and kissed Beth on the cheek. "See, now that's why I love you, my hero."

"That's me, and technically we're both going to be Kate's *heroines*," she checked that Olivia wasn't looking and gave me a peck on the lips before she headed out of the kitchen. "I'm just going to get changed, I'm covered in chocolate, keep an eye on the oven babe," Olivia followed saying that she was going to teach Amelia a song she had been listening to at school and proceeded to practice it as she went upstairs.

About half an hour later we pulled up outside Kate's house and she opened the door before we had even made it up the driveway.

"Hi, I'm so sorry about the phone call Em," she kissed my cheek and then Beth's, before pulling Olivia in for a hug and guiding us all inside. "I just lost it for a moment."

"It's completely fine, no need to apologise," I said.

"I don't know what came over me, one minute I'm changing Amelia's nappy, the next minute I catch my reflection in the mirror and honestly don't recognise the woman staring back at me," she paused and looked at Olivia, "Amelia's in her moses basket in the living room if you want to go through to her." Olivia didn't need telling twice and disappeared in a flash.

"Kate, you're bound to feel a little overwhelmed. You have a new-born baby. You certainly shouldn't be throwing parties!"

"I know, but I miss me. I miss who I was, I never used to look like this Em, I used to wear make-up and have hair that shone from health rather than the amount of grease you could fry chips in. I went to my first 'Mummy and Me' group this week and I thought it would be a chance to escape but all anyone talked about were cracked nipples whilst singing songs about the sun loving me and how to use sign language to say hello. I could think of some other sign language I'd like to have shown them believe me! This one woman does nothing but talk about how everything her baby has is organic and made herself from scratch, and she refers to it all as being 'cobbled together', most morning's I'm just like, alright – I got dressed today! Who are these alien mothers that make it look so easy, where do they come from?"

The whole time Kate was talking I was directing her upstairs and into the bathroom. I ran a bath, put lots of bubble bath in and found her some shampoo and conditioner that had been buried underneath a pile of baby grows and baby shampoo. Kate and I had seen each other in our birthday suits on many an occasion, some whilst drunk on holidays, some whilst putting the world to rights, one of us having a soak, the other on the loo. So I helped her into the bath and then I washed her hair for her.

Once my work here was done, I left her to relax for a while, finding Beth emptying the dishwasher and Olivia singing to Amelia. I found the polish and a duster, and then Beth hoovered. I raced towards Amelia in a panic that she would be woken by the noise, but she never made a sound. I had heard about the wonder of 'white noise' to calm babies, now I was seeing it first-hand it was like a really cool magic trick or baby hypnotism.

Whilst Beth finished off, Olivia and I took the time for some cuddles with Amelia as she stirred, and I wanted to try and soothe her until Kate was ready to put her 'Mum' hat back on. After a few minutes of silence, I heard the front door open, Tom was home. I overheard Beth explaining what we were doing there and then I went to see if Kate was okay. She was snoring. Blissfully, happy, relaxed snores echoing around the bathroom. Smiling, I left her to her sleep and went to put the kettle on.

Tom retrieved a bottle of expressed milk from the fridge and warmed it up. I then fed Amelia, basking in the simple joy of feeding a baby and how much it warmed my heart to hear her tiny little swallows as she guzzled it down.

Half an hour later, Kate appeared as we all sat drinking tea in the kitchen. She was wrapped in a dressing gown with a towel around her head and big fluffy slippers on her feet. But the most noticeable feature was the big smile on her face.

"Oh, Emily Taylor, I could kiss you. Sorry Beth," Kate held up her hands towards Beth and then cupped my face. "You are one in a million, I feel like a new woman. How long was I up there?"

I looked at my watch, "about an hour and a half I think."

"Bloody hell, I don't remember the last hour and a half where I wasn't attached to Amelia or doing something around the house."

"Well, now you're ready to be the hostess with the mostest tonight, and we need to get a wriggle on to ensure we look our best too," I picked up my jacket and gave Tom's arm a squeeze. "Keep an eye on your girls, Tom," I said under my breath as Kate gathered up Amelia from Olivia. "I've not seen her that wound up in a long time, is she okay?"

"I know," he paused and looked at his wife and daughter, "she's been a bit teary, but Amelia is not fond of sleeping. At. All. We're both exhausted, but obviously I'm at work and so Kate's taking the brunt of it all."

"Well if there is anything I can do then please just ask, we're here if we can help."

"Thanks, Em. Appreciate that, hopefully Eve is sticking around for a bit, she's having some 'life issues', whatever that means, she's in no hurry to go home anyway," I smiled and then we all moved to the front door. The three of us piled into the car as Kate, Tom and Amelia waved us off.

When we got home it was all systems go. Beth and I began the process of outfit choosing and hair and make-up prep, and Olivia packed an over-night bag for Charlotte's. I called her to let her know that tonight was now a less formal, small intimate occasion, to a slightly larger more sociable affair. She tried to pull out, saying she wasn't ready for socialising with anyone never mind a group of people she didn't know, but I told her she had no choice and that she was coming whether she liked it or not.

I paused for a minute to replay the day in my head. I had tried to check in with Kate as much as I could, but it was hard getting the balance right between letting her enjoy her new baby and her family, and looking like I didn't care at all. I felt a little bit now like I had let her down. I would have to make a more conscious effort to be available more, to not let days pass by before I've asked how everything is. It wasn't about whether she could cope or not, and I didn't think she was depressed or anything like that. She just needed time for herself again, to sleep, to wash her hair, to eat a meal with her husband. They needed a date night.

I would offer my services as a babysitter. Although, as Tom said, with Eve around then that should allow for sharing out the load a little anyway.

We pulled up outside Charlotte's at six thirty, Olivia jumped out of the car, and we beeped for Charlotte to come out to meet us. When she didn't appear after a couple of minutes, I took off my seatbelt and went inside. Beth said she'd call into Tesco Express for a bottle of wine and then come back.

I went inside and found Gran hoola-hooping on the Wii with Amy and Olivia, Mum knocking back what was clearly not her first glass of wine of the evening and Charlie jumping up and down on a whoopee cushion, laughing uncontrollably every time it 'farted'.

"Mum, where's Charlotte?"

"Upstairs. I've tried to help her, Emily, but she won't even open the door now. You'll have to try yourself," Mum took another sip of wine, and I went up to Charlotte's bedroom. I knocked on the door and pushed it open.

"Charlotte? Are you okay?" she was sitting at her dressing table, clothes all over the bed, the floor, shoes discarded everywhere, drawers and wardrobe doors wide open. And she was crying.

"I'm sorry. I am coming, I am. I'm just not quite ready."

"What is it? What's wrong?" I sat beside her and placed an arm around her shoulder.

"I'm being ridiculous. But, it's just that... everything reminds me of him. Every outfit I try on that I think I look good in, is an outfit I bought to look good for him. Then it triggers a memory of when I last wore it and I start to cry. I can't control the tears, they're unbearable, and I thought I was done with crying over him, so then I get mad because he's still making me cry."

"Oh sweetie. I hate to say it, but you're probably going to cry about lots of things for a while. It's still so soon after... well, after he..."

"Abandoned his wife and children?"

"Well, yes."

"I've heard nothing from him, Em. Not a word. Nothing about the kids, not even asking how they are doing. That's what hurts the most," I took a minute to think and watched as my baby sister dabbed tears from her cheeks, desperately trying to not have to reapply make-up for probably the tenth time.

"Okay, I have an idea. Take off your clothes."

Fifteen minutes later, Charlotte and I reappeared in the living room and the only person who really took any notice was Beth.

"Umm. Okay. I am fairly certain that that is not the outfit you had on when we left home..." she was confused and I smiled, kissing her cheek.

"We had a change of heart on our attire, and I decided to give something different a try, Charlotte liked what I had arrived in, so we traded."

"Okay... well, for the record, you look hot. I'm not against clothes swapping with your sister for any and all future nights out," I grinned at Beth as her hand slid down from my shoulder blade to gently rest on my bum. A small squeeze and I looked up at the suggestive twinkle in her eyes.

"Later," I whispered.

We moved to the front door, Mum the only person to come and see us off. I could hear Gran getting cross at her Wii remote, blaming it for why she had just fallen off her skis. A little part of me wished I could stay and be a fly on the wall as the evening here played out. Mum and Gran were staying, and Charlotte was coming home with us, I was worried about Mum drinking so much, but then when I heard Gran shout at the TV, declaring that the little obese Wii Mii was a 'feckin' gobshite', I realised Mum would need the wine to survive until morning.

As we pulled off the drive a little part of me couldn't help but think Mum would have loved to join us, but even as the nonpaternal parent of any of the minors involved, I would not be comfortable leaving Gran in charge. We would have arrived home to find they had all gone out to get tattoos and take a ride on the back of a motorcycle.

Chapter 18

We pulled up outside Kate and Tom's, struggling to find somewhere to park. We ended up having to walk from the next street due to the number of cars that were parked at the front of the house. I wasn't entirely sure how Kate and Tom's neighbours were going to feel about this impromptu party, or the lack of ability to get onto their own driveways, but it wasn't for me to worry over.

I knocked on the front door and went straight in. There was music playing in the living room, which I soon realised could also be heard in the kitchen via Bluetooth speakers. It was a playlist of up to date chart music and songs that had been around over the last couple of decades. We moved through the house, keeping an eye out for Kate or Tom, and then I felt an arm land on my shoulder. I spun round to find Eve standing behind us.

"Emily!" she threw her arms around me as if we were old friends reunited. I really didn't know her that well, we had only met a few times at the usual events: Tom's 30th, Kate's 30th, Kate's hen night, the wedding. We weren't at the 'great big hug' stage of our friendship, if you could even call it that.

"Hi, Eve! Good to see you, you look great."

"Thanks, you too, I was so surprised when Tom and Kate offered to do this tonight, but it's great to see so many familiar faces."

"I'll bet. Well, umm, this is my partner Beth, and you remember my sister Charlotte."

"Of course," she gave them both the pleasantry air kiss by the cheek and then placed her hand on Charlotte's arm. "I was so sorry to hear about your husband, I mean, Kate asked me not to say anything, but when I heard what he did to you I was determined to make sure you had a great time tonight!" I managed a quick wide eyed exchange with Beth. "And we can't do that if you don't have a drink!" Eve grabbed Charlotte, who grabbed me, and I grabbed Beth's hand as we were dragged into the kitchen for drinks.

Eve certainly hadn't been shy about her passing comment. I wasn't sure that getting drunk would solve any of Charlotte's problems, but then it had been my idea to bring her along, so I suppose provided she had a good time there wasn't really anything to worry about...

There were probably around a dozen people in the kitchen, and from the glimpse of the living room I had managed as we walked in, around half a dozen more in there. The back door was open and there were maybe another half a dozen people or so outside. I thought for a second about whether I thought they were crazy or not, we were a few days shy of May, but it was a warm spring night and I supposed that it wasn't unrealistic to think people would filter outside, it was very warm in the house.

Drinks in hand, Eve kidnapped Charlotte to introduce her to some of her friends, and Beth and I found a place to sit in the living room. It was then that I spotted Kate walk by and head upstairs. We had struck up a conversation with someone Beth knew from an old job (pre working in education), so I excused myself as they reminisced and went after Kate.

"Kate! Hey, everything okay?" I followed her into Amelia's room, and she picked up the baby monitor off the chest of drawers.

"Forget my head if it wasn't screwed on, I must keep this attached to myself at all times, I feel like the world's worst mother having a party when there's a baby in the house. She's not old enough to be out of my sight for a single second!"

"You're allowed to be Kate tonight, don't worry about Amelia, she's fast asleep."

"For now!"

"Yes, and there are plenty of us here to keep checking on her and share the nappy changing and feeding so that you can have a good time."

"Emily, since when do you lactate? That doesn't usually happen until after the baby is born, not when you've only just decided to get pregnant," she winked at me, and I laughed.

"I'm fully aware of that."

"I'm so happy for you Em, it's the best news I could have heard. I can't wait for our kids to grow up together and be best friends just like us."

"What if it's a boy?"

"Then they can get married and have their own babies one day, you'd make a boy into a good and decent man. Nobody else would ever do for my girl," I rested my head on Kate's shoulder and we both stood watching a sleeping Amelia. It was hypnotic and made me wish I was curled up asleep somewhere too. Our hypnosis was broken when Tom came in laughing.

"I thought tonight was about being non-parent people?"

"Tom! She's still here, she's not gone away just because we've got some friends round. Although friends is stretching it, I don't know most of the people who are here. I could kill your sister."

"I know, sorry, she got a little bit carried away," Tom apologised and then disappeared as his name was shouted up the stairs.

"Well Eve's certainly taken Charlotte under her wing, pounced on her as soon as we got here."

"Sorry about that. We were talking earlier, and she was asking me who I had asked to come along, so I mentioned Charlotte and it all just came out."

"Well, Eve was certainly very outspoken! But it's fine, I suppose Charlotte can't pretend Chris is still around, she needs to try and forget him as soon as she possibly can."

"Well, she's a hot momma, she'll meet someone else. And speaking of hot momma's, can I just say how mightily hot you are looking this evening."

"Oh shut up," I shoved her aside and we headed out of the nursery, the baby monitor firmly attached to Kate's hand.

"I'm serious, you are dressed for trouble, miss," she smacked my bum and laughed as we went downstairs and re-joined the party.

I found Beth talking to Tom in the garden, Tom was seeking advice on whether Amelia was ever going to sleep during the night-time, and then a friend of his ran over with a shot of something green, apparently every time he mentioned Amelia tonight, he had to have a shot. As Tom walked away with his friend, I took the opportunity to kiss Beth. It was a good one. Soft, but meaningful, loaded with promises of where our night would end. I hadn't planned on drinking much, I wanted a steady head and would rather have made sure that

Beth and Charlotte had a good night, not to mention elevating any stress I could in tending to Amelia so that Kate and Tom had a great time too. But I knew exactly how I wanted my evening to end once I got my fiancée home.

The party was really quite wonderful. I believed it was largely down to the age of the people in attendance. Had we been ten years younger, then I think the volume of both the noise and alcohol consumed would have been very different. Everybody was mindful of their responsibilities the following morning. So once Amelia had had her eleven o'clock feed, there were only about a dozen people left. It was at this point, however, that things got a little messy. Somebody suggested playing the games 'I have never' and 'would you rather'.

For those of you unfamiliar with how they work, 'I have never' is when each person takes it in turns to say something that they have never done, and anyone who has tried the activity must have a shot. 'Would you rather' was just a silly game, which we decided everyone should have a drink after each person had a turn. You had to decide whether you would rather do things such as: eat dog shit or wash yourself in dog shit, or watch a porn film with your parents or watch a porn film with your parents staring. Unbearable questions that were impossible to not feel physically sick at the thought of doing. 'I have never' proved to be very interesting though, and definitely the more popular of the two games.

Beth was very drunk, as was Charlotte and her new best friend Eve. The three of them were sat giggling like little school girls, and I sat with Kate, considerably more sober than the others.

"Okay, I've got one," Eve held her shot glass up, "I have never done anything sexual with a woman," there were loud cheers around the room, and I rolled my eyes, taking a sip of my wine. I looked around as I watched all the men, Beth and Eve have a shot.

"Eve!" this was Tom's exclamation. He obviously was not aware of his sister's dabbling.

"Oh Tom, lighten up, there's a lot you don't know about me big brother," she winked and leaned towards Beth. I watched her move and it made me prickle slightly. Beth was completely oblivious and poured herself and Eve another shot. I wasn't sure I had ever seen her this drunk, but she was having a good time and that was the main thing.

"Okay, my turn," this was Kate, "I have never had a threesome," there were raucous cheers and squeals of shock as one or two people necked their shot, none more so than my own surprise when Charlotte knocked hers back!

"Oh my God, Charlotte!"

"I know. For fuck's sake don't tell Mum, and definitely don't tell Gran, she'll want a blow by blow account," she rolled around laughing and Beth and Eve reached delirious heights of laughter too.

"But, you and Chris…"

"Yes, yes, he was my first, blah, blah, blah. Do you remember that week away I had in Ibiza for my twenty-first? Well, let's just say, I had a *very* good time celebrating! Just me and two guys we spent the week hanging out with, it was our last night and definitely the most memorable…" laughter again erupted around the room, and I excused myself to go and get some fresh air.

"You okay?" Kate followed me out.

"Yeah, sorry, feel like I'm being a party-pooper. I just didn't know that Charlotte had led that kind of life!"

"She had a threesome Em, it's not like she's just confessed to being a high priced prostitute or serial killer," we both laughed.

"I know. I know, I'm being silly."

"If I'm being honest, I was more surprised that Eve has been up to no good with women than your sister's three-way, no offence! I mean that was a real shocker, I don't think Tom will be able to remove those mental images from his head for a while!" we laughed again and then Kate hooked her arm through mine. "Come on, let's go back inside it's bloody freezing out here, you can help me politely ask everyone to leave, I'm fucking knackered and just want to curl up with my baby."

"Tom or Amelia?"

"Definitely Amelia. Tom can take the sofa the amount he's had to drink," we walked back inside to hear Tom saying goodbye to a small group at the front door.

"Emily, Beth has gone upstairs with Eve to check on Amelia."

"Christ, Tom, they've got enough alcohol in them to open their own brewery, one breath on our child's face and she'll be as drunk as they are!" Kate was not impressed with this parenting decision, she was about to go upstairs when a smash was heard from the kitchen. "Shit."

"You sort the glass, I'll check on Amelia and the drunks," Kate blew me a kiss and I turned to go upstairs.

As I approached Amelia's bedroom door, I could hear Beth and Eve talking. I am not one for eavesdropping on other people's conversations, despite my gene pool, but as I reached out to push the door fully open, I couldn't help myself but to stand back and listen for a moment. Just for a giggle at the ramblings of two drunken women really.

"She's so beautiful when she's sleeping. Remind me, you have just the one daughter, is that right?" Eve asked.

"Yeah, Olivia. She's ten now. I can't believe it, she's growing up so fast."

"You don't look old enough to have a ten-year-old."

"Ha! You are drunk."

"You are more drunkerer."

"Am not! What about you anyway, got kids? Want kids?"

"Umm, got, no, want, not sure. They make life so... different," Beth laughed and then Eve echoed her, "I mean my brother is a changed man. And Kate? She's not the woman I knew a year ago, I just don't know if I have it in me to devote my whole life to raising another human being. They're so needy."

"Yes, exactly they are needy, they are needy and small and loud and messy," they both giggled, and I smiled at their drunken honesty.

"But I mean, Emily, she must want to be a mother, she's got that thing, that… that…"

"Quality."

"Yes! She's got the quality. The Mummy calling," they both laughed again. "So, do you think you guys will have a baby together?"

"Well, we're sort of missing some of the key ingredients and resources for that to happen," Eve burst out laughing and I heard a murmur from Amelia, "shh, shh, shh," they choked down laughter through noisy 'shh's.

"Okay, I know that, but there are ways of making it happen, you must have talked about it, especially now you're planning on getting married!"

"Sure, sure we've talked about it."

"And? I'm right aren't I, Emily wants to be a Mummy."

"Yep. She wants the sleepless nights, the worry, the stress, the restrictions and limitations on your freedom, the tied to your house with nappies and the smell of regurgitated baby milk surrounding you and embedded into everything you own…"

"Wow, if I wasn't sure about becoming a mother before, then you've definitely helped me to make my mind up now!" more sniggering from both women.

"Now, now don't say that. I love Olivia, it's not like I wish I had never had a child, because that's not true, I would never change that. But Emily, she wants a baby, and I don't… I don't want to go through all that again, but she'll change her mind, she'll… she will… we'll get married, and she'll be happy and that will be enough. Once she is my wife then I can finally put this silly baby stuff to bed, which I'm actually thinking is where I should be right now."

"Are you propositioning me, Elizabeth?" they both burst out laughing and Amelia started to cry. "Ssh, quick, before Kate or Tom hear," I didn't know what to do and I don't know how I got my feet to move, but I hid in the doorway of Kate and Tom's bedroom, and once Beth and Eve were safely down stairs, I went into the nursery and picked up Amelia.

What the hell had just happened? I couldn't keep my legs upright beneath me and half sat, half fell into Kate's nursing chair. It couldn't be true. She didn't mean it, she didn't really feel

139

that way. She said she loved me and that she wanted to do this with me, she couldn't possibly have been playing me all along, just to get me to marry her and then hold me at my promise of 'til death do us part', no matter what that meant I had to give up. How could she do this?

I looked down at Amelia as she lay blinking up at me in my arms, and just as sure as I had been that I had cried my last tears over not being able to have a child of my own, a fresh set worked their way down my cheeks. Silently stealing into the night, taking my happily ever after with them.

I had to put it down to the amount of alcohol she had had. I mean, we all say things when we're drunk. And yes, there's the whole thing where people say 'you speak the truth when you're drunk' but that wasn't the case with everything that anyone ever said. If that were true, then people would be saying the most awful things to one another as soon as they had breached their drink limitations. I mean, for all those girls' nights out when you've helped a friend drown their sorrows over a bloke that you knew all along was a total dick, but you still sympathise and support your friend in their grief over the end of a relationship. Or when you've had one too many cocktails and your best friend bends over and splits her trousers, and you thought they had looked a bit snug in the first place, but you tell her that they mustn't have been stitched properly. We all do it, we all protect people from what is unkind and, frankly, a little bitchy. This is because we care, and I knew that Beth cared about me.

After I had pulled myself together, I got Amelia back to sleep and then went back downstairs. Everybody had gone apart from me, Charlotte and Beth. They were talking with Eve in the living room, Tom was snoring on the sofa and Kate was in the kitchen clearing up. I helped finish off the tidying as much as I could whilst listening to Kate go on about how much she had enjoyed the night but that it had confirmed for her that she was past drunken nights and indecent conduct (not that there had really been any of that) and she couldn't wait for her house to be back to normal and to carry on being a mum. I smiled and nodded in agreement and then she saw that as an opportunity to talk about my own supposed impending journey to motherhood.

I switched off at this point and could not tell you one word that she said to me. It was safer to not listen whilst I processed what I had heard upstairs, rather than try and share the excitement I could hear in Kate's voice, albeit muffled like a playground full of laughing children. You know they're there and they are making noise, but you can't pick up specifically what anyone is saying.

Kate very kindly drove us all back to ours and I managed to get Beth and Charlotte out of their clothes and into bed. Charlotte was in Olivia's room, and it took me about twenty minutes to stop her obsessively watching the fish swim around the tank before I could convince her it was time to go to sleep. It was getting on for one o'clock and I was way past ready to try and get some rest. Mostly I was desperate to sleep in order for my brain to stop thinking. The problem I had was that I couldn't bring myself to get into bed beside Beth.

I took a spare duvet out of the airing cupboard and went into the small bedroom/office. It was an office in the loosest sense of the word. The room held a desk with computer (yes, an old desktop computer complete with monitor, keyboard and mouse, with an X-Files mousepad), a bookcase and an armchair. I climbed into the armchair (it was one of those big round swivel chairs) and I eventually managed to drift off. It was the sound of footsteps running towards the bathroom and the moans of someone throwing up their stomach contents that kept me awake to see light begin to fill the room as the sun eagerly welcomed in a new day.

Chapter 19

By eight o'clock I had given up on sleep. I waited for a break in footsteps, both sets, and darted for the bathroom to have a shower and wake myself up. This was the point I convinced myself that what I overheard last night was all drunk talk. That Beth loved me and wanted a child with me and that everything was going to work out just as it was supposed to. A small part of me wondered if maybe Beth could have been showing off to try and impress Eve with her carefree and high-spirited view of life, not wanting to have those 'restrictions' as she called them, making Eve think that she liked to live life on the edge and have adventures. Beth was the least adventurous person I knew, but I could see why she would want Eve to think otherwise.

After my shower I made both Charlotte and Beth some toast and got them a bottle of cold water each from the fridge. Both women thanked me, but only Charlotte managed to keep hers down and announced that she was beginning to feel more human and less walking dead. Beth, however, did not manage to eat much before needing to bring it back up. I waited so I could make sure she drank some water, and then I heard the shower go on.

Once Charlotte was ready to face a short car journey, I took her home. My car was still at Kate and Tom's, so I asked Mum to take me in hers to go and fetch it. When she asked if I was going back to Charlotte's or straight home with Olivia, I didn't hesitate in saying I would return to Charlotte's house. Beth was sleeping it off and would do far better by having some peace and quiet rather than Olivia and I pottering around.

When we had all returned to Charlotte's Mum made some sandwiches for everybody (Charlotte may have been present in body but she certainly was not in mind, the kids had hugged and kissed her, she had then taken to the sofa underneath a blanket where she proceeded to fall asleep). Mum enquired as to how the evening had gone and I managed to tell stories of fun and laughter, I may have even overshared, as Gran was keen to try out the game 'I have never'. I was terrified about the things I might find out about her if we did.

"It's more of a drinking game Gran, you know, when your inhibitions have been lowered and you don't care how honest you are."

"I don't need a feckin' drink to be honest about my life. I've never kept any secrets about myself," we knew this already, "sure I don't mind sharing things with my family."

"Mm, it's more over-sharing that I would be concerned about..."

Mum lifted her head and looked at Gran, "there's not enough alcohol in the world to numb the pain of what playing a game like that with you would cause!" it was rare for Mum to speak out like this, she saved these outbursts for when they were absolutely necessary. The thought of 'I have never' made her go pale and she quickly sat herself at the table.

"Well now, Jane, I can't help but wonder if it's mine or your own confessions that would trouble you so..." Gran winked at me, and Mum scowled. To be fair to Gran she had a point, but after the revelations about being dropped down the toilet as a baby I wasn't sure I was ready for any more stories like that.

"Eve is apparently sticking around for a while," my change the subject tactic.

"Oh well that's nice for Tom," Mum was thankful with her response, Gran sulked and gnawed on a cheese and pickle sandwich.

"Yes, she certainly enjoyed partying last night!"

"If I remember right, she was always a bit of a party girl, soon as she was old enough to go out drinking, she was off!" Mum said.

"How would you know that? Kate and Tom weren't together when Eve would have been that age."

"I know, their mum used to come to the yoga when it was all the craze. I tried my best, but I just couldn't relax my body enough to get into those ridiculous positions."

"There's nothing ridiculous about being a downward facing dog when a feathered peacock comes strutting your way," Gran. Even I rolled my eyes at her for that one.

"So, you knew Tom and Eve's mum well then?"

"I wouldn't say I knew her well, we talked whilst waiting for the instructor to begin each week. She would talk about trying to get Eve to come along with her to try and calm her soul and refocus her energy on something other than drinking and partying."

"Crikey, I had no idea. I guess Tom has never shared that side of Eve with Kate."

"Well, you wouldn't would you, I mean he's such a lovely young man, he wouldn't necessarily want Kate knowing about his sister's shenanigans as a young woman!"

"I bet he's got a nice set of peacock feathers," Gran again. "What does his sister do anyway? Sure she can't be that bad."

"I'm not sure, Gran. I think she's between jobs as they say."

"Well that's just a polite way of saying someone can't feckin' be arsed to get off their backside and sort themselves out a job. I never had a day where I was 'between jobs', feckin' lay abouts."

"Gran! You can't be so presumptuous of someone's circumstances."

"Sure I can, I worked my whole life, and I still get the odd phone call from the men in black, needing my expertise to stop the latest terrorist threat."

"Mother, you did not work for MI5, will you please just stop with that."

"I did! Ah you're all gobshites, I know what I did with my life, and I don't have to prove me-self to anyone."

"They would never employ an Irish woman to do that sort of job."

"Ha! Is that so? Did you never wonder, Jane, where I was some nights? Why I was gone for days at a time? Why your father was the one doing the school runs and making sure you had clean clothes to wear?"

"You were just one of those wives who wanted to make sure that their husband did housework, you never were one to conform to traditional roles. Everybody knows that you worked in publishing and had to travel with your job. Now let that be an end to it!"

"You ungrateful little... If it wasn't for my work with the MI5 then none of you would be here today, you mark my words! Now if I told you anymore than I already have I'd have to kill you, so let that be the end of it," with that she slunk off into the living room and proceeded to try and wake Charlotte. Good luck Gran.

Gran always spoke with such conviction when she talked about working for MI5. It did make you wonder for just a second whether there was actually any truth in it. It also made you wonder if she was suffering with some form of dementia. It all brought my mind back in a full circle though to Beth, and how convincing a person could be when actually they are telling you a complete and utter lie just because they know it's what you want to hear.

I was due to have some of my blood tests done this coming week, I was going to wait and see how involved she became in those before deciding whether to confront her about what I overheard. Obviously I know there isn't much anyone can do to be 'involved' in a blood test, but I wasn't a massive fan of needles, so the hope would be to have her at least come with me to hold my hand. It's what any caring spouse would do isn't it?

At the point Olivia appeared in the kitchen to sit beside me because she was bored, I knew it was time to go. The day had disappeared into nowhere and nothing, tomorrow back to work and to another week that would go by in a whirlwind. We said our goodbyes and got into the car, waving off the small crowd at the door. Charlotte had insisted that she was fine, and that Mum and Gran could leave too, but Mum insisted she get the kids their tea and then she would go. Charlotte didn't argue and said she was going for a lie down.

We got home and the house was dark. It wasn't yet dark outside though, dusk was sitting comfortably in the sky and light wasn't quite ready to give its time up to the night. Olivia went straight upstairs to check on the fish, I pulled some take away menus out of the drawer and wondered what I fancied to eat. I couldn't be bothered to cook, and I didn't think Beth would be all that interested in food anyway.

"Liv, just stick your head in our bedroom and see if your mum is awake," I shouted up the stairs. My shouting alone would have woken anyone sleeping, but I was just trying to establish dinner plans. I listened to the footsteps pad across the landing and our bedroom door open. A muffled sound of voices in conversation and then the door closing again.

"She's awake, she said she'll be down in a minute."

"Okay, pizza for tea, Liv. That alright?"

"Yes!" she did a little fist pump at the top of the stairs and then disappeared back into her bedroom.

I hadn't expected Beth to want anything to eat, but when she saw me perusing the menu of my preferred take away establishment, she pouted her lips and rubbed her belly.

"I need stodge," she sighed and kissed my cheek. "I'm so sorry babe, I can't believe I've lost a whole day."

"Well I can, you were hammered. As was my sister."

"Shit, yeah, is she okay?"

"She's home, she's tired, but she's okay. Mum and Gran are doing their best to take care of the kids without annoying her and getting under her feet, but I don't know how successful they are in their mission with that one."

"Ha, no. I can't imagine Nancy being particularly patient and understanding."

"She's not a bitch."

"No, I know, I wasn't saying she was a bitch, I just meant she's not the most subtle of people," Beth took a sip of a glass of water, and I smiled at her apologetically. I knew she hadn't meant anything bad about Gran. I snapped because the sound of her voice took me right back to hearing her conversation with Eve last night. Also, I was also incredibly tired and after pizza and a soak in the bath I would be ready for bed.

Menu choices made, dinner was ordered, delivered and consumed within an hour. Olivia went for a shower, and I waited patiently to hear her bedroom door close so I could make my way up for a bath. It was usually the one place where I could get lost in a good book, knowing I was free from interruption and distraction, but tonight I wasn't in the mood for reading. I just needed to close my eyes and let the hot, soapy water wash over me. I was absolutely worrying over nothing. Beth was fine, she was being perfectly normal with me, we were getting on with one another, we had talked over dinner, Olivia made us laugh filling us in on the card games that Gran had tried teaching them all after giving up on trying to win anything on the Wii. Although we were a little concerned about their ages and the fact that they were all now pretty skilled at poker.

After my bath I popped my head into Olivia's room and she was already fast asleep in bed, I dread to think what time they were up to the night before, probably later than we were! I went into our bedroom and Beth was sitting up looking through the paper. We had had the Mail on Sunday delivered to our house ever since I can remember. Evidently today it had taken Beth a while to feel up to reading it. It was usually thumbed through thoroughly on a Sunday morning whilst I got up and did some school work before we did anything else with the remainder of our weekend.

I climbed into bed and kissed her briefly on the lips before turning over to get comfortable.

"Is that the best I get? A peck on the lips?"

"Sorry, I'm knackered. Just need to get a decent night's sleep or the kids will run rings round me at work."

"Are you okay?" she quizzed.

"Yes, I'm fine. Why wouldn't I be?" did she have a sudden memory of what she had said and was about to confess the secret thoughts she shared with Eve?

"No reason. You've just been a bit off tonight."

"I'm just tired, yours and Charlotte's footsteps dashing across the landing through the early hours wasn't exactly conducive to sleep," I turned back round to face her again and smiled reassuringly, "there is nothing wrong, honestly."

"Okay," she leaned down and kissed me again. She lingered longer than I had, and then I rolled back over.

"By the way, are you going to be able to come to the Doctor's with me on Thursday for my blood tests?"

"That's this week?"

"Yep. Out of our hands I'm afraid, this part is all down to Mother Nature and her monthly visits."

"Okay, yeah, of course I'll be there with you," she put the paper down on the floor and curled up behind me, I believe it is called spooning. "I'll be there every step of the way, and I know how much you hate needles." See, she was wonderful. She was wonderful and loving and with me all the way. I was worrying for no reason whatsoever and my mind was completely convinced of this as it finally drifted into a peaceful sleep.

Chapter 20

Thursday arrived so quickly I could have put money on Monday through to Wednesday not actually happening. Life couldn't have been more 'normal' and it was almost unsettling at how everyone in my life seemed to be harmoniously ticking over in their own little way.

So when we sat in the waiting room about to have my blood test, I was remarkably calm. It was a lovely sensation and one that I was completely open to becoming accustomed to. When my name flashed up on the screen, however, that sensation left my body so fast I felt as if I was just a shell sitting on the hard red chairs and my body and everything that makes me me, had ran out of the door so fast I could see it swinging back and forth on its hinges.

Beth squeezed my hand, and I came back to Earth. The door wasn't swinging on its hinges, and I wasn't an empty shell. I was here and this was a necessary step that I just had to grow some balls (ironic when you considered if there were actual balls involved then there would be no need to have a medical intervention to make a baby) and get on with it.

The nurse always tells you that you'll feel a little scratch, and it usually is, and this was no different. I sat with my eyes closed, Beth holding the hand of the arm that wasn't being stuck with a needle, and I went to a happy place in my head. Imagining the end result of all of this. The baby that I would get to hold in my arms and raise together with the woman I love. Just that simple image in my head and that was that. Job done, blood taken, trauma over.

We went for a celebratory latte from a small cafe a few streets away from home and I made the most of the pampering and looking after that Beth was offering after I had been so brave at the doctors. Pathetic, I know. We went home with a happy bounce in our step and somehow Eve came up in conversation. I think the link had been talking about Kate and Amelia.

"Apparently she's still staying with them," I said.

"You're kidding?"

"No, I spoke to Kate yesterday and she said that Eve was an absolute God send and really helping them out with housework and stuff."

"Wow, that's not the Eve that we spent last Saturday night with!"

"No, it certainly isn't." I had a window of opportunity here. Beth and I hadn't talked about Saturday night at all, so I couldn't bring anything up about conversations that may or may not have happened that Beth may or may not remember that she may or may not know that I overheard. Wait, did that make sense...

It was now or never, I either brought it up or I put it to bed for good. "Do you remember disappearing off upstairs with her last weekend?"

"Who? Me and Eve?" I nodded," God, no. Not really. I mean, I remember saying I'd check on Amelia, I think you were outside with Kate... and I might remember Eve being there... she could have been, I honestly don't know babe. It's been a long time since I've been that drunk and I'm in no hurry to do it again! In fact, once you're pregnant, then I'm going to stop drinking too," we stopped walking and I looked at her in disbelief.

"What?"

"Yes. I've decided. If you can't drink, then I won't drink either," she kissed me and pulled me into a big bear hug. I wrapped my arms around her and squeezed as hard as I could. That was the end of that. This was all just nonsense in my own silly head. Beth had been drunk and let her mouth run away from her, probably for the purpose of entertaining the woman she was with at the time. Maybe even a small flirtation? Whatever it was, I didn't care.

I couldn't afford to keep these unnecessary stresses or worries in my head. They were foolish and had no basis for any legitimate fear. From this moment on I was going to focus on the future, and what Beth and I were now heading towards. Raising our baby together and getting married.

When we got home, I set about finding something to make for dinner. As I've said, I wasn't historically the cook in our house. I had some issues regarding high standards of cleanliness, and good housekeeping. So, Beth was the cook because she cooked better, and I was the cleaner because I cleaned better. I'm not sure how much of my thought process on these roles Beth was actually privy to, but I didn't enjoy cooking as much as I enjoyed the sight of a clean kitchen once it was all over and done with. Beth was a messy cook, she would happily own up to this fact, I was a tidy up as you go along kind of cook. I had taken some chicken out to defrost that morning, so I just had to figure out what to do with it now. Fajitas were usually my go to dish, I saw no reason to change the cooking habits of a lifetime, so fajitas it was.

I was a couple of minutes from dishing up – the salad was in a bowl on the table, there was sour cream, guacamole, grated cheese, salsa, peppers and a pile of tortillas to load up with fajita goodness – when there was a knock at the door. Beth answered it and I cursed under my breath whoever it was to dare interrupt my culinary masterpiece. I was rather surprised to then discover Beth stood in the hallway with Eve. She looked like she had been crying, and this was confirmed when she burst into tears, Beth put her arm around her and guided her into the living room. I went into the kitchen and turned down the heat on the chicken, I sensed dinner would be delayed.

"I'm so sorry to just turn up like this, but I didn't know where to go and I hate people seeing me like this, but I knew you wouldn't judge, I've had a huge row with Kate and Tom, well, more so Tom, but I had to get out of the house."

"Of course, we are the last people who would ever judge anyone," Beth provided the consoling friend role, I sat down on the armchair opposite the two of them. "What happened? What was the argument over? I'll bet it was something really daft and it will all sort itself out."

"I wouldn't be so sure about that," Eve half laughed through her upset. "I umm, I didn't know how to tell them about why I was really back when I first got here. So, I just said it was to meet Amelia and spend time with my family. But that wasn't the truth," she paused, and I could see she was processing in her mind the best way to tell us whatever it was she had been hiding.

"Eve," I smiled, "if you don't want to tell us that's okay," I knew that Kate would fill me in if Eve couldn't bring herself to, "but we are here to listen if you feel you want to talk." Eve smiled back and nodded.

"I umm, I got into trouble, I found myself in a situation I didn't want to be in. I just, I wasn't ready, I wasn't ready for everything that comes with it, I couldn't do it. I don't know why I came back here, I mean seeing Amelia was never going to make it any easier. I guess maybe I wanted to see if I felt any differently around a baby, but I didn't. I knew that I had done the right thing, just by seeing how crazy life was now for Kate and Tom, they never stop doing things for Amelia or linked to Amelia, I can't do that, I'm too selfish. It wouldn't have been fair on... on the baby..." she burst into tears, sobbing onto Beth's shoulder.

She may not have explicitly said the words, but I was in no need of further explanation from Eve about what she had done. Her 'situation' had clearly been a pregnancy. And she had got rid of it. She had had an abortion. How ironic it was our house that she saw as a sanctuary. I am not a judgemental person, but my road to pregnancy was not going to be as simple and easy as hers had been. I couldn't sit here and pretend that I thought what she had done was okay, when my own selfish needs made me want to scream at her.

I stood up and announced I would make us all some tea, when I got into the kitchen, I stared at the chicken getting dry and stuck to the pan. I filled the kettle and waited for it to be loud enough to mask the sound of my anger, my anger as it was released through a glass I smashed down into the sink as I mourned the loss of Eve's unborn child.

I did make us all a cup of tea, and I managed to sit intermittently in the living room with them, but Beth was doing an amazing job at being a supportive friend, I wasn't in a place where I could do that.

"I take it, Kate and Tom were not supportive of your decision?" I asked.

"That's an understatement. I mean, I get it, they're new parents, but that doesn't give them the right to make everyone else feel like they should be parents too. They're obsessed with it, it's their whole world, but I'm not ready."

"Does the father know?"

"No. We just fooled around a few times, we weren't serious. He's an old friend, we go back years, and I didn't see the point in ruining my friendship with him by complicating matters any more than they needed to be. Kate wasn't the worst one, which surprised me, it was Tom. He was so disappointed in me, I think that's why I was so upset. He's my big brother and I would never want to let him down. But how is it fair to bring a child into the world who wasn't planned for or wanted? A child needs love and stability and two parents who love each other, I have nothing to offer a baby right now," Eve started crying again and I took the empty mugs out to the kitchen.

Standing at the sink (the broken glass having been safely removed), I stared out into the garden. This was all requiring a lot of deep breaths and self-control on my part to not reflect my own current wants onto Eve. We're not all the same, we don't all strive for the same things, and ultimately, my anger and upset was all rooted in jealousy. That she had been able to get pregnant and have a life starting inside her and then she chose to get rid of it. I just couldn't wrap my head around it, but that was the head of someone trying to get pregnant. If I wasn't at the place in my life that I was, then maybe I would be able to demonstrate more sympathy and understanding.

I busied myself in the kitchen, tidying, sorting, it seemed like as good a time as any to have the routine clear out of some things that were past their use by date. Beth was not as stringent in following these recommended dates, I struggled not to. In my mind the date was there for a reason. Past the date, pass the bin.

After a while of making myself scarce, I made my way back to the living room. I paused as my hand reached out to open the door, I was puzzled. I didn't remember shutting it when I left them. I took a deep breath and told myself I was being ridiculous as all sorts of reasons for the door being closed ran through my very overactive imagination. It wasn't closed exactly, just pushed close. I could see them both through the gap, their voices were quiet, I struggled to hear at first what they were talking about.

"I knew you'd understand, when we talked at the party at the weekend, I could see in you exactly what I feel in myself. When you said about not wanting another baby," Eve paused, "I knew I could talk to you. But I am sorry to just barge in like this."

"It's fine, don't worry. Of course you can talk to me."

"Does Emily know yet? About you not wanting a baby?" Beth didn't speak, but I couldn't be sure if she shook her head, the gap in the door wasn't wide enough. She glanced over towards the exact spot I was stood in, and I shot backwards, being very thankful of having no creaky floorboards. She was checking the door was closed and that I was nowhere in earshot.

"I'm going to push for a quick wedding, that's the only thing I can think to do. Then once we're married, I'll be able to make her see that she doesn't need a baby. That Olivia and I are all the family she needs, and I know Emily, she won't take the commitment of wedding vows lightly, she'd never walk away from Olivia and I, not after everything we've been through. Her sister's done me a huge favour too by her marriage breaking up, Emily would never bring that to her parents' door after seeing how it has affected her family rallying around her sister and her kids. So that would be the end of that."

"But she doesn't technically need you to have a baby. What if she just goes ahead and does it anyway?"

"Emily? No way. She wouldn't do something like that. We love each other, that'll be enough. She'll see. I've just got to play it carefully to make sure I get it right, and the first thing once we're married will be to move away from here."

"Wow, really?"

"Yeah, it's time we bought somewhere that was ours. This place is Emily's, she bought it before I came along, and it's never really felt like home to me. I need to get her away from people who will encourage her to pursue things that as far as I am concerned are not part of my plan for our life together."

"Bloody hell, Beth. How very James Bond Villain of you."

"I'm not doing anything wrong. I'm protecting my family, and I'll do whatever it takes to keep us all together."

I had half leaned and half fallen into the wall as I used it to work my way back to the kitchen. Once I was in there I sat down on a chair and just stared. I didn't cry, I didn't make a sound. My whole life was unravelling before my eyes, my plans and hopes for the future were being kept out of my reach by a woman who protested she loved me. I had been a fool. A big, stupid fool.

Eve didn't stay much longer. I managed to say goodbye to her and smile politely, I let Beth see her out whilst I tried to salvage dinner. They certainly weren't my best attempt at fajitas, but we managed to eat them, and Beth kindly implied they were just as tasty as if we had eaten them an hour or so earlier. I struggled to swallow every bite. Once I had tidied up the kitchen I went for a bath and then I got straight into bed. I had no idea what Beth was doing, and I didn't care.

I somehow managed to fall asleep and when I woke the next morning I got up and ready before Beth had even stirred. I couldn't bring myself to look at her never mind talk to her. I had no idea what I was going to do but I knew that for the time being I needed to be as far away from her as I could make possible.

When she came downstairs for breakfast, I was putting my bags into the car.

"I have a meeting this morning with a parent, and then a training thing after school, so we'll go in two cars today, I'll catch you later tonight."

"Oh," Beth looked confused, "you never said."

"I know, been preoccupied though, of course," I smiled. At least I hoped it came out as a smile, I was a bloody good actress when I had to be.

"Well what about dinner?"

"You and Olivia eat; I'll pick something up on my way home. Got to go, see you later," I shut the door behind me and leaned on it momentarily before forcing my legs to carry me to the safety of the car.

The drive to school was quick and one of those routes you take so often that just happens. One minute you're at home, the next you're at work, with no idea of how you actually got there. I busied myself quickly and easily once I was shut away inside the haven of my classroom. It was the arrival of Lucy that forced me out of my happy work bubble.

"Morning! How glad are we that it's Friday!" It was a statement rather than a question; Lucy liked Fridays and was probably going to be out most of the weekend with her boyfriend.

"Mm, lots to do here though, could do without the weekend to be honest."

"Rubbish! Bloody hell, Emily, if that's the case then you're not using your weekends very wisely! What plans do you have?" Lucy asked. I mulled the question over and wondered what this weekend would look like. I would spend as much time as I could with Olivia and as little time as I could with Beth. I would think things over until my head could unravel the new information that had unfolded, and I would likely pretend it just wasn't happening.

"Not much," I replied. "The usual, marking, planning, preparing resources..."

"Well that sounds like an exhilarating thrill. Why don't you come out with me tonight?"

"What? No, I couldn't." Could I?

"Why the hell not? My brother and his boyfriend are having the opening night of their new club, it'll be right up your street," she winked at me, and I rolled my eyes. Obviously this must be some sort of gay bar, which of course meant that it would be perfect for all gay people across the country in the eyes of all straight people no matter what their targeted market was.

"You do know I'm engaged? Not really looking for dangerous liaisons in dark corners of clubs, I'm a bit past that."

"Oh, Emily, you are depressing! You're a woman barely into her thirties and talking like you're about ninety! Yes, I know you're engaged, but that doesn't mean you can't come and let your hair down and have a bit of fun. What else are you going to do tonight?" I thought for a moment. She had a point. What was I going to do tonight? I wasn't sure if I could bring myself to fake smile all weekend, and once Olivia was in bed what was I to do to avoid Beth then? I have never had to deal with anything like this before. I didn't know what I was supposed to do – every scenario moving forward involved people I cared about getting hurt. Myself if I stay put and Olivia if I walk away.

"Okay. You've convinced me. I'll come." It was as good a way of avoiding my life as any right now.

"Yay! Beth can come too if you want a night out together?"

"She can't tonight, we have Olivia this weekend, so she'll be at home with her."

"Okay, no worries. It's going to be epic! We'll pick you up from yours in the taxi at about nine," Jesus, nine? At night? I was usually in my pyjamas ready for bed by then! "We can have a few in the pub before heading to the club."

"Sounds great, I'll see you then," Lucy almost skipped out of my room, and I smiled to myself at her excitement. She was still in that mid-twenties part of her life where she enjoyed clubbing and late nights. She had tried getting me out on many occasions, but I had always found a reason (an excuse) to not go. What better reason though for a night out than the opening of a new gay bar to avoid my fiancée who has been lying and manipulating me for goodness knows how long?

Chapter 21

I got through the day with a smile on my face and the ability to teach without any of my personal issues creeping to the front of my mind. As all good teachers should credit themselves for, we put our game faces on and just deal with it. Despite all of my hesitation and usual avoidance, I found myself looking forward to going out. I hadn't had a good night out in years. Kate and I had always enjoyed a good time when we were younger, but we were more sit in your pyjamas with a glass of wine, a bar of chocolate and a couple of microphones for karaoke kind of girls, than go and jump up and down in a deafening club until you throw up your insides.

I had found Beth at lunch time and told her I was going out. She had been surprised and it made me want to slap her across the face. She was smiling, as if she knew how I was feeling inside, and she was trying to make amends and suck up to me. Of course that isn't the case, but I couldn't help but feel like she was creeping. Maybe she planned on putting an impromptu wedding date in our diaries this weekend and she was working her charm. Or perhaps I'd wake up tomorrow morning and we would be married. That's the amount of control it seemed I had over my future currently. Well, I was past the powers of her charm, there was nothing she could say or do to make me want to be anywhere near her right now.

A shower and some faffing with my hair before choosing from my very small collection of suitable club-wear, and I was ready to rock. Olivia had spent most of the time I took getting ready sitting playing around with my make-up in the bedroom with me. She was full of puppy tales to share, and I couldn't help but laugh and smile as she raved about how happy she was. I was beyond joyful hearing her like this, I wished it could be just me and her like this every time she was here. I had never seen her so animated and spontaneously giggly, and with everything going on in my head right now, it was comforting to know that whatever happened, she would be okay. Her dad was a good man, he had found a good woman and together they had made a happy life for their children.

Heals were not historically good friends of mine, but I pulled out the nicest pair of shoes I owned and managed to hobble in a very Bambi-like way down the stairs. Beth was stood in the hall fishing in the pocket of her coat, and she did a double-take as she caught sight of me coming down towards her.

"Wow! You look, amazing. Seriously, I mean… my fiancée is hot!" her eyes were wide and sparkly, I was flattered I had that effect on her, but it didn't register as a meaningful compliment as it would have before. I unexpectedly panicked at the thought of things never being the same for us again.

"Thanks," I stuttered, "I wasn't sure what to wear, but I figured this might do the trick."

"Seriously, babe, you look stunning," she leaned towards me and was about to kiss me when Olivia ran out of her bedroom and shouted down the stairs.

"I think Joy is sick," she looked upset, and I hesitated for a fraction of a second. I couldn't go back now. "Mum, come and look," decision out of my hands, she wanted her mum. I was free to continue as planned.

"You better go and take a look, I don't know what time I'll be home."

"Okay, well have a great time," she smiled, and I faltered slightly. I couldn't just walk away from her, I couldn't actually bring myself to hate her. I loved her. Even now, I still loved her, knowing she was lying to me.

I looked at her and thought about how happy we were, how happy I thought we were going to be for the rest of our lives. I leaned in and kissed her softly on the lips, slowly my tongue found hers and I leaned into her slightly so she had to steady herself on the wall behind her. My hands slipped around her waist and up her back, hers ran up and down my spine, skimming my bum.

The sound of a car horn beeping outside and Olivia shouting for her mum from her bedroom pulled us apart.

"If you feel like you need to wake me up for any reason when you get home, then please feel free, I won't mind in the slightest," Beth grinned. I picked up my bag from the telephone table and turned away from her.

"Don't wait up," and then I closed the door behind me.

Never let it be said that I can't hold my drink. But then it had been some time since I had gone out with the biggest intention of my life to get absolutely bladdered. I know my limits,

I know when I've had enough and when one more will be one too many, but tonight none of that mattered.

Lucy was a bad influence, which coupled with the fact I did not need any encouragement made for a highly intoxicated evening. She was all about two-for-one cocktails, shots and double spirits. We hadn't even made it to her brother's club before I was feeling the after effects of several Pornstar Martinis and a couple of Whiskey Sours. Her friends were fun, they made me feel very welcome, but I did attach myself to the only other person from work who was with us, familiar face and all that.

The club, 'The Basque Lounge' (apparently it was supposed to be a play on words, as in basking to be lounging around, and Basque, the ever-so-slightly sexy lingerie attire), was heaving when we arrived. Lucy had said the only publicity they had gone for was word of mouth and a few leaflets dotted around the busiest areas of town, its reputation preceded itself before it had even opened.

We ordered more drinks and a very flamboyant young man ushered us to a private seating area behind a rope. It was like being a VIP at a film premier, it was wonderful, and I was having the most fun I had had in years. The drinks kept coming and the music kept playing. I danced, I sang, it was exactly what I had needed, and when I thought about the fact I had believed my partying days to be over, I felt a little sad. The nostalgia of my twenties had taken over my entire body and I wasn't prepared to let it go. Not tonight.

Time stands still when you're in a nightclub, I am sure of it. I had no idea how long we had been in here, but I did know that there was a woman who had been watching me for quite some time. A woman who had caught my eye hours earlier and had made my pulse race more than it should have as she watched me dance and move around the club.

Our little group of groovers (I can't believe I used the word 'groovers', I was trying to prove I wasn't past my sell by date for clubbing and I was using a word my mum would use to describe a night at the community centre for bingo and nibbles), had diminished in numbers somewhat. Lucy had made her exit when her boyfriend called to say he was missing her. Puke. The other woman from work had gone home to her cat at least two hours ago, so I was left with two or three of Lucy's friends who were all single and all straight. They were here for the cheesy music and fun atmosphere. What was I here for?

I was drunk, more drunk than I think I had been in years. I was still aware of my surroundings and what was happening around me, but any inhibitions I had were completely washed away and I simply wanted to stay here forever.

The woman who had been watching me was now on the dance floor and we were both subconsciously (I think) moving ourselves closer towards one another. She was the complete opposite of dark haired and hazel eyed Beth, a blonde with blue whirlpools for eyes. Her smile was bewitching and once our eyes finally locked, I couldn't take them off her.

We were side by side, our bodies so close you could feel the heat between them without having to touch. The dancing continued and the music allowed us to carry on with moving closer until our bodies were working in perfect sync with one another. Every movement was like it had been choreographed and I could feel my heart race faster and faster with each beat of the music.

When her hand wound its way around my waist I gasped. You wouldn't have heard me over the noise, but I heard it, and I was sure she did too. I placed my hand round the back of her neck, and we pulled each other closer, the space between us felt like the vast Grand Canyon, but it was seconds before there was no space between us at all. I didn't even know her name, I had no idea who this woman was, I had no idea what I was prepared to let happen, and I had no idea at what point I would stop it.

Our lips met quickly, and our tongues entwined instantly. It was hard and fast, and I grabbed her long, loose hair at the base of her neck, pulling her into me. She pressed her body into mine as we continued to kiss, the lust rising and the desire for much more overwhelming. I don't know how long we were stood like that for, but when we parted, she smiled at me and took my hand. We walked towards the exit, and I had never been more afraid or excited in my life. I had no idea what I was doing, and it was thrilling.

Chapter 22

Before I knew what was happening, we were in a taxi, it had stopped right in front of us as soon as we left the club. Our hands began exploring each other's bodies, we continued to kiss, our mouths only parting to take in small amounts of air. I had never done anything like this before, and I mean *never*. Not when I was a reckless teen, and not when I was partying away my twenties. I had never had a one-night stand. Oh shit. I'd said it now. Those words, 'one-night stand'. So I was clearly thinking it. I was making it real in my mind and the fact that this woman was reaching underneath my top and rubbing my nipples made it physically real too.

I couldn't think about this morally. I was drunk, I had barely been able to put one foot in front of the other without falling flat on my face as we left The Basque Lounge, I felt completely out of control of my body. Yet, at the same time something inside me felt like I was finally taking control of my life. The taxi stopped and she grabbed my hand, launching a note (I have no idea how much for) at the driver, she didn't wait for change. She fumbled for a key in her bag, I think it was the first time we had stopped kissing for more than a few seconds, but once the door was open, she continued to lead me through a corridor and into a lift where the kissing began again. My hands were everywhere, I couldn't cover enough of her body at any one moment in time, I wanted every part of me to be touching every part of her.

The journey from the lift to her front door was a blur. I couldn't tell you what floor we were on or what number was on the door, but as soon as we were inside and the door shut behinds us, there was absolutely no going back.

Afterwards, I've no idea how long. Seconds? Minutes? Hours? She rolled over and looked at me. Her eyes swam over me, and I was intoxicated by them.

"Anna," she smirked and held out her hand. I took it in mine.

"Emily," she smiled again and leaned towards me, kissing me. I returned my hands to the contours of her body, and it wasn't long before we were discovering each other all over again.

I couldn't tell you how many times that happened. I suppose it repeated itself until I was sober. When you finally sober up and you're lying naked next to a woman you've only known for a few hours, life slaps you in the face quite viciously. Fuck.

Gathering my things as quietly and quickly as I could, I managed to find a bathroom and make myself look marginally human. At least enough to get out of here without too many inquisitive or judging looks from the people I would pass as I walked by. I couldn't go home. I had to wash this whole experience off of me, I had to come up with a story as to where I had been all night. I had to figure out what I was going to say. But what worried me more than any of that was how desperately I wanted to crawl back into bed beside this stranger rather than go back to the life awaiting me at home.

It was of course Kate I turned to. It was her front door I was knocking on at six thirty in the morning. I knew she'd be awake, Amelia was still not a great sleeper and so I could rely on them for being up and amusing one another with silly faces and cooing. When she opened the door, she took one look at me, a sleeping Amelia in her arms, and I burst into tears.

Chapter 23

The first thing I asked Kate to do was call Beth. I hated doing it, but I had to let her know I was okay. The time of day didn't matter, what mattered was her freaking out that I hadn't come home. I asked Kate to lie, she told Beth I had turned up at hers drunk and that she presumed I had told Beth where I was so didn't think she needed to contact her. It was all done via speakerphone, and I listened attentively as Beth expressed her relief that I was okay and that she had never known me to do anything like this before.

I felt like the absolute worst person in the world. It was as if the devil himself had decided to have a bit of fun by taking over my body and making it do things that I would never have done without his influence. How was I supposed to deal with this? What was I supposed to do?

It wasn't until I had showered and had a cup of coffee and a sausage and egg sandwich in front of me that I was able to even form the words to tell Kate what I had done. I relived the whole thing, every last detail. Although the part where I actually left the club and ended up at this 'Anna's' home was a bit blurry. Everything that followed I could remember, but I wished that I couldn't. I wished that it would all go away or that I could somehow undo it. I cried a lot as I sat with Kate, and she simply listened, like the very wonderful friend that she is.

"Oh, Em," were her first words. "What a fucking mess." The understatement of the year.

"I don't know what to do, Kate. I can't believe I risked almost throwing my whole life away."

"Well, yes, this is true. It was a stupid and reckless thing to do, and I'm not for a second condoning cheating, but the lie that Beth is spinning you about wanting a baby is pretty ruthless. It's a low move for someone who asked you to marry them and supposedly loves you."

"She does love me! Of course she loves me, that's why she proposed. And maybe she's right. Maybe I am a fool to want more, I could lose everything if she finds out about this. I need to just go back and tell her it's okay."

"That what's okay?" Kate eyed me suspiciously and I swallowed hard. I wasn't sure if the lump in my throat was due to my over emotional state or trying to stop myself throwing up.

"That I can let it all go, I don't need a baby…"

"Em…"

"No, I mean look at what I've done. I could have thrown my whole life away on one stupid, drunken mistake, the likes of which I have never done before, why would I do that? I want to get married and have a family to take care of and feel secure and loved. Beth gives me all of that. Beth and Olivia, they are my future."

"Em, please. She wants to move you away from us all. Keep you from being with the people who know and love you most. Please think about this before you rush into something you'll regret…"

"The only regret I will have is if I let this tear us apart. Beth can never know. I will somehow get round to dropping the baby issue. We haven't gone so far that we can't turn back. I have to do this for her."

"And what about what she should do for you? I'm not being funny Em, but it's her lies and deceit that have led to you jumping into bed with another woman, you've said yourself you were so drunk you didn't know what you were doing."

"That doesn't make it right."

"No, but it doesn't mean that what Beth is doing is right either. She's lying to you, she's made promises to you and never had any intention of keeping them."

"And is that not what I've now done? I've committed the worst betrayal of all!"

"Cheating is shit, yes. It's an awful thing to do to someone and an awful thing for someone to have done to them, but Beth wants to marry you to trap you into giving up a baby and then take you goodness knows where so none of us can spend time with you! You may be able to overlook and forgive that, but I'm not so sure that your family will. Nor do I think that I can."

"Well I'm not asking you to, you're not engaged to be married to her."

"No, but my best friend is, and I can't stand by and watch her make a mistake."

I sighed with irritation. I was grateful that there were not more people who knew about any of the things that had been going on because Kate just didn't understand. Which meant neither would anyone else and it was exhausting figuring out how to reconcile myself with the future I claimed I was now happy with without fighting to help others make sense of it.

"The only mistake I might make is if I let this tear me and Beth apart. If I lose Olivia, I don't know how I would survive that."

"I know you love Olivia, and she's an amazing little girl, but she's Beth's daughter. You can't stay with Beth and give up everything you want to keep Liv in your life."

"I will do whatever it takes. I have to make up for what I have done."

"I'm not comfortable with you taking all the blame for this, Em. Has it not crossed your mind that the reason you ended up in bed with this woman was maybe because you were subconsciously looking for a way out?"

"So I went out looking for someone to sleep with so I could walk away from my future with Beth? How could you say that? Why would I want out? I love her! I want to marry her!"

"Well I'm sorry, but I can't support you in the decision you're about to make."

"Well I don't need your approval. This is my life, I know what I have to do," I stood up from the kitchen table and picked up my jacket. "I have to go, thanks for breakfast and the shower. I'll call you later," I walked away convinced that I was the one who was making sense. That my best friend was letting me down by not seeing that I knew what was right for me. I instantly felt very alone. I needed to get home. I had to see Beth.

When I stepped in the front door, Beth was standing at the bottom of the stairs. She looked at me and for a split second I thought she knew. I had no idea how she could, but I was so scared she could see what I had done. I rushed over, Beth opening her arms as I buried my face in her shoulder. I breathed in her familiar and comforting smell, and I wondered if I smelt different to her. The scent of adultery.

She guided me into the living room, and we sat down on the sofa. I was desperate to talk to her and pretend the last twenty-four hours had not happened, but I couldn't get a read on what she was thinking. I needed her to break the silence so I knew it was okay for me to speak.

"So, you had a good night then?" finally. She spoke and I was able to relax slightly.

"Yes, from what I remember... I'm so sorry to have worried you. I don't know what happened. One drink just followed another, and I don't remember much until waking up at Kate's this morning..." I could feel my pulse racing and my temperature was through the roof.

"I would have appreciated a call. Even from Kate, I mean I know she said she presumed you had told me where you were, but even so. I'd have let Tom know if she turned up here too drunk to find her way home."

"I know, and I really am sorry."

"Where did you even go?" I waited whilst my brain tried to decide whether to tell her the truth, I hadn't mentioned the opening of a gay bar as I knew she wouldn't like it. "I mean, when you said you didn't know what time you'd be home, I didn't expect that time to be within a new day."

"I didn't go out until nine…"

"That's not the point. A few hours having a drink and dance, then you could have come home."

"I wasn't aware I had a curfew." I was starting to get wound up and yes, I was completely aware of the irony. What possible right did I have to get annoyed with how Beth was being? "I hadn't expected to be that late. We ended up going to an opening of a new bar that Lucy's brother has just opened."

"You never said it was a special occasion," she said sulkily, she obviously now felt she had been left out of something.

"It wasn't. I've never even met her brother before; I don't remember if I actually met him last night."

"It's not a very dignified way to conduct yourself, Em. I just hope none of the parents from school saw you."

"In a gay bar?" shit.

"A gay bar?" double shit. Hadn't meant to share that. "So let me get this straight, you disappear all night, you don't call me or let me know where you are or that you're okay, and the whole time you were surrounded by women of whom you could have taken your pick?"

"Hardly! Jesus, Beth. It was a gay bar, yes, but I didn't think you were one of those people who fell for the stereotype of all gay people being promiscuous and offering themselves up on a plate." Oh I am an awful, awful person.

"I don't think that, I just don't like that you weren't open about where you were. If I'm honest, Em, the whole thing has really baffled me."

"I know," I started to soften again, and I reminded myself that this was supposed to be me making amends for something Beth didn't even know about. I wasn't doing a very good job.

"I don't want us to fight. I just didn't like it."

"I'm sorry. It all just got out of control," that was the biggest of all understatements.

"Well, I'm hoping you've got it out of your system, whatever it was you needed to drink yourself stupid over."

"I didn't need to drink myself stupid over anything, it was just a night out. I don't need to get having fun with friends 'out of my system'."

"When Kate called this morning, and I knew where you were and how drunk you must have been it made me certain that I want us to have a joint hen night!" Christ. Here I am just desperately trying to see myself survive the next few hours and she was straight back on the wedding. But that was a good sign. I hadn't blown things, my relationship with Beth would be okay and we would get married. Crisis averted.

"What else have you been considering about hen nights?"

"Nothing much. Other than maybe having a whole separate one where your mum and Gran can let their hair down!"

"Surely you're not embarrassed by my perfectly sane family?" I was half joking, but also slightly offended if she genuinely didn't want my family around our friends. Especially when most of our friends know and willingly accept the lunacy that runs in the Taylor's.

"No I'm not embarrassed. I just get a bit twitchy over my family being with your family. I swear last time we got them all together I came out in a rash."

"That was a mosquito bite."

"Whatever, it is not advisable to create scenarios like that."

"Says who?"

"Me," she laughed, but I was biting my tongue at the message she was trying to get across to me. She stood up and I knew I just had to let it go.

As Beth left the room and went into the kitchen, I finally let my body sink into the familiar curves of the sofa. I could relax now, it was all over. I just had to give her what she wanted, then we would be right where we were supposed to be. Most importantly we would be together. I tucked my legs up underneath me with a cup of tea and a plate of jammy dodger biscuits, and Beth and I enjoyed an afternoon of rubbish telly before I cooked us some dinner. Olivia spent the afternoon in her bedroom doing homework and reading Harry Potter. Again.

We had a wonderful weekend after its slightly unexpected start. On Sunday we picked up Margot and took her for a walk through the local park and woodlands. I had never seen Olivia laugh and smile so much, it was a wise decision to bring this little fur ball into her life. Even Beth seemed to warm to Margot by the time we had had a coffee break and made our way back to take the dog home. Maybe there was some hope yet that we could add our own four-legged friend to our brood.

We had a full Sunday roast for dinner, and I pulled out all the stops. The whole day would have been fit for a scene from the Walton's or some other more modern perfect family. It was like those cheesy Christmas films that are on the Hallmark channel every year. You know they're ridiculously trite, but you love them none the less. That was how our Sunday went. Trite but perfect.

I had decided to just not mention having a baby for the time being. I couldn't imagine for a second that Beth would bring it up in conversation. All I had done so far was have some blood taken. So as far as she was concerned that could be the end of it all. I couldn't bring myself to say the words, that I didn't want a child, let's face it I was doing enough lying for the time being. So we would just tick over as we were, except now we had a wedding to plan too. Plenty to keep me busy.

Monday morning was a bit frantic as we forgot to set an alarm. So it was Olivia shouting up the stairs asking if we had any bread because her cereal was all gone that woke us both up. This was approximately forty-five minutes later than we would normally have been getting up and ready. Needless to say, we rushed around getting in each other's way and starting the day in the most stressful manner possible.

I drove us to school, each of us feeling like we had already worked a full day just with how exhausting it had been to actually get ready. Beth took her phone out of her pocket and read a text to say the teacher in her class wasn't in today. Ill apparently. So there would be a supply teacher in, great. Beth was not a fan of supply teachers and struggled when somebody didn't know what they were doing and she needed to offer a little more patience. She had experienced a wide range of supply teachers, those who chat with you and make sure the marking is done and the classroom is tidy before they leave, and those that walked out the door with the kids at the end of the day. I hoped that today's teacher would be of the first category!

I couldn't deny that I was a little apprehensive about seeing Lucy. I hadn't heard from her all weekend, and I had no idea how much of my behaviour she had seen on Friday night. I had to speak to her before she relayed anything to Beth. I couldn't risk things being destroyed now that we had so smoothly moved past the whole thing. Luckily, Lucy was in my classroom when I arrived.

"Morning, Lucy."

"Morning! I've been waiting for you to arrive," she winked at me, and I think I threw up in my mouth a little bit. "I'm so sorry I left you Friday night. I felt really bad, but I checked with my mates over the weekend, and they said you seemed to have a great time!"

"Yes!" Christ, I think I'd stopped breathing for a few moments, "it was fine, you had to leave. It was a great night, from what I remember!"

"Yeah, from what I've heard from my other friends that seems to be the general outcome of the evening! Not many memories, but that just means a good night! My brother and his boyfriend were buzzing about it all weekend."

"Oh I'm really pleased it went well for them, it was a great place."

"Yeah I thought so, it was a terrific night," she stood up from the table she had been sat on and walked towards me, "well, back to reality now! We should do it again soon though, I promise I won't ditch you next time," she laughed and then walked out of the room. I half sat, half fell onto the nearest chair and took some very deep breaths. I couldn't believe I had managed to get away with this pretty much unscathed.

I hung my coat up and put my bag away, and as I reached for my phone to make sure I had turned the volume off, I pulled Beth's out of my bag. She must have dropped it after reading her text this morning. Phone in hand, I headed to her classroom down the corridor and heard her talking to someone as I got closer.

"You've got nothing to worry about here today then if you're used to inner city year six kids!"

"I hope that's the case! I've only just moved to the area, so supply work was the most obvious option until I can find something permanent."

"Well I'm sure you'll be fine with this lot today."

"By the sounds of it the teacher you normally have might be off for a few days or so. Put her back out or something I think your headteacher said."

I stopped in the doorway and froze. This had to be some sort of mistake. Somebody's idea of a joke? Lucy. It must be Lucy trying to get a laugh. How was this possible?

"Emily?" Beth's voice startled me as she approached.

"Mm? Oh, umm, you left this in my bag," I handed her the phone. I couldn't bring my eyes to meet the voice of the woman who was working with her today. If I saw her then I would have to accept that she was really here.

"Thanks. This is the supply teacher working with me by the way, I'm so sorry I've forgotten your name already," she laughed. They both laughed.

"It's Anna. Anna Lowe," I lifted my head, but my eyes didn't follow for a few seconds, still refusing to face what was happening. But I couldn't could I? I couldn't ignore it.

It was her.

Chapter 24

Never in all my years of teaching had I kept as low a profile as I did that day. I ignored every adult conversation I heard start up in the corridor. I let boys fly past my door at the speed of light, racing to the toilets, without making them come back and walk. I asked my teaching assistant to see the children out at the end of the day and pretended I had a meeting I had to rush off to with the head. I did whatever it took to stop our paths from crossing.

I would say 'what have I done to deserve the Gods treating me this way?', but I knew exactly what I had done. And if my mother knew, there would not be enough signs of the cross she could make for the rest of her life that would erase my actions. Gran would probably want a fully detailed account of what happened, which was a really weird thought, but it was Gran.

Beth came into my classroom once the building had fallen quiet and I smiled, not knowing whether to ask her how her day had been or not. Which would be the least unusual behaviour?

"Good day?" she asked.

"Yeah, same old, same old. You?" I waited. I watched her face, desperately looking for a read on her.

"Yeah, good actually. Which is unusual when a supply teacher is in!" bugger. She likes her. "She was really good, back tomorrow as well apparently, she's just come back from asking Marie if she needs her again," Marie was the headteacher, "she spoke to me at lunch time."

"Who? The supply teacher?" I couldn't bring myself to say her name. And why would I have remembered it as far as Beth was concerned anyway?

"No, Marie. She wanted to know what I thought of her, you know she likes to have a bank of reliable supply teachers."

"And what did you tell her about this one?"

"Anna? I said she was great. Good with the kids, didn't take any crap but had a good rapport with them too. I think she's gone back into the classroom to finish the marking! Not many supply teachers work like that."

"Well, I'm sure there are plenty of other supply teachers out there who have the same work ethic."

"None of them have ever been sent here if there are," Beth was clearly besotted with the high quality of teacher she had had the pleasure of spending the day with. It was the night I had spent with her that was causing me heightened levels of anxiety.

"You may as well go, I'm going to be a while."

"Oh, okay, are you sure?"

"Yeah. I'll walk home, could do with some fresh air."

"Okay, well if you change your mind just give me a ring and I'll come and get you. I'll go and start dinner," she smiled, and I smiled back. It didn't feel particularly natural, but it was the best I could offer right now. There wasn't a single part of me on the inside that could find anything to smile about but I had to keep convincing Beth I was fine.

She left the classroom with a sneaky wink in my direction, and I was alone again. I wasn't even being honest with her now. I was not going to 'be a while', I had very little to finish off before I would be ready for going home, but I couldn't leave until I had spoken to *her*. Maybe she didn't remember me? Maybe I was worrying for nothing, and she was as drunk as I was and this whole thing is really over because the other woman doesn't even remember it was me who she went home with.

I know. It was highly unlikely that it was going to be as simple as that.

"Emily?" her voice filled the room, and I was catapulted back to her flat. I turned to look at her and I instantly replayed our evening together in some sort of triple time speed. I immediately started to sweat; my hands were clammy as I tried to continue stacking exercise books.

"Anna. Hi." She stepped into my classroom and closed the door behind her. Something was very wrong in my head because now rather than replaying Friday night I was imaging what I could do with her inside an empty classroom.

"So, do you often run out on women that you spend the night with? Or was I the first?"

"Anna. I... I don't even know where to begin..."

"It's fine. I get it. You needed to let your hair down, you were looking for a good time," she was walking towards me the whole time she was speaking, and I was finding myself backed into the corner, "at least I hope you had a good time…"

"Anna, please…"

"What's wrong? Am I making you uncomfortable? You didn't seem to mind on Friday…" she grinned a very knowing grin. I had a sneaky suspicion she was doing things in her mind to my body that I was blushing about without even needing to know what they were.

"It was a mistake, a moment of weakness and so, so, so out of character for me, I don't do things like that, I've *never* done anything like that."

"It's a shame because you are very good at things like *that*," her body was getting increasingly closer to mine and I think my breathing became heavier than it was sixty seconds ago, although I wasn't sure if I was actually breathing at all. There were only a few inches between us, and I couldn't figure out what I wanted to do about that.

"It was a mistake. It cannot and will not happen again."

"I'm not asking you to marry me, it's just a bit of fun." Oh and it had been fun…

"Well it's not fun for *me*, I don't want to hurt anyone. I don't want *this*," I waved a hand between the two of us, "to happen again."

"Is that what you really want?" she pressed her body against mine and I was suddenly reminded of where we were. It was as if my conscience had finally decided to start it's next shift or was back from a coffee break. I was in my classroom for God's sake.

"Yes," I gently pressed my hands against her waist, and she stepped back, "it is what I want."

She looked at me, she was surprised, and I was scared that I was going to change my mind and rip her clothes off where we stood.

"Well, then I suppose I'll go. See you tomorrow, Emily," she turned and walked towards the classroom door, my heart was pounding. She stopped as her hand reached out for the handle, and then she turned back around. "If you change your mind, I'm hoping that I will be hanging around here for a while… so, just let me know." She left the room, and my body sank into a chair.

Shit.

Anna worked at the school for the rest of the week. I hid in my classroom as much as a could, but ultimately, I couldn't do my job properly if I didn't speak to and interact with other members of staff around school. It wasn't as bad as I thought. I decided I just had to get on with things and pretend that last Friday never happened. It was the best option and the only one that allowed me to feel remotely in control of my life again.

The upcoming weekend saw a family roll call at my mum's, she was worried about Charlotte. She was always worried about Charlotte. Although to be fair, I had been a little slack on the checking in with my recently separated from her husband sister this last week or so. I could use some time to feel the unconditional love of my family around me, no matter what sins I may have committed.

On Friday afternoon, Olivia stuck her head in my classroom door to wish me a good weekend and then disappeared again. I walked over and watched as she skipped out across the playground with Sarah, who had her arm around Olivia's shoulder, pulling her in and laughing with her. I loved Olivia with all my heart, but even watching her with Sarah made my womb contract, desperate for the time when I would have that relationship with a child of my own. No. I had to let those thoughts go now. I had taken too many risks and making Beth have a baby when she didn't want one was not something I was going to push at the cost of our relationship.

I gathered my things together and I went into the walk-in cupboard where I supposedly keep resources and folders, but in reality, it houses all of the things that I don't know what to do with. As I reached up for a folder that I needed to take home with me I heard the door close and turned quickly, dropping the folder to see Anna behind me.

"Jesus Christ! You scared the shit out of me."

"Sorry, absolutely not what my intention was by coming to see you."

"Well, whatever your intention is, you need to leave."

"See, now that's where we have very different opinions. I have been on my best behaviour all week long, I've stayed away from you whenever I can, I've been friendly, but not *too* friendly with your girlfriend... I would say I have earned a reward for all my hard efforts," she had left as much space between us as was possible in my tiny walk-in cupboard. I felt the corners of my mouth move to form a small grin at her remarks, but I managed to stop it before she noticed.

She thought *she* had been good? I had been on my best behaviour all week! I stayed away from her, and I was *very* friendly with my girlfriend! Where was my reward? Here and now in a storage cupboard? Wait. Shit. There was a part of me that wanted that to be true. I had to get out of here. Right. Now.

"You're crossing so many lines right now, Anna," I moved towards her and reached for the door handle.

"Emily, wait," she put her hand on mine, I lifted my eyes to meet hers and I felt her other hand slide around my waist.

Before I knew what was happening, she leaned in and kissed me. It started soft and light enough for me to pull away, but then I found her tongue with my own and for a few seconds I was back in her flat. Hands wound their way inside waist bands and underneath clothes to locate bare skin. Her touch was like a live wire, running through my whole body. We grabbed at one another as if we were drowning and reaching for buoyancy aids. All I could think about was how much I wanted to feel this woman's naked body pressed against my own, it was greater than my need for air.

It took longer than it should have for me to come to my senses, and I pulled back quickly, surprising us both at the distance I tried to put between us.

"I can't do this, you need to leave." I reached for the door as we both froze at footsteps on the other side.

"Emily?" we stopped and stared wide eyed at one another. Beth was in my classroom.

"Stay here and wait until we've left before you come out." I pulled open the door enough for me to slide out and I shut it quickly behind me.

"There you are, you ready to go? I thought we could go out for dinner tonight if you fancy it?" Beth asked.

"Sounds lovely, let's go."

"Now?"

"Absolutely, I'm ready, let's get out of here," I picked up my things and ushered Beth towards the door, closed it behind me and practically raced us out to the car.

"You're either really hungry or really glad that it's the weekend."

"Both. It's been a crazy week, I'm ready to put it behind me and just enjoy some time together."

"Sounds good to me," we got in the car, and I quickly turned the engine on, I had to get as far away from here as possible. "Oh, by the way, Anna said she was at that club opening you went to last Friday, I wonder if you saw each other at all. Small world!" She had no idea.

Chapter 25

We arrived at Mum and Dad's promptly at one o'clock, and once she'd got over the panic and stress of seeing we didn't have Olivia with us and so had set one place too many at the table, Mum welcomed us in and ordered Dad to get us a drink. I don't know if there is a special shop somewhere where Irish families can buy dining tables, but every time I ate at my parents and we were all there, I swear the table got longer and longer. Chairs were not so well supplied, however. Dad was on his fishing stool and Amy and Charlie were sat on two deck chairs out of the shed. The rest of us got proper dining chairs, but pretty much no elbow room or the ability to cut anything up that was on our plates.

Polite conversation was made around the table, Mum asked about school, Charlotte asked about Olivia, Gran complained about the inflation on street prices for Marijuana and Dad never said a word.

After lunch we went to sit in the living room. Dad took the kids outside to make a wormery, which Charlie was not too sure about whilst Amy was standing at the window waving around half a dozen worms she'd already managed to capture. The women sat talking about the unusually warm spring we were having and if any of us had plans to go on holiday this year. It all seemed very calm and not at all Taylor like, even Gran was keeping quiet. It wasn't until Mum appeared with fresh tea and slices of the Victoria sponge she had made the day before that her motives for today's lunch became clear.

"So, Charlotte. Have you had the sex again yet?" Mum blurted. I spat my cake out like sprinkles of snow, Beth choked on her tea and Charlotte simply bit into her slice of cake and I wondered if she had heard the question at all.

Nobody said a word. It was creepy for my family to be so quiet, but how on earth are you supposed to respond to that question? Charlotte finished her cake and was enjoying her cup of tea, I don't think anyone else had moved an inch.

"You've no need to be embarrassed, we all do it. Not your father and I so often anymore, but on birthdays and anniversaries everything does what it's supposed to do, in a fashion."

"Oh God! Mum, I beg you please stop talking. Are you drunk? Or high?" I couldn't help myself, I was not prepared to listen to any more details about my parents' sex life.

"I am looking after my child's wellbeing. I spoke to Helen at the bingo, and she said her daughter had been through a similar thing as Charlotte, and that she wasn't really herself again until she had some company in the bedroom. So I wasn't sure if that had happened yet for you, and I want to help you find someone if you need some assistance. I'm very handy on Tinder now, your gran doesn't swipe without me anymore."

"It's true I'm afraid. I'm one of those feckin' women who won't go on a date without their daughter's approval." I couldn't understand why she said she was 'one of those women', I was fairly certain that a group of women who didn't choose an online date without their daughter's approval didn't actually exist. "A sad state of affairs, but I haven't been disappointed with a single yoke, if you know what I mean," she winked. I was a little sick in my mouth.

"I'm sorry to just blurt it out, Charlotte," still my poor sister never said a word, "but I am worried about you. I want you to be happy..."

"I am happy!" she screamed. "For the first time in my life I am *really* happy! I'm spending more time with my kids, I'm working more hours when they're not home, I'm talking to friends more, I'm exercising, I'm eating better, I'm not waiting around for a fucking arse hole of a husband to contribute anything to the running of my home and I am completely and totally satisfied when I enjoy some time alone in the bath or shower with wonderful products that bring a little buzz to my day!"

"Is she smoking pot?" Gran 'whispered' to Mum.

"No! I'm not!" The room fell quiet. Still, nobody really moved. Mum started to fiddle nervously with the hem of her skirt.

"Well... I umm, I'm going to make another pot of tea."

"I'll help," Mum and Gran disappeared into the kitchen. I looked at Beth, who was already looking at me, and then we both looked at Charlotte, who was staring out of the window.

"Well. That was a surreal three minutes of my life," she said as she turned to face us both. Then she started to laugh before swallowing down sobs and being overridden with sadness, "oh God it was all lies! I haven't orgasmed in eighteen months. I'm going crazy. I don't have baths or showers with vibrators, I barely have time to have a wash before there's a child knocking on the door asking for a poo or to tell me they're hungry. I'm shit at my job, I'm eating crap and every time there is a knock at the door, I think it's him coming back to rescue me from my imprisonment. But I will not have my mother and grandmother thinking I need their bloody advice on my sex life!"

Charlotte left the room and I turned to Beth, who shrugged and carried on eating her cake. I rolled my eyes at her lack of compassion and followed in my baby sister's wake, guessing she had gone out to the kids as that was Dad's turf and she could avoid Mum and Gran out there. I was right. She was standing on the path about half way up the garden watching as Amy chased Dad, who was giving Charlie a piggy back ride, with a handful of worms flapping about in her hand. I gave her a little nudge, shoulder to shoulder and she let out a small laugh.

"Sorry," she exhaled.

"Why are you saying sorry? I think you handled Mum and Gran's line of enquiry wonderfully. If they think you've got a big stash of vibrators at home and are living the dream, then they will leave you alone. For now. Well played," I laughed, and Charlotte managed a small snigger.

"I thought it'd be easier than this. I thought once I knew he was gone and never coming back I would just get on with my life. But it's so hard, Em. I look at you and Beth and I am so envious of the life you have together," oh no. "You clearly love one another."

"Oh, Charlotte, please stop."

"Well it's true. I love you dearly, but sometimes I want to punch you in the ribs for how happy your life is."

"I slept with someone else."

For a second there was nothing. Nothing said, nothing thought. Then she looked at me and she did the weirdest thing. She held her hand up in the air and smiled at me.

"What are you doing?"

"Don't leave me hanging, come on, high five for being a fuck up, come on."

"I always thought that being a lesbian had been my fuck up in life," I managed a grin and gave the requested high five.

"Oh, Emily, you have made my day."

"Thanks! I'm so glad my whore like behaviour can make you feel so good about yourself," Charlotte was now laughing, and I didn't really know whether I was supposed to laugh too. But none of this had given me much to laugh about. After a while the laughter turned to tears, and Charlotte was sobbing into her hands, looking at me with a sadness I didn't like.

"What did you do, Emily? What did you do?"

I gave her an abridged version of that fateful night. And I fabricated some of the details. I told her Beth and I had been arguing a lot. I told her that we had rowed as I had walked out of the door. I told her that Beth had been lying to me about things that I didn't need to bore her with the details of, but that it hurt me, and I was in a bad place and so did something bad as a result of that. I didn't like the way she looked at me, and I knew it was because she was thinking of how Beth would feel if she found out.

In this scenario she could identify with her, the woman who's been cheated on, who has had their love for someone destroyed due to their adulterous behaviour. I hated it, but I had to tell her, she had to know that the life she thought I was leading, the perfect life she saw from the outside, was not at all the one I was living. It was better she knew the truth and hated me a little, than believed things that were false and hated herself.

We stood in silence for a few minutes, watching Charlie try to feed worms to the birds that kept landing on the birdhouse and then flying away when he got anywhere near them. He was frustrated and kept muttering to himself as they took to the sky, but he kept on repeating the exercise, determination running through his core. I smiled and we both let out a little laugh as one bird swooped down and almost landed on his head. This was the end of the line for Charlie, and he dumped the worms back on the soil, looking up at the skies every few seconds to check for any other incoming.

Charlotte reached out and took my hand, I looked at her and she gave it a squeeze.

"I know you've not told me the whole story, I know you've kept things back," she said, "and I know that this is the most out of character behaviour I have *ever* known from you. So, whatever is going on, just promise me you will sort it out."

"I'm trying, Charlotte, I really am."

"I know. But if you know that you made a mistake and it didn't mean anything and you want to keep your relationship with Beth, don't tell her. Don't have some guilt or conscience kick in that makes you confess. Because it won't help her, and it will destroy everything you have. If your relationship is over for whatever reason, then you've got the perfect reason to call it all off."

"I don't want to lose her."

"Are you sure?"

"Of course I'm sure," I said the words, but even I didn't know if I meant them. I had been trying all week to prove I was the perfect fiancée and that I knew what I was doing. But I had Kate's words echoing in my ear, I had a permanent memory of Anna's lips on my own and I couldn't shift the thought out of my head that maybe I actually didn't have a clue what I was doing.

Charlotte and I walked back into the house hand in hand to re-join everyone else, Dad and the kids followed behind us in search of refreshments, and some of Mum's cake. We all sat in the living room and for the first time in my memory, it was Dad carrying the conversation. Mum and Gran wouldn't say a word and kept their heads down in their tea cups. Beth had disappeared to take a phone call and Charlotte was just nodding politely when Dad said anything. I tried to support the topics he raised; the number of fish he caught last weekend on his fishing trip, the cost of his bag of Werther's Originals going up by 3p, the melting of the ice-caps, you know – typical father daughter conversations.

When Beth came back into the room she stayed standing and cleared her throat.

"Sorry to eat and run, but I need to steal Emily away for the rest of the afternoon, if that's okay?" I looked at her and raised an inquisitive eyebrow. "All will be revealed."

"What are you up to?" all I got in response was a grin and I stood up, catching Charlotte's eye as I glanced around the room. I felt myself flush and dropped my head slightly. "Well, thanks for lunch Mum. Always a pleasure," I kissed everyone on the cheek and gave the kids a hug. Charlotte came to the door with us and held me back slightly as Beth got into the car.

"Emily, be careful, okay?"

"Careful? You make it sound like I'm getting into a car with the child catcher."

"I'm serious, you're not yourself. Don't walk down a road that won't lead you to the place you want to be. We all love Beth, but she has always been the one who controls the life the two of you lead. Just remember you should always be free to be the person you are meant to be," I smiled at my little sister and squeezed her hand as I kissed her cheek.

"I'll make things right, I promise," and I turned to get into the car. Charlotte stayed and waited until we were out of sight before she went back inside the house, I sighed, and Beth gave me a quick glance.

"Everything okay with you two?"

"Hmm? Yes, yes of course. I just worry about her."

"I know, but she's okay, she's got lots of people around her."

"I know, I just wish I was around her a little more."

"Well, you need to focus on your own happiness a bit more. Take some time for yourself."

"But that's not who I am. I want to be there to help her, to help all of the people I care about."

"Well, you care about me and Olivia, so maybe it's time to spend some more time being there for us."

I know that the words had come out slightly more dagger like than intended and not how Beth meant them to sound, but I suddenly felt very claustrophobic and trapped. I wound down the window a little and Beth used the controls her side to wind it back up.

"I'm hot," I complained.

"I don't like the blow through, babe." And that was the end of that.

When the car finally stopped, we were about forty minutes outside where I would call 'home'. We seemed to have arrived on a building site in the middle of nowhere. Beth just grinned at me and got out of the car. She started to walk away so I got out and followed. When we'd walked for a few minutes towards what was clearly a housing plot, my breath caught in my throat. She couldn't possibly be putting the next part of her 'plan' in place already, could she?

"Beth, where are we, what's going on?"

"This," she paused for some sort of dramatic effect, and I just wanted to punch her, "is going to be our new home."

Chapter 26

I froze to the spot and I wasn't confident about what my face was showing but Beth wouldn't stop talking. She was pacing around a perimeter that she kept calling 'ours', she was going on and on about the view and the fact that you could hear nothing but birds in the trees and water trickling down a nearby stream, and that mobile phone signals were unreliable and how wonderful that would be, so we could escape from the world together. I felt as if I was going to start hyperventilating.

My entire body was split in half. One half was drowning in guilt over sleeping with another woman and the other half was screaming at me to confront Beth over her lies and run for the hills. Did one equal out the other? Did my cheating level the playing field for the lies she had been telling me? I couldn't believe I was even asking the question. Of course they didn't. There were big problems here and I didn't know where to even begin in fixing them.

"So, what do you think?"

"Hmm? Oh... umm... it's... The view is stunning, of course, and it's certainly peaceful."

"Why do I feel like there's a but coming?"

"It's just," I paused, "I'm not sure why we need to move. I mean, our current home is fine, it has the space we need, a great garden that we neglect year after year, it's perfectly located for school for us and for Olivia. It took forty minutes to get here on a quiet Saturday afternoon, to get to work through rush hour traffic, we'd have to leave the house at a ridiculously early time, Olivia would never be ready, and all of our friends and family would be an expensive taxi ride away if we had any dinners or nights out with them."

"We can get new jobs!" what was she doing? Why did she need to imprison me like this? "It's not about anyone else, babe, it's about us. You and me, our future, and a beautiful home for our baby."

I can't be sure, but I think I hated her a little for saying that. The emotion that ran through every inch of my body was not one full of love or joy, it was complete despair that the woman I had spent four years of my life with was not the woman that I thought she was. I was living with a stranger, who had played me and tried to manipulate me into being someone that I was never meant to be.

"Emily, say something, be happy for us, for our future, it's going to be wonderful, I know it is…"

"I slept with someone else." I said the words without knowing what they would do, but I finally realised I didn't really care. Not anymore.

"I'm sorry? You…"

"Slept with someone. Another woman, I'm sorry Beth, I truly am. I never wanted to hurt you or for things to get to this point between us…"

"Wait, wait, just stop. You slept with another woman?" she stared right at me, and I didn't know what to do. I didn't want to approach her and try to console her, but I didn't want her to hate me either. How ridiculous.

She walked towards me with big purposeful strides, and I wasn't sure if she was going to hit me or hug me. I braced myself but she walked right past me and got into the car. Without a single word, she spun it around and sped out of the site without a moment of hesitation. I stood fixed to the spot. What was I supposed to do now?

Almost two hours later, I was sat in Charlotte's car idling at the curb of my home. My home. I had no idea if Beth was inside, her car was on the drive but that didn't necessarily mean anything. Charlotte placed her hand on my knee and nodded to the house.

"Do you think she's in there?"

"I have no idea. Probably. Maybe waiting with a knife or a gun."

"Emily!"

"Well, she just left me out there in the middle of nowhere!"

"You told her you had slept with another woman!" fair point. I still hadn't told Charlotte the full story, and I had considered calling Kate to come and rescue me, but I wasn't ready for her to have been right about everything yet. I had had to walk half a mile or so to get a signal on my phone that would allow me to make a call in the first place and to find out where exactly I was, but I couldn't think of anyone else to call.

"I suppose I better go in."

"I suppose you better had."

"Will you wait and listen for gunshots?"

"Emily!"

"Sorry. I'm going. Thank you for coming to get me, and for being wonderful."

"It's what sisters are for..." she frowned at something over my shoulder, "and brothers it would appear..." Charlotte pointed over my shoulder as a male figure approached the car. Luke.

We both got out and gave him a big hug. I'd never been happier to see my baby brother and was also slightly freaking out at what he would make of the shit heap I had turned my life into. It wasn't until we let him go that we were able to see he had been crying.

"Luke, what is it? Is it Mum? Dad?" he shook his head, "shit, it's Gran, isn't it?" he shook his head again.

"It's Eve Richards, Tom's sister," Eve? Tom's Eve? Eve who was currently staying with Kate and Tom and who had been unravelling my life through conversations with my girlfriend? That Eve? "She... she'd been staying up in Sunderland, she was working in a club... we only got together a few times, I mean she is fit as, but it didn't mean anything, we both said that... we knew it wasn't a long-term thing... we both said so... but she's... shit, she was... she was pregnant... she got rid of my baby... and I didn't know anything about it..."

We ushered Luke into Charlotte's car and drove back to hers. I wasn't prepared to bring him into my house and the mess I was in the middle of. Charlotte needed to get back for the kids anyway, she had left the teenager who lived next door watching them and wasn't entirely sure which of the three of them had the higher IQ. Luke cried the whole way back and he kept looking at me, and I knew exactly what he was thinking. He was sorry to have brought this to my door when he knew that I wanted a baby, it was written all over his face. We got back to the house, and it was still standing, so Charlotte breathed a sigh of relief and gave the teenager a tenner for her trouble.

Once Amy and Charlie were settled with some cheese and crackers in front of the TV, the grown-ups were able to sit down and talk.

"So, how did you find out about it all? She's still staying with Kate and Tom, isn't she?" I asked the first question and tried to go in gently and disguise the fury I had coursing through my body.

This woman had turned up at my home and sought me and my family out to console her over having gone through this terrible ordeal when she had in fact aborted my brother's baby. As if I didn't have enough reasons to be awaiting Eve's departure from our lives, now this? How did someone have the gall to sit in a person's home knowing the hurt they had brought to their family?

"She called me drunk two nights ago. Rambling apologies and saying how much she regretted it, I had no idea what 'it' was, and that maybe we could have made a proper go of things after all. Then she said we would have made great parents but that it was all just bad timing and that she hoped I would be able to forgive her one day. I wasn't sure, but I pretty much got the gist of what she was confessing to. So I left it and rang her back yesterday. She told me everything," he paused and looked directly at me, "she told me she's been talking to you and Beth about it, but that she hadn't told you who the father was."

"That's right. More so Beth than me, they've struck up quite the friendship, but yes, she told us. And if I ever see the woman again, I'll have a few things to tell her too!"

"She said she found it easy to talk to you after Tom didn't take it well, she didn't know who to turn to."

"Oh Luke, I'm so sorry," Charlotte rested her hand on top of his and he smiled at her, weakly, but it was a smile none-the-less.

"I don't even know why I've come down here. I mean it's not like I can undo it, we can't change it. I guess I just needed to see her, to talk to her in person. I think I wanted to make sure she was okay too."

"You're a good person, Luke," I took his other hand.

"Obviously Mum and Dad don't know, and I don't want them to. And Christ I don't want Gran finding out. She'd probably hunt Eve down and perform some sort of curse on her, or make a voodoo doll or something," we all laughed, and I felt relieved to see Luke manage a real smile.

"Do Mum and Dad know you're here? Where are you staying?"

"No, they don't know, I was hoping I could stay in your spare room, Em?" I looked at Charlotte and she squirmed uncomfortably in her chair. We had each let go of Luke's hands and he sat back, frowning at the two of us. "Okay, so clearly my impromptu arrival has interrupted some other Taylor drama? What's going on?"

It didn't take long to fill Luke in on what had happened in the last week, and it seemed completely pointless to not tell the two of them everything whilst I had a captive audience. I told them all about the conversations with Eve, Beth's lies about wanting a baby and wanting to move me away from my home and the people I love. They were both furious and Luke paced, it reminded me of Dad, he used to pace when he was waiting for Charlotte to get home after it had passed her curfew.

"Well I care about Eve's wellbeing a lot less now!" Luke exclaimed, "I mean she could and *should* have told you! She should have told you immediately that Beth was lying to you!"

"Well it would seem that Eve is in the business of lying to members of the Taylor family for sport."

"Em," Charlotte began, "none of what Beth is doing is Eve's fault…"

"No, I know, but I still don't have to like her anymore. And if anything good can come out of this then I hope it's that you manage to put her behind you," I looked at Luke, "and move on."

"Typical, Emily, always trying to draw out the light from the darkest situations," Charlotte put her arm around me as she spoke, "you did the same thing when Chris left and you're doing it again now. You have spent far too many hours of your life worrying about and taking care of the two of us."

"It's what big sisters do."

"Yes, and we both love you dearly for it," Charlotte looked at Luke and he nodded in agreement with her. "It's time to put yourself first. You need to go and talk to Beth. Sort this out once and for all."

"I know. Time to get my shit together."

"Absolutely," Luke spoke up now and stood beside me, "I am sorry though, Em. I thought Beth was here for the long haul, but I told you someone who loved you would never stop you from having the things you want and being who you want to be. That person is supposed to enjoy the journey and grow with you, not hold you back and manipulate you into doing things you never wanted."

What a wise little brother I had. It was frustrating that people saw the flaws in others before you could see them for yourself. I had to go home and sort things out, I couldn't keep living like this. It wasn't fair on anybody, not me, not Beth and not Olivia. I loved Olivia so much, and if it was over with Beth then I had to let go of her too. The realisation though that she wasn't mine to let go of in the first place suddenly hit me hard and I felt my heart empty where she and Beth had sat for so long. I wiped a tear from my cheek and let out a big, deep breath.

"Can I trouble you for a lift home?" I asked.

"Come on, let's go."

I waited until Charlotte had driven off before opening the front door. It wasn't locked, which made my stomach flip. I wasn't sure what I planned on doing or saying, I didn't even dare call out her name because that would be it, the beginning of the end. I went into each room downstairs and there was no sign of her. I wondered then if maybe she wasn't home and she had left the front door unlocked to dare someone to come in, testing the Gods to protect our home.

I started to walk up the stairs and was about halfway up when I lifted my head and saw her staring down at me. For a second, I thought she was going to push me down the stairs, I almost saw a flicker of the temptation in her eyes too. She didn't. I made it safely to the top and we stood looking at one another, the silence was unbearable.

"Beth…"

"Don't. Please don't say you're sorry, please don't try and make up for what you've done…"

"What I've done? Because you're the innocent victim?"

"You slept with another fucking woman, Emily! So yes! I think the word 'victim' is quite apt in this scenario!"

"Really?"

"Yes! Wow, I never knew you were capable of being such a bitch, I can't believe I didn't know about this side of you…"

"Yes, well it's funny the things that you find yourself thinking and doing when someone spends their life lying to you."

"What?"

"You heard me," she looked genuinely confused, she had no idea that I knew the things I knew. "You're a liar, Beth. And the worst thing is that you're really good at it."

"What are you talking about?"

"I'm talking about you, lying to me! Lying about everything! About wanting a baby, about wanting to get me away from my family and friends – you don't want a baby, you don't want a home to raise a child with me in, you want a prison to lock me up in so you can have me all to yourself! You have hurt me more than I ever knew it was possible another human could," I had been desperate not to cry in front of her, I didn't want her to know I was upset because if you're upset about something then that means you care about it. I didn't want to care about her anymore.

"How long have you known all of that?"

"That's the first thing you want to say to me? How long have I known? No defence? No apology? No pleading and telling me I got it all wrong? Can you do that?" I was broken.

"Please? Just, tell me I got it all wrong?" I crumbled. She closed the distance between us and wrapped me in her arms as I sobbed into her. She was the one who had caused all of this, yet it was only her that I wanted to make it all go away.

The crying subsided but we stayed stood holding each other. Neither one of us spoke a word. I think it was because we knew what was coming. It was inevitable, wasn't it?

"Em, I'm so sorry. I never meant to hurt you, I just... we don't want the same things and I panicked and knew I had to get you away from the people and places that would remind you of things I didn't want us to have. We have each other! That's all we need, we can fix this, Em."

"What?" I lifted my head and looked up at her.

"We've both made mistakes, we've both hurt one another. But we love each other, that's never changed. In fact, that's why we've done the things we've done!"

"What?" I repeated the question because I couldn't understand her, "Beth, people don't lie and cheat because they love one another."

"People do all sorts of crazy things when they're in love!"

I pulled away and created a gap between us.

"Beth, no. This... this isn't how things are supposed to be... do you honestly think we can go back to pretending we're both happy?"

"But I am happy, I have you and I have Olivia, I don't need anything else."

"But I do." I let my words hang in the air waiting for a response from her, but she gave me nothing. "I can't do this anymore, Beth. I can't pretend that I'm happy with my life. I want a baby, I want to stay living close by my family and my friends. I don't want to be trapped somewhere with you and hidden away from the world."

"It's not a trap, Emily, it's called commitment. It's what happens when you're in love."

"You don't make someone you love do things they don't want to do."

"Well then you shouldn't be making me have a baby with you because it's not what I want."

"Exactly." I whispered.

"You've got no idea, have you?" she spat her words out at me.

"No idea about what?"

"About what it's like to try and penetrate the Taylor circle of trust."

"Excuse me?"

"You are all so involved in one another's lives that I don't think you actually know what your own business is and what is not, you can't take a shit without sharing the details with your mum or your sister or your gran, it's exhausting! All I ever wanted was to be with you and for us to make a life together, *our* life. Not their lives, *ours*, mine, yours and Olivia's. But you just can't distance yourself from them, no matter how hard I try to get you to see there's life outside of 'Taylor Land'."

"Can you actually hear yourself right now? Who are you? And how dare you say these things to me. Just because your own family are so emotionally detached from one another doesn't give you the right to tell me my family are *too* close. We care about one another and are there for one another no matter what, which is more than I can say for your family who can go months without so much as a phone call to each other, never mind actually spending time together. You think my family is the dysfunctional one? I wouldn't be so sure about that."

"Really? Because I'm pretty sure that if you asked around, most people would see that the way you all are with one another is unusual to say the least."

"Unusual, maybe, but not wrong. I'd rather have a family who don't know when to step back than a family that don't step forward at all. Tell me something, Beth, if my family have made your life so hard, why the hell have you spent the last four years with me?"

"Because I love you! I want *you*, I don't want them dictating my life, I don't want to go to bed at night beside them or wake in the morning with them, or go on holidays with them, I want you. I don't know why that seems like such an unreasonable request."

"Because they're my family! You knew that when we met, you heard me talk about them at work, share stories about my gran, you were my friend and we talked about them, Beth. They're the same people they've always been, but... I don't feel like I know who you are anymore..."

"So what the hell are we supposed to do now?"

"I don't see how we can move passed this, I just... we aren't the people that we want each other to be... I feel like we've spent four years pretending and trying to make something work that was never meant to happen..."

She looked so small as she stood before me, processing my words. We were unrecognisable, both as individuals to one another and as a couple to the rest of the world. My heart was begging me to take it all back and find a way of making things work, but my head was congratulating me on a job well done. I'd called her on her lies, she'd made her feelings on our life very clear. Neither of us were prepared to change and we shouldn't have to. That's not what love is about. You love someone for who they are not who they could be. I don't know how long passed. I'm sure it must only have been seconds but it felt like hours. We both finally knew the truth. It was over.

Within the next hour, Beth had packed a bag and arranged somewhere to stay. I don't know where, she didn't tell me, and I didn't ask. All I could think about was Olivia. I might never get to see or talk to her again and I hated that. I hoped that Beth wouldn't paint me as the villain. Yes, I played my part in our relationship falling apart but it wasn't all down to me. I'm not saying I expected Beth to tell her everything in full technicoloured detail, but I liked to think we cared enough for one another to not use Olivia as a weapon to cause further upset.

There hadn't been another word said between us, and I stood now in the hallway, watching as she put on her coat and picked up her keys. She fumbled around in her hands for a few seconds and then held out a key to me. The front door key.

"No. I don't want it."

"What's the point in me keeping it?"

"Please. Just hold onto it," she hesitated and lifted her eyes to meet my own, "please?" she nodded and put it in her coat pocket.

Lifting her bag onto her shoulder and opening the front door, she didn't take even one small glance back as she got into her car and pulled off the drive. And just like that. She was gone.

Chapter 27

If it were possible for walls, bricks and mortar to have feelings then those of my home felt betrayed, foolish and heartbroken. A part of me had probably thought we could work things out, just as Beth had tried to do. But when it came down to it, I couldn't even entertain the idea. Maybe my rational mind was finally awake and making a stand against its irrational alter-ego. I had had parked myself the bottom of the stairs after listening to her car disappear into the night. Sitting here I wondered what I was supposed to do next. I hadn't been this alone at night for over four years. It was dreadful, and I didn't know how I would be able to stand it.

Grabbing my car keys off the table, I pulled a jacket around me and reached for the door handle as a knock came from the other side. It startled me, and I jumped before opening it to see who was there.

"Hi, Charlotte called me. Thought you might want some company, and some of this," I looked at the bottle of Jameson's whiskey and then at the person whose hand wielded it before me. Kate.

Once curled up on the sofa beside my oldest and dearest friend, with whiskey for added warmth, I relayed my day to Kate. She sat and listened as only your best friend can, not saying anything, not judging, and not once saying, 'I told you so'. After I stopped talking, Kate pulled me into her arms as I watched the last four years of my life disappear and tried to work out at what point my relationship with Beth began to crash and burn. Perhaps the way we had got together in the first place should have been an indication of the path ahead. A torrid affair some called it. Maybe we were never destined for domesticity. I had really loved the four years that we tried though.

I was so scared about what was going to happen next. Scared to be alone, scared that I still wanted Beth. I didn't know if I would ever make sense of what had happened between us, and the speed at which everything had been destroyed. In the space of a few weeks, we had gone from being engaged, saying we were going to raise a baby together to our relationship coming to a crashing end.

"I can't believe she's actually gone, and I can't believe what she said about your family," Kate hadn't said much up to this point. Listening only. She was now beginning to piece together her carefully articulated response to what she had learned.

"What do I do now? What do I do without her? How does life work?"

"Oh, sweetie, you'll figure it out. And your dysfunctional and overbearing family and friends will be with you every step of the way."

I managed a grateful smile and sighed running my hands through my hair. When I lifted my head back up, Kate was looking at her watch.

"You should go."

"No, sorry, it's fine. I was just wondering if I needed to remind Tom to feed Amelia."

"You have to remind your husband to feed his baby?"

"No," she laughed, "I'm bedtime feeder, then he gets up with her in the night. Although we're both awake and reaching for caffeine drips."

"Wow, so do you have those on a repeat prescription, or do you have to keep seeing the doctor?" I joked, Kate laughed.

"I love my daughter, but when she learns how to sleep a little longer during hours of darkness, then I will like her more," she smiled, and we shared a moment of comfortable silence. "Do you want me to stay over?"

"No, don't be silly. I'll be fine," I was far from fine, but I could at least pretend to be. "You should get home, I'll call you tomorrow."

"Why don't you come over for dinner? Tom does a great Sunday roast, you're more than welcome."

"Yes, okay, that'd be great."

I wasn't convinced that I would actually show up for the dinner invite, but it felt more polite to say yes and then cancel rather than say no to her face. We walked into the hallway and hugged tightly before I opened the door.

"Call me if you need anything, doesn't matter what time it is, just promise you won't sit here alone and miserable."

"I promise."

"Okay," and then she went out into the night.

It felt colder than it had in a while. The stars were shining bright in a clear night sky and a dew clung to the tips of blades of grass. I wrapped my arms around myself as I watched Kate drive into the night. Back to her husband and daughter. Back to her family. I closed the front door and listened intently to the silence that filled my empty home.

I cancelled Sunday dinner at Kate and Tom's. But I had a legitimate reason. My entire family piled through the front door at eight o'clock on Sunday morning. Parents, siblings, niece and nephew, Gran – the works. They had been informed by Charlotte about what had happened, and in true Taylor style, she had told them *everything*. What was the point (she had said) in only telling half a story? Keeping some of the facts back? When it was lies and withholding truths that had led to both the Taylor daughters now being alone. She was right, of course. I just wasn't sure I was ready for a mass intervention.

Everyone busied themselves, Mum started dusting and whizzing the hoover around, Gran started dinner with Luke's assistance, Charlotte changed the bed and 'de-Beth'd' the bedroom. I had lied and told them I slept okay, but Charlotte saw straight through me. I hadn't even made it into the bedroom last night. She removed every trace of Beth, put everything in Olivia's room, she said. I wanted to help her, I wanted to show gratitude for her presence and support, but I couldn't. I just sat drinking the tea my mum kept bringing me and going for a wee every two minutes because of the amount I was drinking.

Dad saw to the outside light he said he'd noticed wasn't working the last time he was round. I smiled gratefully, but then we both seemed to recall with great sorrow the occasion for him last being at my house. The day Beth and I got engaged. We shared a moment of silence, and he kissed my cheek before saying he was going to sort the drip out from the kitchen tap. I could hear Gran cursing him for being in her way as soon as he'd stepped foot in the kitchen, but he persevered, then Luke walked past the door, spotted me and winked.

I hadn't said much during the day. It was now starting to get dark, and Charlie was complaining he was bored and wanted to go home, and as it was a school night, Charlotte soon gathered up her children and left for the Sunday night ritual. Bath, hair wash, clean pyjamas, story and bed. It was the routine we had been raised with and I knew that Charlotte did the same thing with Amy and Charlie. I waved them off from the living room window, Luke had stepped into the goodbye at the door role in my place. I hadn't yet showered or brushed my hair. I had avoided mirrors all day and knew I must have looked dreadful.

Gran whipped out a pack of cards from her handbag and insisted we sit at the dining table to have a game of New Market. I didn't share her enthusiasm, but everyone nodded in agreement, and we all shuffled behind her into the dining room. Gran's skills at card games meant we would all lose anything we put on the table, so the stakes remained low (she complained persistently that what was the point of playing if it wasn't for keeps, but we managed to calm her down by adding some brandy to her tea. I didn't even know I had any brandy in the house, but then Dad reliably informed me he carries a bottle with him for Gran in emergencies such as this. I had a new level of respect for my dad).

A few rounds of New Market later and I started to stifle yawns. It had finally caught up on me that I hadn't really slept the night before. Luke spotted me try to hold another yawn back and then he looked at his watch.

"Is it really nine o'clock? Wow! When did that happen?" he said.

"We should get going and let you have an early night before work," Mum suggested.

Work. Ugh. I couldn't even begin to think about work. She would be there. I would have to see Beth. I had no idea how I would deal with that. Do I want her to talk to me? Do I want to talk to her? Can we remain professional and maintain a relationship as colleagues? Or had it all gone too far for that? Was it too late to salvage anything? My head spun with the possibilities, and I couldn't figure out what I wanted to happen. Luke had asked me earlier in the day if he could stay with me, and I of course said yes. He was going to sleep in Olivia's room, but I had no idea what state it was in after Charlotte had put everything of Beth's in there. I didn't check, he was a big boy and could sort it out for himself.

Once Mum, Dad and Gran had left, I ran myself a bath and let the bubbles and hot water consume me. Literally drowning out all the thoughts that were plaguing my mind. Once I had scrubbed away as much of the weekend as I could, I stuck my head into Olivia's room before going to bed. Luke was already snoring, and I smiled at his still, peaceful silhouette. With everything that had happened, today had completely taken away any opportunity to talk to him about what had happened with Eve. He seemed okay, but I couldn't be sure because I hadn't asked him. I quietly shut the bedroom door and made my way into my own bedroom. It had been my room long before it was 'our' room, so I was hopeful that I would quickly remember how that felt. As I stepped over the threshold and closed the door behind me, all I felt was empty.

I had trained my mind well when it came to the weekday morning routine. I didn't need to think about anything, it all just happened as if I was a Professor at Hogwarts casting a spell to make my will reality. I was dressed and eating breakfast as Luke shuffled slowly into the kitchen, rubbing his eyes and yawning.

"Sorry, did I wake you?"

"No," was the word I think he tried to respond with as he let a loud yawn out. "I've got some stuff to do today anyway."

"Are you going to see Eve?" I wasn't sure how I felt about my little brother and Eve having had a 'relationship', if you could call it that. I watched as he mulled my question over before answering.

"I think so, I think I need to. Even if it's just so I can tell her what I think of her."

"Just don't let what's happened with me and Beth interfere with your feelings towards her. You need to figure out for yourself what you feel without concerning yourself with anything else."

"I know. But I will make it clear that I know what she's facilitated. I can't just let it go."

"And I appreciate that, and I know it's not easy. But just try to separate the two things. Talk to her about what she did to you, not what she did to me," I stood and put my cereal bowl in the sink before giving his shoulder a squeeze.

"What time will you be home?" he asked.

"I've no idea. Around five maybe?"

"Okay. I'm cooking. So don't be late."

"Don't you have anything to do for uni?"

"No, it's fine, I cleared everything before I came down."

"How long are you staying for?"

"I don't know. A few days?"

"Sounds good, stay as long as you want. As long as you can," I put my coat on and picked up my bags.

"Have a good day, sis," he smiled.

"Thanks, you too."

The first thing I did as I pulled into the car park was scan every space for Beth's car. It was nowhere to be seen. I wondered whether the sick feeling in my stomach was caused by relief or worry that she wasn't here yet. I went into school and dropped my things in my classroom. Then I went to Beth's room. She wasn't in there, but the usual teacher was back, no Anna. This time I knew it was relief that coursed through my body, she needed to be gone for good and hopefully she was. I said a quick good morning and pretended to listen as my colleague went into great detail about her back problems. Once she stopped for air, I made my excuses and turned back to my own room.

I set about organising the day ahead and was just about to pop out to the photocopier when Marie, the headteacher, stepped into the classroom.

"Morning, Emily."

"Morning."

"Can I have a quick word?" she was asking a question, but it wasn't one that she was looking for an answer to. She closed the door behind her and sat down, pulling a chair out for me to do the same.

Beth had handed her notice in. She had sent an email yesterday and instructed that Olivia would bring her resignation letter in today. It didn't go into details as to why, citing personal reasons and that she was sorry for any inconvenience. She also wrote that she was aware she was forfeiting pay by not completing her four week notice, but that she had no choice but to not be in school again.

Marie was joining the dots as she sat in front of me and asked if I needed to go home. If I needed my class covering whilst I took some time to process what she had now told me. My answer was no to both questions. I had never thought that Beth would go so far as to leave her job, I couldn't quite believe it was true. I was still waiting for her to arrive and tell Marie it was all a bad joke and she wanted to stay. Deep down I knew that wasn't going to happen, but it didn't stop me picturing it. Imagining her walk through the door so we could put the whole thing behind us. I knew I was being completely unrealistic, but I couldn't just switch off the feelings that had kept us together all these years. It may have turned ugly, but we hadn't always been that way.

I also hadn't forgiven myself for what I did with Anna. No matter what was happening, cheating is unforgivable, and I should have just confronted Beth with what I had overheard her saying to Eve as soon as it happened.

It was a long day. Each lesson dragged on more than the one before it, and yet if anyone had asked me what I taught today I couldn't have told them. I hadn't gone up to the staff room at all, I knew that word would soon spread about Beth leaving and I didn't want any questions or stares pointed in my direction. I gathered up the children's work from the day and loaded up my car. I would do my marking at home and avoid people for as long as possible.

When I got home there was nobody in. Of course there was nobody in. I lived alone now. I had thought Luke might be here, but there was no sign of him either. I went upstairs to get changed and stuck my head in Olivia's room. It was empty. I don't mean that Luke wasn't there. It was empty of Beth. Everything that Charlotte had put in here yesterday was gone, and a lot of Olivia's things were missing too. Including, Joy, the fish. It was all gone, like they had never lived here. Never existed in my world. I sat down on the bed and picked up a jumper from the back of the chair under the window. It had been hanging there, discarded and unwanted, it smelt of strawberries, Olivia's chosen bubble bath from the Body Shop. I held it close and breathed her in. And with each breath I exhaled I could feel them both slipping away.

It wasn't until I went back down stairs that I saw the front door key on the doormat. She was certainly sure about her own future, and it didn't include me anymore. Beth must have pushed the key through after emptying the house. I suddenly had a thought, more of an 'I wonder...' moment really. Stepping into the kitchen I started to open cupboards and then I started to laugh. She had taken her things from here too. Don't get me wrong, she was always the cook, so she had taken her saucepans, frying pans, baking trays, mixing bowls, measuring jugs – they were all gone.

I wandered around from room to room, I couldn't settle. It didn't feel finished, Beth was gone, but I wasn't done, and I knew why. I needed to talk to Olivia. I wasn't sure if it was my place to or if I would even be allowed anywhere near her, but I had to try. I had to know if she was okay and if she had seen Beth. Taking the strawberry smelling jumper, still grasped in my hands with me, I set off to Adam and Sarah's house.

Chapter 28

As my car pulled up at the side of the road, I spotted Olivia and Adam with a very bouncy puppy running at their heals heading in my direction. Olivia stopped for a moment when she saw me, and I tentatively got out of the car.

"Hi," it sounded like such a ridiculous thing to say to her, but I was suddenly lost for words.

"Hi," came Olivia's reply.

Adam smiled at me, almost like he had seen this coming and was now offering his condolences at the death of my relationship with his ex-wife.

"Is it okay if I talk to you, Liv? If it's okay with you and your dad?" I looked at them both, Adam looked at Olivia.

"Is that okay? Do you want to talk to Emily?" he asked. Quite right he should check what she wanted to do. She nodded at him and let go of Margot's lead, which they had been holding together.

"Would it be okay if we went for a milkshake?" I suggested and was given another nod from Olivia and another sympathy loaded smile from Adam. She got into my car and Adam grabbed my arm softly.

"She hasn't seen Beth. She just knows you've split up. Beth bought her things here whilst she was at school. I haven't said anything, and I can't really because I don't know anything. I wasn't in when Beth came round, and she wouldn't talk to Sarah."

"I'm so sorry Adam…"

"Look, I know how much you care about Olivia, just make it right by her. If you can."

"I'll try," I promised. Adam nodded and headed back into the house.

We pulled up outside an American diner that I had taken Olivia to a few times when we'd been over indulgent by ourselves at weekends. She hadn't spoken to me in the car and nor did she speak as we entered the diner. She sat down in the booth we always sat in by the window and I ordered our usual milkshake treats. As I placed them down on the table, she tried to hide the fact she'd wiped her face with her sleeve. She was crying.

"Liv…"

"I know Mum's gone."

"She's not gone. She's just…" She's what? I didn't have an ending for that sentence. "We tried really hard, Liv. We wanted to keep our family together."

"So why did she bring all my things to Dad's? Don't you want me at your house anymore?"

"Of course I do! But, your mum and I... we aren't going to be together anymore."

"So no wedding?" my heart had already been circling the drain, it was now working it's way down through the sewers.

"No, sweetie. No wedding. It turns out that actually, even though we both love you more than anything in the world, there are other things that we both want, and we can't have those things if we stay together."

"Is it because you want a baby?"

I stopped the stirring motion I had been circling around the thick banana milkshake with my straw. How...

"Why would you ask me that?"

"I don't know. I just somehow knew. Like I saw you with Amelia and I just knew, I think I knew because you looked like you would be a good mum. You've been like another mum to me. When it was the Mother's Day morning at school, I told Miss Forrest that I was really lucky to have three mums when some people don't have even one."

Oh, this girl. This wonderful, precious girl. How had we managed to keep her world so happy and positive? And now we were taking all of that away from her.

"Yes," she was too smart for me to try to lie, and what was the point? "I would like to have a baby of my own, and yes, your mum wasn't too keen on the idea."

"Mm. I don't think Mum likes babies as much as you and me, I think she likes children who can look after themselves a bit more," she paused and looked directly in my eyes, "will I be able to still see you?"

"Of course you will! I will always be here for you, if you need me for anything then you just come and find me. Okay?" I wiped my tears away now and held her hand across the table.

"And can I meet your baby when you have one? I'd like that, it would have been my baby brother or sister, and I wouldn't have been the youngest anymore," I didn't have the words for the pain in my chest, my heart felt sick and like each beat was a punch to my stomach.

"If I am lucky enough to be able to have a baby of my own then I would love for you to meet them, and if they are half as clever, kind and wonderful as you are then I will be a very lucky and proud mum," she smiled at me but almost immediately became tearful again. "What is it?"

"Where is my mum? She won't answer her phone when Dad rings, and I heard him talking to Sarah, saying that she isn't going to work at school anymore, and she didn't leave any information about where she is going to live when she brought my things round. Dad rang Nana and Grandpop Walker, and she isn't staying at their house. Is she okay?"

Shit. I had just presumed that Beth had gone to stay with her parents, so where had she gone? If she wasn't taking anybody's calls, then what else could anyone do to find her or check on her? Were we to consider her as a missing person?

"I'm sure she is okay, sweetie, she's sad. We all feel sad right now and when people feel upset, they do and need different things to make them feel better. Your mum is just trying to figure out how to make herself feel better."

"On her own? How can you feel better on your own?"

"Some people like to have time alone, they think better, they can sort their thoughts out."

"I hope she comes to see me."

"She will, she's your mum and she loves you, no matter what."

"Thank you for coming to see me. I was worried that you didn't want to be like a mum to me anymore and that's why you didn't want me in the house."

"Oh, Liv!" I moved from sitting opposite her to next to her and pulled her into my arms, she grabbed me tight, and I breathed every part of her in. "That's not even possible. I have loved being like a mum to you and I will always be here for you."

"Promise?"

"Promise," she squeezed me hard and when we parted, we finished our drinks in silence.

On the drive back to Adam and Sarah's house, Olivia managed some casual chit-chat about school and told me all about Margot getting stung by a bee and her dad having to pay for an emergency vets appointment. She said he had acted grumpy about the cost, but when nobody was looking, he had been giving Margot extra treats and cuddles for being a brave girl. Ultimately Olivia seemed like she would be okay. What more could I do?

I dropped Olivia off and walked her to the door, she held my hand the whole way down the path. Adam very kindly asked if I would like to go in, and I couldn't quite believe that it was possible for the man whose wife I had an affair with to be now inviting me into his house. I politely declined, and after one more reassuring hug for Olivia, I walked back to the car. I took a moment to compile myself before turning the engine over.

I had been so desperate to see Olivia, and I hoped that it hadn't been a selfish need and that I'd managed to make her feel less alone in the world than she had done before we talked. I looked at the road ahead as I was about to start the car and paused. I couldn't be certain, but I thought I could see Beth's car. It sped off as I turned the engine over and then a text came through to my phone:

Thank you for doing what I was unable to. I know she'll be okay now. Beth

Chapter 29

I arrived home and an hour later, Luke walked in and found me with a glass of wine marking books at the dinner table. He didn't know it was actually my third glass and the end of the bottle.

"I'm so sorry, Em, I lost track of time."

"You don't have to apologise to me, I'm not your keeper."

"I know, but I said I would cook, and now all I want to do is call for pizza and veg in front of the tele."

"Sounds good to me. Wine?" I lifted the bottle, and he took it from me.

"It's empty."

"I know, open another," my instruction was clear, but Luke hesitated.

"On a school night?"

"Sod school. Yes, open another bottle and let's get drunk with pizza and Jennifer Lawrence in Hunger Games."

"Ah if only that were a physical possibility and not just a theoretical one."

"Just pour the wine, I'll get the pizza menu."

Sometime later, I have no idea how long exactly, there had been another bottle of wine consumed, two medium pizzas with garlic bread and chicken strips devoured, and we had watched two of the Hunger Games movies. I filled Luke in on my meeting with Olivia, and I told him about Beth's text. He said he felt sorry for Olivia but that it should have been Beth making sure she was okay, not me. I didn't particularly want to analyse any of it. I was tired and a little bit drunk.

"So, did you see her?" I had been dying to know if Luke had visited Eve. I was sure he would have, but he hadn't offered any details all night.

"Yes. I saw her. I told her that I was angry she had the abortion without even telling me she was pregnant. That if she had really wanted to get rid of it then I would have supported her decision, but she should have told me first." He shook his head to himself in thought. "She should never have just done it without telling me, Em. I'm no more ready to be a dad than she is a mum, but it was something we should have talked about first, we should have decided together."

"I know," I rested my hand on his shoulder as we sat on the floor in front of the coffee table, finishing our wine and eating cold pizza. "It will get easier. It will hurt less."

"Are you talking to me or to yourself?"

"I was talking to you, but yes, I will try to take a little of my own advice."

"Wise words. I didn't say anything to Eve about you and Beth. Sorry."

"Don't apologise, I'm glad you didn't, it should have been just about the two of you. At the end of the day, it's not like Eve put the words into Beth's mouth. She meant everything she said, and Eve was just in the wrong place at the wrong time, although for Beth she was probably in the right place, as it was somebody she could discuss her true feelings with." I paused for a second and stared, but not at anything in particular. "How did I miss it? How did I not know how she really felt?"

"I don't know. She had me fooled. She had us all fooled."

"Did she? Did none of you see this? See that she had complete control of us?"

"Well, sometimes I think Charlotte missed doing things with you. You know, sister things."

"Really? Why did she never say anything?"

"I suppose she didn't want to upset you. I don't know what girls do when they get together. But I don't think Charlotte felt the connection she had with you before once Beth was on the scene."

Luke's words made me feel crushed. I had no idea that Charlotte had felt this way, and I can only presume that she had discussed it with our brother at varying points over the last four years.

"I can't believe how wrong I got it. I really thought that I had it all, Luke. Now I have nothing."

"That's not true. You will always have me, Charlotte, Mum, Dad and you know Gran has made a deal with the Devil himself to live forever," we both laughed.

"It will get easier, won't it?" I asked this time.

"Yes. It will," he hooked his arm around my neck and pulled me over to kiss the top of my head. "I'm going to bed. You should do the same, you'll regret your indulgent Monday night shenanigans when the kids pile in tomorrow morning," I laughed and nodded in agreement.

"I know, I'm right behind you."

Luke disappeared upstairs and I tidied up. I had had a wonderful evening with him, but the sadness inside me seemed to grow rather than get smaller. At what point does 'it'll get easier' start to kick in? When does that happen? I sighed as I abandoned the plates and wine glasses in the sink, I could feel a headache starting so got a glass of water and two paracetamol. As I climbed the stairs I wondered where Beth was right now.

Was she asking the same questions that I was? Did she wonder when things would start to feel better? Or had she just washed her hands of the whole thing and was carrying on as if I had never existed? I brushed my teeth, climbed into bed and lay staring at the shadows. Would this darkness ever lift? I hadn't managed to answer the question before I finally fell asleep.

The rest of my week went by a lot faster than Monday had. But I didn't escape more than that one privileged day without people asking me about Beth. I told them the truth, what else could I do? Obviously I didn't tell them everything, but I told them we had split up and that the first I knew of her not coming back to work was when I arrived Monday morning. They were sympathetic, but I know they were desperate to know the reason why. They needed someone to gossip about, someone to blame, someone to side with. But I gave them no more than that. We had simply decided that we wanted different things and that it was time to go our separate ways. None of them believed me, but I didn't care, it was none of their business.

Luke stayed with me until the weekend. We all met for breakfast on Saturday morning and then took him to the train station to head back up to Sunderland. I hugged him for a long time before I would let him go. He squeezed me back and whispered in my ear that he loved me. I kissed his cheek and watched as he walked off to his designated platform. We of course stayed until the train was pulling out of the station and waved until he was about the size of a pin head in the distance. We turned and headed back to our respective cars, and I went home. Alone.

Life goes on. Isn't that what they say? Or is it, the show must go on? Either way, I had to just keep going. It had been a week now and I allowed myself a 'well done' as I climbed into bed each night for getting through another day. The weekend was difficult. I of course had several invites to stop myself having to spend time alone, but I didn't want to get into a pattern where I was never home by myself. Who knows how long this would be my life for? The last thing I needed was to begin being afraid of my own shadow.

Kate thought I was being very brave, but I didn't really like that description. Bravery didn't feel like it had played a part in anything. She had called me every day since that fateful Saturday, and I know she felt bad about what had happened with Beth, but I didn't need to go crying on anyone's shoulder anymore.

It wasn't until the end of the following week that something I had quite forgotten about came fluttering back into my life, clearing a path amongst the gloomy loneliness. I received a call from my GP, they had received my blood test results and were pleased to inform me that everything had come back normal, so we could proceed to the next part of the IVF process.

I went into some kind of baby making auto-pilot and took down a number to call, as I had now been referred to a gynaecologist who would take me through the next stage. Christ. This must be what it's like when Simon Cowell rings you up to say you're through to the live finals of X-Factor.

When I hung up the phone I burst into tears. But it was okay. They were tears of joy. Complete and utter joy. I was going to be able to have a baby. My baby. All mine.

And that was how it happened. That was the day. The day that life started to get easier.

Chapter 30

Each day that followed the 'please proceed with caution' phone call (so named by Charlotte and Kate as they said babies should come with warning labels), was easier than the one before. Suddenly my thoughts were occupied with hormone injections, ovulation and menstrual cycles. Everything that Beth and I had been through was becoming a distant memory. It still hurt if I spent too long dwelling on it, which happened occasionally, but that was the hormone injections. I was sure that the affect they were having on me must be like an addict enduring a come-down. Not that I knew what that felt like of course, but I was not in control of the moods that often left me sat with a tub of ice-cream and a Bridget Jones marathon.

So, when Christmas arrived and I sat in the bathroom at Charlotte's house, with Charlotte sitting on the side of the bath and Kate pacing the very tiny space between the toilet and the door, my breath held for sixty seconds whilst I waited for a plastic stick to tell me whether it had all been worth it or not.

"I'm pregnant."

I'd waited so long to say those words that I kept repeating them, again and again.

"I'm pregnant, I'm pregnant, I'm pregnant, I'm pregnant, I'm pregnant, I'M PREGNANT!" Charlotte jumped up off the bath and both she and Kate flung their arms around me as we bounced around like we were in the middle of a mosh pit.

It was probably the happiest day of my life, up to that point in time anyway. Because the actual happiest day, was when my daughter arrived into the world. A screaming ball of wrinkled pink skin with dark hair, weighing 8lb 1oz, ten toes, ten fingers and one head. The head was important because Gran had been reading horror stories about sperm donors and the things they don't tell the clinics. So she was convinced my baby would end up with an extra toe or a tail. I tried to explain that the stories she read were probably based on clinics that had nothing to do with the NHS, had probably never been vetted and that I didn't need to worry about things like that. But inside I was completely terrified.

And how wrong Gran was, my daughter was perfect, absolutely perfect.

Of course I would expose her to a life without boundaries and over sharing when it came to personal space, I would drive her mad with how involved in her business I would become, but she wouldn't care. She wouldn't care because she would know that I loved her and that that was why I was doing all of the things that drove her absolutely insane.

I named her Sophia Jane Nancy Taylor. It was only right that the two strongest women in my life, who had made me the woman I am today, were a part of making my daughter the strongest woman she could be.

When I took her home, I was accompanied by the whole Taylor family. Which was lovely, I was glad to begin her life the way I wanted it to continue. Surrounded by the people who would love and care for her the most. I had been expecting Kate to come and visit, so when there was a knock at the door I simply shouted 'it's open', welcoming in my best friend to the newest member of the family.

It wasn't Kate. It was the police...

"Mrs Byrne?" known to the rest of us as Gran.

"Who the feck what's to know?"

"Could you come with us please?" I looked at each confused slash concerned face that was turning from the police to Gran and back again, like watching a Wimbledon final.

"And why now would I do that? That little yoke there is my new great-granddaughter. Why would I come with you when I have that little angel to watch over, eejits," I don't know what I was more in shock over. The police being in my home, or Gran calling them eejits.

"Mrs Byrne, we are here on behalf of the MI5 Security Service. There is a pressing matter that requires your attention. I'm afraid we are not able to tell you any more than that in front of civilians, but we do need you to come with us as a matter of urgency."

Gran looked at each of us in turn. I had never seen a more smug looking elderly woman than the one currently sitting in my living room. She stood up slowly, not because she had to (even though she did) but because it added to the dramatic effect.

"Gran... wait... you can't just go..."

"I told you... I told each of you... you fecking little cynics. I don't know when I'll be back," she pulled her coat on and picked up her handbag. "If I don't see you again, then know that I love you, and whatever they tell you about me, I did it for you. I did it for our Queen and country," and with that she followed the two police officers out.

Mum went absolutely nuts. She insisted Dad take her to follow them, but after just a few minutes they had disappeared. The police that is, not my parents. They drove around looking for any hint of which way they might have gone, but there was nothing. They came back to mine, and we drowned Mum with as much alcohol as it took to calm her down. I left her in Charlotte's capable hands and went back into the living room where Luke was sitting with Sophia. He was smitten, and I couldn't blame him one little bit.

"Can you believe it?" he said.

"I know, she's finally here, she's all mine and she's here."

"I meant Gran…" he laughed, and I rolled my eyes as I sat beside him. "All this time we thought it was just a story."

"Not every day MI5 knock on your door to take your gran away on some secret mission," I looked at him and we both suddenly found it less funny.

"She will be okay, won't she?" Luke questioned.

"Gran? Yes, of course. She's the strongest and scariest woman I've ever known. She'll be back in no time," Luke dropped his eyes back onto the small bundle of life in his arms.

"I'm so proud of you, Em. Everything you've been through, and here she is. Worth waiting for?"

"No question," I grinned. Then I yawned.

Once Mum had stopped squealing like a banshee over becoming an orphan (she drank a lot of whiskey) Dad managed to get her into the car and home. Luke went with them, he was staying there now he had completed his degree. Charlotte took the kids home and the house fell quiet. That is until the sound of a baby crying filled every corner of every room, and every space in my very full heart.

Gran never spoke of that day. Other than telling everyone it was the day her youngest great-grandchild came home. Mum tried every tactic she knew, but Gran never let anything slip about what it was she was called upon for. The world carried on turning and we were all still alive, so we would just have to be satisfied with that for now. Dad made a joke about waiting until she gets dementia and Mum cussed him severely, leading to him spending an extra few hours fishing until it was safe to go home. Mum was morphing into Gran at a rate none of us had seen coming, none more so than Dad, who was now fishing with two different clubs and rarely at home during the weekends. Purely for his own safety.

When Sophia was six months old, Kate convinced me that I should have a night off. I couldn't stand the idea of going out and being deafened in a club, with my shoes sticking to the floor and buying drinks that I could enjoy a bottle of at half the price if I was at home. But she insisted, and she was clever because she waited until her birthday and said that it was how she wanted to celebrate this year.

We went to the Basque Lounge. A club that had gone from strength to strength and had branched out opening clubs in Birmingham and Nottingham. I had never returned after opening night, but I must admit it brought an element of closure coming back here now. My life had completely changed since that night, and it was all for the better.

Moving on from the Basque Lounge, we arrived at another establishment, where Kate spent all of her time seeking me out a new woman. More fool her.

"Em, Emily!" I felt a poke in my arm, "she is definitely checking you out."

"You said that about the last two women you've made me look desperate in front of."

"No, I'm serious; she is *definitely* checking you out!" I turned and looked in the general direction my happily-married-therefore-rubbish-at-dating-best-friend was motioning, to see a tall slim blonde looking our way. I blushed immediately and then felt a shove against my shoulder. I heard a mumbled apology come from a woman who had bumped into me and watched the glamorous figure walk by. I continued to watch as she approached the woman supposedly making eyes at me and kissed her. Of course she did.

Kate, reached for her drink and took a very quick slurp whilst avoiding my eye. I knew that she had my best interests at heart, but we had been at this for hours and so far, I had managed to scare away anyone that had actually dared approach me for conversation.

"Can we please go home now?" I pleaded to Kate's better nature, but she just eyed me up suspiciously.

"Why?"

"Why? Because I feel like I've aged about ten years during the delightful time we've spent in this bar… what's it called again?" Kate paused and took another sip of her drink before answering.

"Les-be-friends," I buried my face in my hands and groaned.

"I cannot believe I let you talk me into this! We need to leave, right now."

"But I have three phone numbers, if they see me leave with you then they'll think that we've you know, become scissor sisters," Kate made the action with her hands, and I gave her my stern 'you need to listen to what I am saying' face and I grabbed my jacket. (I am in my thirties it is no longer acceptable to go out clubbing without the security of a jacket to take the chill off when you leave.)

I started to walk away, rummaging in my bag for my phone to call a taxi. As I turned around, I collided with someone at a ridiculously high level of impact and the contents of my bag proceeded to scatter across the floor. Well, I say floor, it felt like I was walking on double sided sticky tape every time I tried to lift my foot up, I kept checking to see if I had left my shoe behind.

The person responsible for my handbag contents now sticking to the ground like Amy Winehouse to a bottle of Vodka, began to collect up various things and hand them back to me. I was in such a foul mood by this point I did not care for chivalry and just wanted to get the hell out of here. I took the items belonging to me and finally looked up into the eyes of my collision. I paused. I think I may have blinked and possibly allowed my jaw to drop slightly. I was completely lost, swimming in a pool of dark brown sultry eyes and my heart began to race. She smiled. At me. Feck.

"May I offer you a word of advice?" Oh bugger, now she was talking to me.

I tried to answer but when nothing but: "mmfffshhppp" came out of my mouth I motioned to the DJ box, implying I couldn't hear over the music, and I think I got away with not looking like I was completely demented. She leaned in close and spoke right into my ear, the left one, not that that's relevant, just trying to paint an exact picture.

"Don't make your opening line 'I'm a single mum whose partner ran a mile when faced with the prospect of raising a baby with me'," Jesus, how long had she been watching/listening/STALKING me? "I mean, it didn't put me off, but you might want to try out a few new lines before you tackle going out looking for a date again," she moved back and smiled at me, and I swear I became a puddle on the floor.

I turned to look for Kate to rescue me and as I clocked her, she was already heading over. I turned back and the woman was gone.

"Who was that? Are you okay?" I nodded that I was fine and pointed to the door, I was fed up of shouting, I was fed up of rejection, I was fed up of mysterious women offering me 'advice' with a creepy hint of 'the call is coming from inside the house' about it. I shoved the rest of the fallen items back into my bag and as Kate and I headed for the exit I felt around in my bag and pulled out a piece of paper. I read it a couple of times before I actually understood what had just happened. It read:

Callie: 07712378910, for when you work out some new pick-up lines x

Oh...

Epilogue

No. No. No. That's not right either. I reached for the seventh top out of the wardrobe, threw the one I had on across the bed and yanked the new one down over my head. I had no idea why I was getting so nervous. I mean, this was our... umm... wow, fourteenth date? Is it fourteen? No. Wait. Does it count if all you did was... never mind. We'll stick with fourteen. Fourteen dates in two months. Was that a lot? It's been a while since I've counted dates.

After the first week with Callie, we spoke on the phone almost every day. This date was different though. I knew why I was getting into such a flap. Callie was meeting Sophia for the first time.

We had been talking about it for a while, and I had finally decided it was the right time. I mean, we hadn't used the 'L' word yet. Love that is. Not lesbian. But I felt strongly enough about this woman who had opened her world up to be a part of mine, and all of my wacky baggage, that I knew it was time to take that next step. I had hit that nervous/exciting point of the relationship where you can picture a future, possibly the rest of your life, with a person. Of course, I wasn't about to tell her that, she would likely run a mile.

This would have to do, I was running out of time and Sophia was likely to wake any minute. I took one last look in the mirror and sighed. I hadn't scared her away so far, so fingers crossed this was all going to be fine. I had considered asking Kate to come round with

Amelia, safety in numbers and a toddler running round, plus Kate and Callie had already met so it would be an ideal opportunity for more 'getting to know you' time. However, I decided against it and that today was about family.

Sophia was my whole world, and it was a big step for me to introduce Callie to her. All those years that I had watched on and wondered, dreamed of what it would be like to be a mother and now I know. There are no words.

I skipped quite fast down the stairs and went into the living room. Sophia was awake in her travel cot and staring at me as if she had heard me coming down the stairs and was now watching the door expectantly. I picked her up and sat with her on the sofa. She looked at me as if she could sense every nerve and pang of anxiety that was running through my body and then she smiled. I don't know why or how it works, but I swear that smile was to tell me that everything was okay and that she knew what was about to happen. At that exact moment, the doorbell rang, and I jumped up, startling Sophia, who I think gave her head a little shake as if steadying her brain. I took a deep breath and stood up to go and answer the door.

As I opened it, Sophia turned and looked at the person standing on the other side. I smiled and took a deep breath.

"Hi. Sophia, this is Callie. Callie, meet Sophia," I stepped aside to let Callie over the threshold and closed the door behind her.

"Hi, Sophia," she reached out and took Sophia's little hand in a 'how do you do?' sort of way and we went through to the living room. I offered Callie a seat and sat myself and Sophia beside her. We talked about mundane things for a few minutes, passing the time of day as if we were old friends who hadn't seen each other in a while rather than two women who regularly saw each other naked in bed.

Sophia started to squirm, and Callie held her arms out. "May I?" she asked. I nodded and handed Sophia over. She didn't seem to mind at all, that someone she had never met before was now holding her in their arms. Callie picked up a toy off the floor and started talking and entertaining Sophia, who lapped up the attention with giggles and smiles. My whole body felt as if it slumped into the sofa as all of my anxiety and nerves disappeared into the sound of my daughter's laughter.

I left them to it to go and put the kettle on, and I could hear Sophia giggling and Callie talking in silly voices. When I popped my head in the door to see if we were ready to have lunch, they had moved to the floor and were playing peek-a-boo. I laughed and headed back to the kitchen just as the doorbell went. I stopped and turned, I was hoping it was perhaps the postman with a parcel or next door saying their car was blocked in on the drive. But deep down, deep, deep down I knew who was at the door.

"Mum, Gran, what are you doing here?" I had made the huge mistake of talking to Charlotte about today, thinking that the unspoken sister code meant she would keep it to herself until after the event had passed so that I may share the success of it at my own leisure. It was like I didn't know my family at all to even consider that would be possible.

"We wondered if we could borrow your car," Mum was talking but I knew Gran was pulling the strings.

"My car?"

"Yes. Your car."

"What's wrong with your car?"

"It's in the garage."

"So how did you get here?"

"On the bus," wow, they had rehearsed this well. I was impressed.

"What number bus do you need to get here?" a flash of panic flew across Mum's face and Gran interrupted our little back and forth.

"Oh for feck's sake, it's the number 9, now where is that beautiful great-granddaughter of mine?" just at that moment, Callie appeared in the doorway to the living room with Sophia in her arms. "Oh, well sure, we didn't know you had company, Emily. Won't you introduce us to your friend?" Gran winked at me, and I rolled my eyes. Unbelievable. Actually, it was so unbelievable that for my family it was entirely believable.

"Mum, Gran, this is Callie. Callie, this is my mum, Jane and my gran, Nancy."

"Well, sure it's nice to meet you Callie, we've heard so much about you, nothing intimate mind, we're close but not that close, although I dabbled once with Shirley O'Neil in her dad's shed, so I have a fair idea of what ladies and the like do in that department," Gran sidled past Callie and into the living room, Mum followed with a polite nod and Callie came over to me laughing.

"I am so sorry, I didn't know they were coming over, I will kill my sister when I see her."

"Emily, it's fine," she laughed.

"I warned you my gran was nuts."

"I like her. And I really like you, so let's go and get to know each other," she leaned in and kissed me softly and I rested one arm on her waist and the other on Sophia's back. As we parted I looked into her eyes as she smiled at me.

"I love you," I said it. I said it out loud. I'd thought it in my head for a while, but I just said it. In my voice, my voice that she could hear. Alarm bells were ringing in my head, and I didn't quite know what to do. I looked at my baby girl in her arms and diverted my attention to her, but she wasn't interested in me, she was pulling at Callie's ear (a new trick she had learned) and I tried to pull her hand down and away. As I did so, Callie reached out to my hand and held it in her own.

"I love you too," she beamed at me, and I think I might have laughed a little. Not in an 'I was only joking' kind of way, in an 'I'm so relieved that you said that' way. "I've been waiting for you to say that for weeks," she kissed me again and it was the melodic sound of my gran's shouts from the living room that made us part.

"Have you been robbed Emily? Because I can't hear the feckin' kettle, did they take anything else?" I rolled my eyes and the three of us re-joined Mum and Gran.

"I'm just doing it now Gran."

"We were about to have lunch too, Nancy, Jane, if you would care to join us?" Mum and Gran looked at each other, then at Callie, then at me, and then back at Callie.

"Lunch would be just lovely, Callie. Thank you," I smiled as conversation started to flow through the room. I was still going to kill Charlotte a little bit, but as first meetings go, this was quite alright.

I went back into the kitchen and started making sandwiches and putting crisps and nibbles into bowls. Sounds of laughter came filtering through the house and I was confident that finally my life looked exactly the way it was supposed to. I had been waiting for a long time to be able to say that. As I started to take lunch and cups of tea through, I ignored the questions I could hear Gran firing at Callie, it was nothing too sinister at this point. Just about her family and job. They were safe questions. For now. I wasn't nervous anymore though. I had done it. I had moved on and made my life *mine*. It felt pretty good too.

Acknowledgement

I've always wondered what I would write if I ever got to do an 'acknowledgement' page in my very own published book. And now I haven't got a clue where to begin.

I'll start at the very beginning by thanking every teacher who ever taught me at school, read any of my school work, and made me believe I was good at English.

Thank you to my family who have always encouraged me to follow my dream of sharing my books with the world (well, further than a group of great proof-reading friends anyway).

And to those friends who have read every word, some several times, and always been the critics and supporters I needed most, I am so grateful to you.

Thank you to Kate, for guiding me into the world of self-publishing. Our paths were absolutely meant to cross at this point in my life. Thank you to Katie, for reading this book probably almost as many times as I have. And thank you to Beatrice, for napping enough for me to have finally figured out how to get this book into the world.

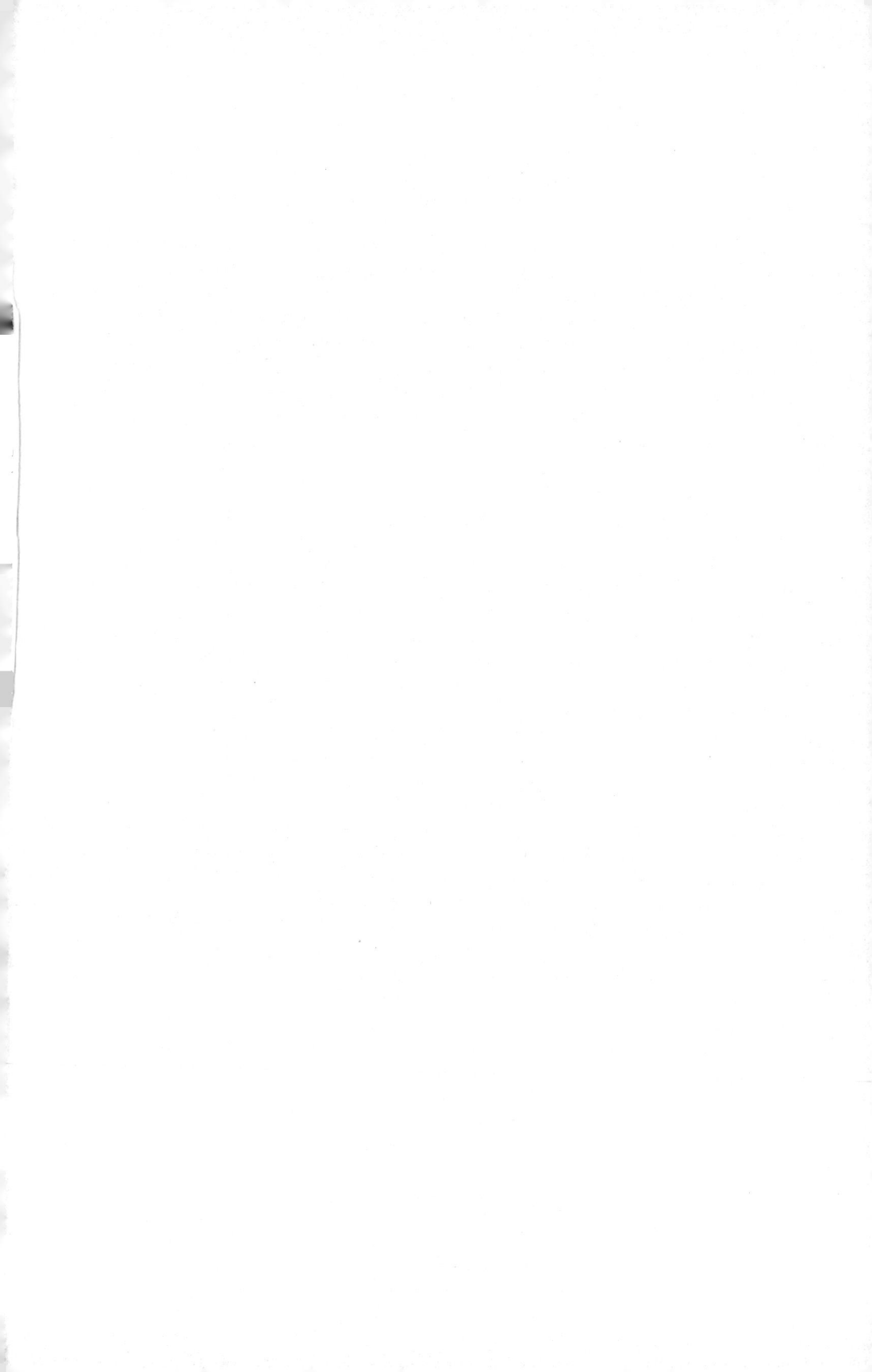

Printed in Great Britain
by Amazon